I0789012

HOW TO STEAL A STAR

Geonn Cannon

Supposed Crimes LLC • Matthews, North Carolina

All Rights Reserved
Copyright © 2021 Geonn Cannon

Published in the United States.

ISBN: 978-1-952150-15-9

www.supposedcrimes.com

This book is typeset in Goudy Old Style.

PROLOGUE

THE FIRST time Margot Sullivan failed to fly, she started at the top of the steepest hill in her neighborhood. It was reportedly the steepest in the entire county, maybe the state, but that information came from a fellow third-grader and his fact-checking was suspect at best. The only thing that mattered was the incline worked for her purposes. An 18.4% slope with three good plateaus before ending in a washed-out bridge. It wasn't a wide gap, but she wasn't interested in distance. She wanted height.

To that end, she'd convinced a classmate named Walter have his brothers build her a ramp. He agreed in exchange for a kiss; a small price to pay in her eyes. The ramp was in place and well-secured, and Walter's three older brothers were sitting in the back of a pick-up drinking from shiny silver cans.

Most of Mrs. Black's class was also there, either to cheer her on or watch her fail. She didn't care either way, it wasn't about them. She would have done it even without an audience. This was just about her. No one had told their parents, she made sure of that. No teachers were alerted. She'd used her allowance to buy what she needed to build her car, taken what she couldn't afford from garages and workshops of her friends' parents, and did her build in the shed behind the school.

Now she was ready. No nerves, only excitement. Every minute of her eight years on Earth had been leading to this moment.

Goggles, check. She reached up and hooked a finger under the strap to make sure it was sitting properly.

Helmet, check. Her hair stuck out of the bottom like stalks of dry straw.

She wore fingerless gloves, the better to grip the wheel. Her dad's thick leather jacket would protect her from any accidents, but she still had pads on her elbows and knees just in case. She rocked side to side in the seat to make sure it was bolted in right. It was. The car was as sturdy as it could be, given the circumstances, and she was confident it would survive the trip.

Margot inhaled, blew the air out through her lips, and held up one hand. Her classmates hushed, and the older kids also fell silent. Her best friend Terry came running over and crouched next to her.

"You sure you wanna do this?" He looked down the hill. "It seems an awful lot bigger than it did when we walked it."

"It's now or never," she said, her hand still in the air, "and never isn't an option. Let's go."

Terry gulped and picked up the rope. He moved back to the side of the road. Margot dropped her hand. Terry pulled the rope, and the chocks in front of her wheels skittered away across the pavement. She heard one of the teenagers say, "Oh, shit, she's really gonna do it!" as gravity took hold and started to pull the cart forward.

Margot's breath was trapped in her chest, and she was very aware of her heart sitting stationary behind her ribs. She tilted forward and she saw the grey ribbon of track ahead of her. The tall pines on either side of the road seemed to lean out, as if they were creating a tunnel for her passage.

She felt it, the pivot moment, and then...

Speed, the wheels growling on the ancient asphalt, her body shaken and rattled inside the cage she'd made. She kept her arms as relaxed as possible because keeping them rigid would be a quick break if anything happened. Eyes forward, watching for stones or cracks that could trip her up. Lips in a firm line, chin down, eyes narrowed behind the goggles. She could see the ramp now. She could all but feel herself rising, cut free, soaring.

And then something cracked, the wheel jerked in her hands, and everything in her seemed to twist one way while gravity pulled her the other way.

She didn't remember hitting the ground or the four times she apparently bounced on the road, or the ruins of her car smashing into the ramp. She never heard the sound as both tumbled into the ravine or the shrieks of her classmates as she finally came to a stop fifteen yards from her intended destination. Her goggles were cracked, her lips bloody from being cut on her teeth, and her father's jacket was completely shredded.

Hours later, she woke in the hospital. One of the teenagers risked his freedom by taking her to the hospital and owning up to his part in the events. Her father was sitting by her bed, one of her hands wrapped in both of his.

"What were you thinking?" he whispered as he hugged her tightly.

"I know what I did wrong," she said.

"I would hope so." Then he pulled back and looked at her. "Wait... you know what you did *was* wrong, right? That's what you meant to say, baby?"

Margot didn't answer. She was already imagining what she would do differently next time.

The second time she failed to fly, Margot Sullivan once again thought she'd cleared all the hurdles in her way. She met the physical and mental qualifications to be an astronaut - degree in computer science, completion of flight school, 20/20 vision, she was five foot eight, the whole ball of wax - and she had secured a place on the next shuttle mission. She got the news six days before her birthday and drove four hundred miles to tell her father in person.

She showed up at his house looking like a recruiter for NASA, their logo emblazoned on her shirt, jacket, and cap. When she told him she was going to space, he grabbed her around the waist and lifted her off the ground, carrying her into the house. She laughed and squirmed to get away, but his arms were a vise even at his age.

He planted her in front of the wall where he'd framed all her achievements and took out his phone. "You'll be proud of me," he said as he poked at the screen. "I'm even figuring out Instagram."

"I know, I've seen the filters." Margot cocked her hip and lifted her chin as he lined up his shot. "You made a great basset hound."

"Hush and pose," he said.

He grilled up steaks on the back porch while bugging her for details about her mission. When she was leaving, how long she'd be gone, what the goal was, who else was on the team, on and on and on. She was exhausted by his interrogation but also touched that he was so proud.

After dinner they watched the sun go down, slowly draining beers, finally silent after all his questions dried up. He reached over and patted her hand.

"My little girl going to space. How many fathers can say that? Ten?"

"We may have taken an embarrassingly long time to put a woman up there, but there's still been a couple more than that."

He shrugged. "Either way. Take that, Jerry 'my daughter was on *The Bachelorette*' Murphy."

Margot laughed.

While she was laughing, her phone rang.

She picked it up and saw Tracie's face on the screen. Her laugh morphed into a groan.

"Something wrong?"

She pushed up out of the chair and headed inside. "No, just... it's whatever..." She answered the phone and pushed the patio door shut behind her. "Hey, babe. Can I call you back? I'm at my dad's..."

"Are you watching the news?"

"What? No." She looked around but didn't see a television. "Why?"

"Turn on the TV."

"Babe, I'm with my dad..."

Tracie sniffled. "It's the space station, Margot. Something's happening on the space station. I don't know what, but they're saying it's really bad."

Margot felt cold. "Let me call you back."

She hung up without waiting for an answer. She went to that most-reviled but also fasted updated source of information, Twitter, and immediately saw ISS was trending. Her finger trembled as she tapped it and began scrolling through the meager updates and misinformation to get an idea of what was going on. At some point her knees gave out and she sank onto the couch. Her arms felt disconnected from her body, like they were floating inches away from her torso.

There were photos, streaks of fire in the sky. She blinked away tears and watched quick video clips that showed the pinprick of light flaring.

She didn't know how long she spent refreshing the feed as the news solidified, conjecture was replaced with facts, but by the time her dad came in, the light had changed enough that she knew the sun had gone down. The phone's screen shone on her face, blinding her as she watched the video again and again and again. Magnified who knew how many times. A flash. That flash was lives, it was billions of dollars lost, it was hope crashing.

"What happened?" her father asked.

"The International Space Station just blew up." She tapped the phone against her palm, her rage and anger and sorrow so overwhelming that no single emotion could produce the tears that were making her voice shake.

Her father swore quietly in the darkness. Then he said, "What now?"

Margot clenched her jaw so tightly that it made her throat ache. Her eyes were burning but the tears still wouldn't fall. She had some idea of the politics that would happen, the science that would happen, what the experts would say as details of the disaster came to light. But she knew her father didn't give a damn about that. He was asking about her. How she would deal with this, what her next steps would be, now that every hope and dream she'd ever had was currently burning up in the atmosphere somewhere over the Atlantic Ocean.

And now the tears finally did flow, because she honestly had no damn idea.

Chapter One

Ten Years Later

MARGOT SLIPPED on her aviators as she walked out into the sun. She moved like a gunslinger, straight back and rolling shoulders, like she was about to saddle up a horse and head out to wrangle some outlaws. But the only ride ahead of her was the small Cessna and, if it was a horse, it probably would have been shot and put out of its misery a long time ago. A woman in a pale blue jumpsuit was standing under one wing, head tilted back, hands out of sight within the wing's structure.

"Tell me something good, Knapp."

Rosie Knapp finished what she was doing before she dropped her hands. "In terms of good news, you're going to make some repairman very, very happy."

Margot winced. "Okay. Break my heart."

"Leaking wet wing."

"Plug it."

Knapp shook her head. "Sorry, boss. Wing has to come off and get sent away."

"Off?" Margot could feel her chest constricting at the imagined price tag. She pushed her hair out of her face and faced the plane. The sun glinted off of the windscreen, almost like it was winking at her. It was her primary plane, Hawkeye, and she hated the idea of it being 'injured.' "That doesn't sound like a cheap proposition."

"Or quick," Knapp said. "We'll be down to one plane, but it's better to get it taken care of now."

"I know, I know."

Margot looked past the plane at the foothills beyond the runway. They'd be down to one plane, Hunnicutt, but fuel problems had been making Hawkeye less reliable with each passing day. The pain and the price tag were inevitable, and she knew if she waited, both would only get worse. She pictured their calendar, tried to imagine how much emergency funds they had, and tried to calculate the losses. Finally she reached out and patted Hawkeye's body.

"Call around. See if you can get us a deal with one of your pals."

"Always," the mechanic said, already moving toward the hangar. "I'll let you know who I find."

"Thanks, Knapp."

She started back toward the terminal. She almost made it before the door flew open and Linnie Payton, the company's other pilot came running out. Her phone was in her hand, so Margot braced herself for some new fresh hell to start raining down on her.

"The ODIE is crashing!"

It was such an unexpected statement that Margot stopped in her tracks and took a second to process the words. Linnie stopped next to her and held up the phone, cupping her palm over the screen to block the sun. Margot squinted and leaned in. It seemed to be a weather camera, aimed at a sky full of thick fluffy clouds. A light streaked across the sky, like a shooting star but much lower.

"Whoa!"

"It's breaking news on every channel. They said the ODIE is crashing."

Margot understood now. ODIE, the Orbital Debris Independent Eradication engine, was the one-person spacecraft Astraea Aviation built in an effort to clear some of the debris around the planet. Colonel Noa Laurie had spent the past year and a half orbiting the Earth destroying anything large enough to puncture a hull or tear a spacesuit. So far the mission was successful, and several companies were already planning future excursions to the Moon, Mars, and rebuilding the lost space station. The future of space exploration was brighter than it had been in a decade.

But if it was failing...

The video was looping. "Are there any live shots?" Margot asked.

"No, this is all stuff from YouTube and Facebook. The TV news are just showing stock images from before the launch. It's moving too fast for anyone to track it very long, but... here." Linnie backed out of the video and went to another page. "This person has marked the sightings of it."

Margot looked at the map with the eye of a pilot. "This is not a crash. Look, there's a course correction here and here." She pointed. "If she stays on this trajectory, she can land in the Mojave. Unless she's aiming for the Pacific."

Linnie was confused. "So... so, what... the mission ended early? Why not make an announcement?" She groaned. "Maybe they did and I just didn't see it. Shit." She turned her phone and began searching. "No one is acting like this was planned. That lady on Channel 4 was practically crying."

Margot started walking back to the terminal. "There could have been a problem with the ship that required an abort. The colonel could have a medical issue that needs to be taken care of. There are a thousand reasons that ship might be coming in for what's sure to be a very hard landing, but we likely won't know the whole story for a while. Right now, I have a plane that's out of commission. I have way too much money going out, and Knapp just cut our income in half."

"You're going inside? But..." Linnie looked at the sky. "The ship might go over here any second."

"The odds of that would be—"

"Astronomical?"

"Not worth calculating." She held the door open. "Want to come help me, or...?"

Linnie reluctantly went inside. Margot thanked her with a nod, then paused on the threshold and looked up at the clear, cloudless sky. Colonel Laurie and the ODIE had been doing a good job so far from all the articles and reports she'd seen. She only hoped it would be enough to get mankind off the ground again. But that was someone else's problem. She had more terrestrial flights to figure out.

Two minutes after Margot went inside, Knapp caught a flicker of something coming in fast from the east. She craned her neck and watched as a very low-flying craft zipped across the sky like a bird hunting for prey. The sun glinted off its hull, a blinding white spark, and then it was out of sight.

"Huh," Knapp said.

She waited for a sonic boom and, when none happened, she went back to her work on the engine.

St. Elmo, Colorado, started life the same way a lot of towns did in this part of Colorado: miners. An initial burst of successes caused the town to bloom up from the foothills almost overnight, but the gold dried up and the people who had arrived in search of their fortune had nowhere else to go. The town was born from a mixture of false hope, shattered dreams, and resignation that Margot found appealing, and she'd always liked the mountains, so that was where she decided to settle in every sense of the word.

She liked flying, but it was always a means to an end. She liked Colorado but it was never where she wanted to end up. She always planned to live in Pasadena near JPL, or Johnson in Texas, or Kennedy in Florida. Colorado wasn't in the plan. A ceiling of fifteen thousand feet wasn't in the plan. But she had a job where she could leave the ground from time to time. She could spend a lazy afternoon cutting clouds in half if she wanted to. It was good enough to settle for, even if she did still sometimes dream of breaking atmosphere and seeing what weightlessness felt like.

When the ISS exploded, when NASA confirmed her mission was scrubbed and was unlikely to be rescheduled in the near future, Margot slipped into a depression and started thumbing through the stages of grief. Anger and shock got a lot of play. She didn't give herself the luxury of denial or bargaining. This had happened, it wasn't going to change because she wanted it really, really badly, and raging wouldn't get her anywhere. She felt trapped, as if Earth was a prison and space was her only way out. She could only think, "What the hell do I do now?"

She never would have imagined a tiny charter service would be her salvation. David Larkin, her mentor from NASA, made the deal happen for her. He was aware of how lost she would be in what some people were calling the "post-space era." He also knew the airline's owner was looking to sell, and Larkin convinced him that finding the right owner was more important than getting the right price. They came to an arrangement, and Magpie Air & Charters was born. Margot was still paying him installments, but she was making good progress on the debt, and the airline was slowly starting to find its legs.

At least it would, if Hawkeye wasn't having problems. Hunnicutt was reliable, but the idea of being down to just one plane made her itchy.

That night, at her dinner table in shorts and a T-shirt, she ate her dinner while she went over their finances. The news was playing on the TV behind her but she was only paying attention subconsciously, too focused on the numbers to listen fully. She only took notice when she caught the name "Laurie," and she paused to twist around the look at the screen.

"~home safe and sound following a year and a half in orbit." There was footage of Colonel Laurie being recovered from the crashed spacecraft, which bobbed in the water like a futuristic raft, and then giving a thumbs-up from a gurney as it was loaded into an ambulance. The anchor was still speaking. "~recovery and recuperation after spending so long in a zero-g environment. Astraea founder Enver Crane had this to say."

The footage cut to an attractive man smiling and squinting into the sun, the landing site visible over his shoulder.

"We consider this mission, while unfinished, to be an enormous success on many levels. First and foremost, Colonel Laurie has returned to Earth healthy and unharmed, which is the most important takeaway from this whole endeavor. And also, in terms of her, ah, objective, we're still crunching the numbers, but, ah, they're looking very, very good indeed. Agencies have been making plans ever since we launched eighteen months ago, and I'm confident those plans can, ah, begin moving forward very soon.

The stars belong to us once more."

The hairs on Margot's arms stood up. She swiped her left hand from wrist to elbow on her right arm until the chill had passed. She wasn't going to let herself get excited. She wasn't going to get her hopes up just to let herself be crushed all over again. She flexed her hands and turned around. The numbers in her bank book may be bad, but at least they were real. They were in her control, and any problems with them could be fixed.

Behind her, the news transitioned to *Wheel of Fortune*, and she let the bells and applause drown out any thoughts she might be harboring of how open the skies had just become.

Rosie mutilated Hawkeye to ship off its wing, leaving the plane looking forlorn and abandoned in the hangar. Margot tried to keep her mind off it by thinking about the alternatives instead. Their situation looked horrible, but it wasn't a crash. They could recover from this. Hawkeye would be whole again, and soon, and the peace of mind would be worth the expense. She and Linnie worked out a new schedule. Neither of them would get close their preferred flight hours but both would get plenty of time in the air.

Once that was settled, Margot took Hunnicutt out for a quick spin just to confirm it was in perfect working order. Having two planes out of commission at the same time would be horrible, but crashing their backup would be infinitely worse. They wouldn't be able to come back from that.

Hunnicutt was a fine plane, absolutely top-notch, but it wasn't her baby. She loved Hawkeye, doted on it, always chose to take it up if she had a choice between the two. It was the first plane she flew when she got to Colorado, and it held a special place in her heart for reliably getting her into the air whenever she wanted it to. Well, most of the time.

When she reached altitude, she relaxed into the cushion of her seat. There were eight seats behind her for passengers but, since the FAA didn't require a co-pilot on this particular plane, she could fit a ninth in the seat next to her if she needed to. She banked west toward the Rockies, letting the rolling land below pull away into a patchwork quilt. From this height, she could see pretty much every kind of landscape: mountain, plain, river, and forest. It reminded her that no place was any one thing, no matter how it might look on the surface.

Margot loved the feel of being in a cockpit, the yoke in her hand, feet resting on the rudder pedals, the hum of the engines comforting and all-encompassing.

As she relaxed, she thought about a conversation she'd had with a passenger not long ago. A beautiful woman: thick chestnut hair, big green eyes, accent, killer body. She had asked if she could sit next to Margot during the flight, even though other seats were available. She sheepishly said, "I get car sick if I ride in the backseat. This is close enough that I'm afraid it may be an issue." Margot agreed and, as the woman fastened her seatbelt, she'd added, "Plus the view is much better from here."

She didn't know if the comment was innocent or suggestive until a few minutes into the flight.

"Have you ever joined the Mile High Club?"

Margot's lips twisted into a smile. "Not really advisable when you're in the pilot seat."

"But other flights, surely..."

"Nope. Can't say I'm a member."

The woman had made a sound of disappointment and looked out the window for a few minutes. Margot risked a glance over. The passenger's hands were resting on her thigh, fingers loosely spread below the hem of her skirt.

"Four times," the woman said.

"Pardon?"

She looked over. "I've joined the club. And renewed my membership. Four times." She repositioned herself in the seat and faced forward, chest out. "Six if you count solo entries."

Margot had cleared her throat. "Oh. I think that counts."

"You're extremely attractive. I like your jaw."

"My *jaw?*"

"You are a handsome woman. You should find a way to make love while you're in the air. It's a magnificent feeling. Promise me, Handsome."

Margot couldn't help but laugh. "Fine, if you insist."

"I do. One hundred percent." She leaned in. "You should at least take off your clothes and fly naked sometime. I imagine there's no freer feeling."

At the time, Margot had laughed it off. She *was* a handsome woman, and she'd been hit on plenty of times. But the suggestion of flying naked had occasionally popped up, but there was always a passenger or some other consideration that kept her from taking the risk. But now... she could consider it a christening, a way to make herself feel as at home in Hunnicutt as she did in Hawkeye. She bit her lip, tried to think of a reason not to, and decided she'd never have a better opportunity.

She flipped on the autopilot and quickly unbuttoned her shirt. She shrugged out of it, heart pounding, smiling like a goon as she tossed it onto the passenger seat. Her undershirt followed quickly, then her bra. She kept an eye on the controls as she unfastened her belt. A few seconds later she stood up just long enough to get her pants, shoes, and socks off. She kept her briefs on, because she had issues about sitting on anything completely naked, and took control again.

"If I crash now, I'm going to be really... *really* pissed off."

But she couldn't help smiling as she banked again, angling to see Pikes Peak in the distance. On a clear day, when she got enough altitude, she imagined she could see all the way to both coasts, though she knew there was no way it could be possible. The sun was setting, perfectly casting into the windows to gild every surface with the last light of day. Margot looked down and saw her own skin was golden, and she laughed, sweeping a hand through her hair.

"This could be the beginning of a very dangerous habit," she said, warning herself against enjoying it too much.

She gave herself ten minutes of naked flying before she set a course for home. Hunnicutt not only proved itself worthy of taking the lead, now she felt a personal connection to it. She'd never flown Hawkeye naked, and she had a feeling she'd remember that for a long time.

"We're going to get along just fine, Hunnicutt."

She brought the plane in without issue, switching to autopilot to get her clothes back on before she got anywhere near the airport. Night seemed to fall unnaturally fast as she came down below the mountains. She thought about calling Rosie to let her know she was coming in, but she would just ask how Hunnicutt had performed. Then she'd ask again on the ground. Margot preferred not to have the same conversation twice.

She was surprised Rosie wasn't waiting for her in the spacious hangar, one quarter of which had been transformed into a mechanic's version of a dragon hoard. Tall shelves filled with every tool and small spare part imaginable marked the boundaries. Three red tool cabinets stood like sentries in random parts of the room, their shadows merging with oil stains on the concrete. Stacks of spare parts created landmarks in Rosie's sanctum, tall obstacles that an uninvited guest risked getting snagged on if they dared trespass where they didn't belong. There was also a basketball hoop that she and Rosie occasionally challenged each other on.

Margot put Hunnicutt to bed before she went out into the darkened terminal. It wasn't much of an airport; small waiting area combined with a baggage claim, Magpie's ticket counter, a bank of phone booths, and three vending machines. A food truck serving burgers and tacos parked outside from mid-morning to late afternoon, and it was responsible for a much higher percentage of Margot's meals than she cared to quantify. She went to one of the vending machines and bought herself a bottle of grape soda.

As she passed the Magpie offices, she heard a chair scrape across the floor. She changed direction and went behind the ticket counter, intending to tell Linnie that Hunnicutt had passed its test, but she paused at the door when she heard Rosie's laugh. She leaned closer, her ear almost touching the fogged glass, and listened closer. Another scrape, then an unmistakable kiss.

Margot stepped back and winced at how close she'd come to walking in on them again. It wasn't their fault; they probably expected her to spend a lot longer up in the air. And once things were underway, they might have been too preoccupied to hear her come back in. Although the amount of distraction required to miss a plane landing a few feet away was... impressive.

She wasn't jealous. She refused to be jealous. She would never sleep with someone she did business with, and neither of them was her type. She was happy for them. They deserved to have a little fun, blow off some steam at the end of the day. If she was jealous of anything, it was the situation. It was her desk. She should be the one moving it across the floor with some hot, horny woman.

But she only had time to meet passengers, and they were as high on the no-go list as colleagues. She really needed to get out more. Expand her figurative horizons, meet some new potential partners. It was either that or relax her standards, and that was a~

Rosie moaned.

Margot spun on the ball of her foot and retreated, waving over her shoulder as if they could see her. "Have fun, ladies," she whispered, much too quietly for them to have heard, and hurried out into the night. Once she was outside she stopped and craned her neck to look up at the stars. It was a beautiful and clear night, with so many stars it was truly awe-inspiring. She'd gotten so close, so incredibly close, that she could almost taste the thin atmosphere.

And now the way was clear. Colonel Noa Laurie had done her job, and scientists all over the world were hatching schemes to make humanity's triumphant return to outer space.

Tears pricked Margot's eyes. It was like Linnie and Rosie in the office. She was so close to something she wanted so damn much, right fucking next to it, and for some reason it was out of reach.

Margot raised her bottle in a toast.

"Whoever goes up there," she said, "I hope you fucking appreciate it."

She took a drink and continued to her car. Tomorrow was another day of skimming the edge of her dream.

Chapter Two

Margot waited two weeks for a call. She didn't know who it would come from, maybe some higher-up she'd never even heard of, but she still expected some kind of contact. It wouldn't be a mission, not this far out, but it was abundantly clear that pieces were being put in place in anticipation of locking in plans. It wasn't a complete fantasy to think they might want her back. She was still in shape, still young enough to qualify, she'd maintained her flight credentials, and she had actually gone through astronaut training. She was more prepared than anyone else they might get. She occupied her mind with work, flying tours and charters, taking graduates and honeymooners up over the Rockies, witnessing engagements and arguments among the passengers.

Tuesday and Wednesday were her weekend, and those were the days when she really let the anxiety in. She wandered her house, stared out the window, tried to imagine what was happening in Washington or the Mojave desert or wherever the new breed of spacefarers were plotting their trips. Her home was small, but she loved it. She loved the little covered patio, the high adobe brick walls around her postage stamp backyard. She paced from the bedroom, cluttered with clothes and books, to the kitchen on the other side of the house where she prepared meals she wasn't hungry for, and occasionally came to rest in the living room long enough to watch most of something on TV.

But she always ended up back at the patio door, craning her neck to look at the wedge of sky between the mountains and the pergola. She always had the phone in her hand, though it was loud enough and her house small enough that she couldn't have missed its ring no matter where she left it.

She tapped it against her thigh, chewed her lip, and waited. And waited.

On the second Wednesday after Colonel Laurie's mission was declared a success, Margot realized she had no clue what the current world of space flight looked like. Some people had stayed put after the crisis, riding desks in an agency most politicians considered defunct. Others were like her and moved on with their lives, found new dreams, put aside their crazy hopes and dreams for something more practical.

She waited until it was mid-afternoon in Florida before she dialed a familiar number and paced her kitchen as it rang.

Ward Hawkins picked up on the third ring, declaring his name into the receiver like it was the answer to an unasked question.

"Commander," she said, unable to drop the rank or the smile that popped up when she heard his voice. Hawkins would have been the commander of her mission, and she'd gotten to know him extremely well during their training. Hearing his lazy Wyoming drawl was like hearing from a beloved high school teacher. "Sorry to bother you at home. This is--"

"I know damn well who it is, Sullivan. You've got a lot of nerve taking this long to call me."

"Sorry, sir. Things kept coming up."

He made a dismissive sound. "Where'd you end up?"

"Colorado. A little town called St. Elmo, right up against the Rockies. It's beautiful. I fly planes."

"Good to keep your head in the clouds," he said. "Can you see Pikes Peak?"

She said, "Every single day."

"Don't take it for granted, Sullivan, not even once."

"I'll do my best. What about you? Did you ever make an honest woman out of Kate?"

Ward made the sound again. "More like pulled her down to my level. But however you want to call it, we've been married six years now. You can send her your condolences later."

Margot laughed. "It's good to hear your voice again, Hawk. You know, um, one of my planes... my best plane... is named Hawkeye. It's sort of a MASH reference and sort of an homage to you."

"I think Alan Alda gets more credit on that than I do, but I appreciate the thought." He paused. "Look, kid, I know why you're calling. I watched every bit of footage Colonel Laurie had, and I paid attention to every single thing she did while she was in space. I even marked on the damn calendar when she passed the threshold to make launching feasible. So I know what you want. But I can't help you get it. I left not long after you did."

She tried not to feel too crushed. "They have to be open to the idea, right? Everything on the news is about how people are racing to be the first ones back up there. Surely choosing from the existing astronaut pool is the best option. It will save time, and–”

“Sullivan,” he interrupted. “Look, the simple fact is that you were twenty-nine when you got our mission. It's been ten years.”

Margot frowned. “Don't you dare say I'm too old.”

“Ordinarily, no. But age means different things in different circumstances. You wouldn't expect me to start playing pro-football at my relatively ancient age.”

“Noa Laurie is in her late forties,” Margot said.

“Enver Crane chose her to make a statement,” Hawkins said. “She was the sole survivor of the ISS, so it meant something for her to be the first one back up to clear the way for everyone else. It was a narrative. It had to be her to open the door. What's the narrative of sending us up there now?”

Margot said, “That we're picking up where we left off.”

Hawkins' voice was compassionate. “It's the past. Looking backward, not forward. I've had a couple people call me to help them recruit the new ASCANs. They want young, Sullivan. The astronaut candidates they're looking at are twenty-five, twenty-six. A new generation taking the first steps into the future. I hate to say it, but the window closed on us.”

Her cheeks were wet, and she used the cuff of her sleeve to dry them. She hadn't realized how much hope she'd been putting into this day until it was snatched away from her.

Hawkins, bless him, kept his mouth shut to let her cry silently. She rested her forehead on the glass of the patio door and got her breathing under control, inhaling deeply and letting it out before she spoke again.

“So there's no chance.”

“Hey, never say never. John Glenn was almost eighty when they let him go back.”

Margot scoffed. “I'm not John Glenn.”

“No. Me neither. I know it's not the same, but if you want to join this committee the agency is putting together to vet the new crop–”

“Choose the people who get to live my dream? God, no. That would be...” She shivered. “No, I can't do that.”

Hawkins said, “I understand. I'd probably feel the same way.” His voice softened. “I really am sorry. It sucks what happened to you. It was cruel. Maybe one of the cruelest things I've ever seen happen to someone.”

“Thanks, Hawk.” She wiped her eyes again. “Look, um. I... I have to get going... Give my love to Kate, all right?”

“Will do. Stay in touch, all right?”

“Yes, sir.”

She hung up and went to the dinner table, sank into a chair, and covered her face with her hand. She finally had to admit how much of the past ten years had been biding time, waiting for the moment to return to the life that had been kept from her. The idea of handing the airline off to

Linnie was always at the back of her mind. She'd avoided relationships because it wouldn't be fair to drop her partner the second a mission opened up for her. She didn't even have a pet, for crying out loud. She crossed her arms on the table in front of her and put her head down.

She'd kept herself on standby for ten years for absolutely no reason.

Margot was sitting on the back porch of her father's house when he came home from work. She heard him put his things down, the rustle of take-out bags as he prepared his dinner, and the sound of the fridge door as he grabbed a beer. She didn't say anything, she just lay on the chaise lounge and watched the color fade from the sky. It was like seeing paint wiped away to reveal a true masterpiece underneath. A vast spray of stars from horizon to horizon. Her father lived far enough from the city that light pollution wasn't much of a concern, but it would pale in comparison to...

To a viewpoint she'd never get to see.

He finally spotted her outside and opened the door. "Hey. I didn't see a car parked outside."

"I walked."

"From... from where, the airport? That's got to be, what, ten miles."

She shrugged. "Sounds about right. I stayed in shape. Perfectly qualified astronaut candidate. ASCAN. Now I really am an ass-can."

"Oh boy." He came out and sat on the other chair. He was holding a white box of Chinese food in one hand, a beer in the other. He put the beer down between his feet and started opening the box. "I didn't get any extra, but I'm willing to part with the eggroll."

"No thanks."

"Fortune cookie?"

She laughed harshly. "Yeah, sure. Tell me what the fucking future holds."

"Okay," he said. "What happened?"

She sat up and put her feet down on the patio. "I'm never going to space."

He carefully weighed his response. "I know it's been a really bleak time... but~"

"Hawkins basically told me no one will want me on a crew. Too old. They want... young, fresh, hopeful. Apparently forty is ancient in terms of astronauts. In what world is forty old?"

"Well. Football players~"

She grunted and shot to her feet. "What is it with guys and football analogies? Noa Laurie is forty-seven, okay? Why does she get to go back up when I never got the chance? And don't answer that, I know it was symbolic, okay, so just spare me." She put her fingers to her temples, pressing hard as she started pacing.

Her father started eating, giving her the silence she needed.

"I-I..." She stopped and threw her arms out to either side. "I have a good life. The airline is fine, it's fine. Linnie and Rosie are amazing coworkers. I get to fly every single day in one of the most beautiful places in the world. It's the kind of life a lot of people would kill for."

He thought. "Do you want to be President?"

She stared at him. "What? No. Of course not. What a terrible job."

"Same," he said. "Seems like the ultimate no-win scenario. And yet, there are people who spend millions upon millions of dollars running for the job. I don't want to be a movie star, either, even though I absolutely have the looks for it. Don't say a word."

Despite herself, Margot smiled.

"You can't judge your life based on someone else's dream. Magpie Air might be someone else's fantasy, but it's not yours. Of course it's going to seem a little... uncharming. But that doesn't have to make it bad. No one dreams of being a single dad to a little girl who liked hurling herself down hills in soapbox derby cars. There were times, back then, when I would rage about how unfair life was. But looking back, it's my life. This is my life. And it's not something to be sad about or ashamed of, just because it's wrong."

Margot came back and sat down across from him. "I'm sorry I insisted on being a daredevil."

He shrugged and winked at her. "At least you wore a helmet and pads. And you were going to lose those teeth anyway. The real horror would have been having a boring daughter."

She hunched her shoulders and looked down at her shoes.

"You can spend the night here, and in the morning I'll drive you back to the airport."

Margot looked at the takeout box. "Is that from Laurel Lee's?"

He looked offended. "Why would I get Chinese from anyone else?"

"And you're really not going to share? With your daughter? Your *sad* daughter?"

"Cry me a river," he said, "you'll take your eggroll and you'll like it."

She said, "You're cruel."

"*You're* uninvited. Play your cards right and I'll take you to IHOP on the way to the airport."

She smiled. "I love you, Dad."

"Yeah, yeah, yeah, you're still not getting my dumplings."

After her return to Magpie, Margot buried herself in work. She took extra flights and kept her eyes straight ahead whether she was on the ground or in the air. There was no point in looking up anymore. So what if she never made it to space? Billions of people never got the opportunity, never even thought about it, and at least she got to fly. That was something. She confirmed with Linnie that her afterhours activities with Rosie only happened on her desk, never Margot's, and reminded her to lock the door to avoid any uncomfortable situations. Life was fine. Life was normal. Normal was good.

Hawkeye's wing came back and soon her boy was whole again, as ready to get back in the air as she was to be behind the yoke once more.

Margot was in the hangar with Rosie preparing to take Hawkeye out for a shakedown flight when the phone that only received calls from the ticket counter rang. Rosie trotted over to answer, which she did with an affected Scottish accent.

"Aye, Captain, engineering here." She listened, then put the phone against her shoulder. "Hey, Margot, Linnie says a passenger wants to have a word with you."

"Complaint?"

"Didn't sound like a complaint."

"Fingers crossed." Margot put down the clipboard with her checklist and headed for the door. When she and Rosie passed each other, Margot said, "That *Star Trek* thing. You guys do that behind closed doors, don't you?"

"I'll never tell."

"She insists on being Kirk, doesn't she?"

Rosie grinned and did the Vulcan salute.

Margot chuckled to herself as she headed out into the terminal. Linnie was at the ticket counter talking to a woman whose back was to the room. Long black hair, a leather jacket, jeans, a nice ass. She had her elbows resting on the counter, and was currently laughing at something Linnie said before she spotted Margot.

"Here's the big boss lady now."

The woman turned and Margot nearly tripped over her feet when she recognized Nazanin Shirazi, Nina, one of the Mission Specialists from her scuttled mission. She was smiling, but her eyes gave away her anxiety about just dropping in without warning. Margot returned the smile, hopefully without the trepidation, and closed the distance between them.

"Oh, great, probably complaining about the in-flight snacks."

Nina rolled her head back in exasperation. "Well, how can anything compare to the feasts we had at NASA? We've been spoiled."

Margot offered a hug, and Nina accepted. "Good to see you again, Nina."

"You too. It's been way too long."

"Did you two meet?" Margot asked, gesturing at Linnie.

Nina nodded. "We did. An all-lady airline? I like it."

Margot said, "It wasn't really my intent, but I decided to hire the best and things just sort of worked out. So what are you doing here?"

"Just passing through. Relocating, and St. Elmo was only a few miles out of my way. I heard you were out here now, so..."

"Heard from Hawkins...?"

Nina feigned innocence. "Oh, you know, he might have been the one who brought it up, now that you mention it."

Margot laughed." Uh-huh. Old busybody. You can buy me dinner to apologize for talking behind my back."

"Deal!" Nina leaned closer to Linnie, lowering her voice to a stage whisper. "See, when you're in a new place, the trick is to offend a local and then offer to buy them dinner to make up for it. That way you're guaranteed to eat at the nicest place in town." To Margot, she said, "When are you free? I can kill some time if you need to take a flight or something."

"Actually," Margot said, "I was just about to take Hawkeye up for a test drive, to make sure everything is working right. Wanna come up with me?"

"Is that allowed?"

"I'm the boss, so yeah, if you want."

Nina tensed with excitement, hunching her shoulders. "Boy, I haven't been in a plane in forever. I'm driving back and forth between my new place and the old one. I'd love to go up if you're sure it's not a problem."

"Absolutely. It'll be nice to have a copilot who doesn't bug the crap out of me for a change."

Linnie said, "Hey!"

Margot aimed a finger at her. "Talk behind my back, get roasted. Them's the rules." She slung an arm around Nina's shoulders and walked her back toward the hangar. "You know, before I knew that was you standing there, I checked you out a little."

"Oh yeah? What was the verdict?"

"Nice ass."

Nina laughed and put her arm around Margot's waist. "From you, I'll consider that the highest of praise, my dear."

"I'm surprised you went with Hunnicutt for the other plane," Nina said once they were in the air. "I would have thought Houlihan, for an outfit as female-centric as this."

"We thought about it," Margot admitted, "but we didn't want to risk any kind of boy-plane versus girl-plane competition even among ourselves, so..." She shrugged. "We decided it was easier to stick with the dynamic duo."

"Makes sense."

Margot leaned closer to Nina's seat. "The secret is, I recast the whole show in my head. Houlihan's a dude, Hawkeye and Hunnicutt are both women."

Nina laughed. "Now *that's* what I'm talking about! Who did you recast?"

"Hawkeye is Julia Louis-Dreyfus, Hunnicutt is Aisha Tyler."

Nina applauded. "Okay, now I want to see that version."

Margot grinned. "Anything in particular you want to see while we're up here? Pikes Peak?"

"Absolutely. Just no barrel rolls."

"And you call yourself an astronaut."

Nina laughed again, but this time it was an uncomfortable sound. Uncomfortable enough that Margot looked over to make sure her passenger wasn't about to throw up. She remembered Nina's comment about driving to her new place instead of flying.

"Are you okay? I know if it's been a while since you were in the air, it can be a little..."

"Oh, it's not that." She cleared her throat. "I was hoping for a better, uh, situation to bring this up, but maybe it's better to just do it like a band-aid." She lowered her head, chin on chest, and very low and soft, said, "Shi-i-i-it."

Margot stared at the mountains ahead. She braced herself. "This ought to be good."

"You should know that I... I didn't..." She looked out the window. "Hawkins found out and called me, and he said it should come from me. You know due to the circumstances they're not doing the normal candidate selection, and it's a bit more of a free-for-all. Anyone with the proper training is eligible for missions. I thought face-to-face would be the best..."

"Come on, out with it," Margot snapped, although by now she could guess what Nina was about to say. "Band-aid, right?"

Nina exhaled and seemed to deflate. "I've been assigned to the first shuttle to go back up."

"Of course you have," Margot muttered. "You're a fantastic astronaut. You're younger than me, too, so... two whole years. But still younger." Her voice had grown louder and she sounded almost manic to her own ear. She couldn't even imagine how she sounded to Nina.

"It doesn't hurt that I'm Iranian. Having a brown face aboard–"

"Hey, no," Margot said. "I may be hurting, but I won't let you pull that shit. You were chosen because you're a good astronaut and a fucking brilliant engineer."

Nina looked sidelong at her. "Yeah, but if there was another Iranian woman who was a little younger than me in the program... who knows, right? If this was entirely about merit, you would be the one leading the mission."

Margot looked over. "Wait, you know who's leading the mission?"

Nina looked out the window, giving Margot the back of her head.

"Who?" She waited. "Nazanin, who is leading the mission?"

Nina took a deep breath. "Doc."

Margot couldn't help but laugh. She slapped her hand on the side wall. "Doc. Sure. So that's their type of..." She forced herself to calm down, even as she wanted to guide the plane into the sheerest rock face she could find.

Earl "Doc" Bennett was an old guard, cigar-smoking pilot with a macho swagger. He could make "ma'am" sound like an insult because, from his mouth, it probably was. He had to be in his fifties now, but even as infuriating as it was, she could understand the logic behind putting him on the crew.

"Hawkins said they were looking at kids in their twenties."

"To fill up the Astronaut Candidates group, yeah," Nina said. "But they're also very aware of the media circus it's going to be. It's more like casting a movie than anything based on true merit. They want people who look good. They want 'personalities', and Doc will give the kind of interviews that go viral. Get people talking. Get people interested."

"Right. Well. Nice to see who they're willing to make exceptions for."

"I'm sorry. Hawkins told me what you were going through. If there was any way–"

Margot cut her off with a wave of her hand. "I don't want you to waste any time feeling guilty about me, okay? I trained with you. I don't care what the brass was thinking when they put your name on the list. I know for a fact you belong there, so I'm happy for you. I want to make that absolutely clear. Clear?"

"Yes, ma'am."

Margot squared her shoulders. "It just..."

"It fucking sucks," Nina said.

"Fucking, fucking sucks."

They flew on in silence for a few minutes.

"I'm still taking you out to dinner."

"I thought I was supposed to be treating *you*."

Margot shook her head. "You're going to space. I'm buying you dinner. It's going to be a celebration." She held out her hand between the seats. "Congratulations, Astronaut Shirazi."

"Thank you." Nina gripped Margot's hand. "If I have an opportunity to leave Doc on the Moon, I'll do it in your honor."

Margot laughed. "Deal." She withdrew her hand, wiped the back of it across her cheek, and pretended to check her instruments as an excuse to blink away her tears. "Everything looks solid right now. I think I can give Hawkeye a clean bill of health. Are you ready to head back?"

"I'm up for another loop of this little horseshoe."

"One more spin," Margot said. "You got it."

She banked around to take another lap.

CHAPTER THREE

MARGOT'S GROUP of astronaut candidates were nicknamed the Magpies by the previous group. The bird was considered good luck in Eastern culture, a reference to the selection of Deborah Kim, and it was also widely regarded as the smartest animal on the planet. Margot had been skeptical about that claim but the internet backed it up. A magpie could recognize itself in a mirror, mimic human speech, use tools, play games, and work in teams. Once she learned that, Margot was more than happy to accept the bird as their mascot, and to use it as the name of her airline once she was a civilian again.

Magpies also held funerals for each other.

The night after Nina's celebratory dinner, Margot went into her closet and removed the box of NASA mementos she'd tucked away when she moved into the house. She sat cross-legged on her bed and laid the mementos out on the duvet in front of her, considering each one before moving on to the other like she was dealing herself a poker hand, rearranging them in chronological order.

She had the official group photo they'd taken in their flight suits, all high school yearbook smiles and perfect postures. She was standing beside Nina at the far right of the photo and she distinctly remembered the buzz of conversation while the photographer was getting the shot ready. She looked out over the group: seven pilots, twelve mission specialists, and four specialists from international partners: France, Italy, and two from Canada.

She had looked at their faces, all full of hope and excitement, and she'd known in her heart that not all of them would go to space. They were candidates, not official crew, and NASA had learned early on that disasters could happen at any second. But she'd been confident. She'd looked at her fellow Magpies and wondered which of them would have their dreams crushed, never imagining it would be her. They'd all dreamed of this moment, sure, but hadn't she *earned* it? She was here, she only had to be patient and wait.

She picked up her mission patch and ran her thumb over the stitching. A bird spreading its wings over the globe, with its beak aiming at a small red dot in the distance.

Edward Jarosky had seen her eyeing the other candidates and flashed her a smile. "Can you believe one of us might actually be the first person to set foot on Mars?"

In the years since, she decided everything that happened afterward was his fault. She could have called him Jinx Jarosky if she'd been in the nicknaming mood.

Margot put aside the official portraits and picked up the Polaroids she'd taken. Everyone had a smartphone, but there was something about the training facilities that insisted on a more analog approach. It was counterintuitive, since they were dealing with some of the most advanced technology available, but that didn't stop her from getting a camera from a pawn shop and carrying it everywhere.

A shot of Nina's head crowned by a shuttle model.

The backs of the other four women in their group, all suited up, walking across the runway toward the Vomit Comet. She really loved that shot, and she picked it up to look closer. Nazanin, Joyce Hetrick, Deborah Kim, and Katie Lindal. Five women out of twenty-three candidates wasn't exactly a great ratio, but it was better than it could have been, and it definitely helped them all feel less alone. Katie had suggested they do everything in their power to make sure they all ended up on a mission.

"Maybe even the same one," she said.

"Yeah, like that will happen," Joyce laughed.

Katie held her arms out. "Why not? It's bound to happen someday, so why not now? With us? We're qualified and we're ready. I'd be happy to take any one of you to Mars with me."

It really was a joke, but Margot had taken it to heart. She would also have gladly flown with any of those five women, so having them all on a shuttle with her was definitely something to hope for.

That night, she'd gone to Katie's hotel room after they were dismissed for the night. Over pizza and beers, slouching together on the bed, Margot casually said, "There's one flaw in your scheme for us to be the first women on Mars. Eventually we're going to get lonely."

Katie had shrugged. "Desperate times. I'll have to pack some really good movies to get me through those long cold Martian nights."

Margot had casually brushed her finger over Katie's arm. "What if the times get really desperate? Or the nights are colder than you thought?"

Katie tensed. "Oh. I'm not..."

Margot shrugged. "I'm just saying, if women are literally the only people on the whole planet, it might be nice to have an alternative."

"Yeah," Katie said. "Sure." She laughed and looked away, her cheeks reddening. "But you're... I mean, are you actually attracted to me?"

"I am," Margot said, reaching up to tuck a stray hair behind Katie's ear. "Very much so."

Katie took a drink of her beer, then leaned across the open pizza box and kissed Margot. It was a violent, experimental kiss, and Margot kept her eyes open until Katie withdrew.

"Well?" she asked after a silent minute had passed.

Katie ran her thumb across her bottom lip. "Well," she said slowly. "Kissing is fine... what else would we do?"

Margot had spent the rest of the night demonstrating. In the morning, they came up with lame jokes about "space style" and "becoming Marsexual." They went back to training as if nothing had changed, and a couple of nights a week Margot went to Katie's room to help her with a more private kind of training. They were lying in bed after a few weeks of meetups, and Katie had kicked Margot's hip with one bare foot.

"If I find out I've actually been bisexual my whole life right before I leave a planet full of women, I'm going to be pissed."

She was safe, as it turned out. The International Space Station was destroyed, their mission was scrubbed, and they went from being astronaut candidates to has-beens. Never-was, to be more accurate. They were standing at the threshold when the door was slammed in their faces, and no one gave them any idea where they were supposed to go or what they were supposed to do next.

The last Margot heard, Katie was teaching in San Diego. She pulled out her laptop and did a little digging on social media. It turned out Katie was married to a man, but had enough posts about Pride that it seemed clear she really did have an awakening. Margot was happy that something good had come out of their essentially useless training period. She considered sending a message, the prompt was right there, but she closed the tab without succumbing to temptation.

Magpies held funerals for each other, and it was time to say goodbye to these birds. She gathered the photos, only saving one or two that she truly thought were special beyond their meaning to her, and carried them into the kitchen. She had a metal trash can and she placed the photos and papers into it and found a box of matches in the drawer. She struck one, touched it to the corner of a photo until it curled, and then dropped it in.

She watched as the pictures burned. Most of the group was happy, she knew. Jonathan Colman died in a car accident four or five years ago, and

Michael Kidd was in prison for assault, but otherwise the last group of potential astronauts ended up leading relatively unremarkable lives. Marriages, divorces, new careers, families, lives that had nothing to do with strapping themselves to a rocket and flying farther than any human ever had before. They seemed to have accepted they would never leave the planet.

Except for Nina and Doc, of course. They were finally going to live the dream. She was happy for them, really.

Maybe not Doc.

She doused the burning mementos, got up, and went to the bathroom. She shed clothes as she went, letting them lay wherever they happened to fall. She turned on the shower and let the spray hit her, flattening her hair before it cascaded down her face. This was something she wouldn't have been able to get on the ISS, or even Mars. Water would have been a precious commodity. That was something to be grateful for. Long showers. Wasteful showers. Except, she realized with a twinge of regret, the state was currently in a drought. She turned off the water and got out of the stall, wrapping herself in a towel.

The truly sad fact was that her trysts with Katie had been her last relationship. After the disaster, after NASA was all but shuttered, she was too depressed to even think about dating. Then she was too preoccupied with Magpie, and then busy with work, and eventually having a relationship just wasn't something she thought about.

Of course now she was thinking about it. Now she was thinking about how nice it would be to have someone lying behind her on the bed. Someone who could say all the things a partner was supposed to say. Comfort her, make her feel better about everything. She looked back as if a woman might have magically appeared, but the mattress was still empty.

She untied her towel and laid back on the bed, letting her skin dry in the cool air-conditioning. After a minute she reached up, grabbed her pillow, and moved it between her legs. She squeezed it between her thighs, held it in place with one hand, and closed her eyes as she began moving her hips against it. It wasn't really about sex, although having a partner instead of a pillow would have been nice. She was mainly after the endorphins, that burst of sweet feel-good static that came with a climax. She was close. She was—

Her phone rang.

She swore. Her whole body tensed. She reached for the phone and breathed through her mouth as she looked at the unknown number. She debated ignoring the call and tossing the phone, but she was annoyed and frustrated enough to make the person on the other side regret calling so late at night. She swept her thumb across the screen and put the phone to her ear.

"This better be good, I was about to come."

There was silence on the other end of the line. Margot cringed and opened her mouth to apologize to the poor telemarketer or wrong number who had the misfortune to call her.

"Well, don't let me stop you."

Margot opened her eyes and stared at the ceiling. She didn't recognize the woman's voice, but it was sexy. Deep without being husky, light enough to sound like she was on the verge of either a laugh or breaking into song. The amusement may have come from the situation, but she also sounded intrigued. Margot remained still and silent, almost convinced the woman had hung up.

"Are you really this quiet?" she asked.

"No." Margot closed her eyes and began moving her hips again. She grunted and moaned, playing up her pleasure now that she had an audience. "Mm, yeah."

The woman said, "That's more like it. Are you in bed?"

"Mm-n," Margot said. "Naked. Just took a shower."

"Nice. Very nice. Are you using your hand or a toy?"

Margot's cheeks were on fire. Who the hell was this woman? "Pillow."

"Oh, I like that. Very clever, Margot."

Her eyes opened. It was one thing when this was a wrong number or some cold call, but the woman knew her name? She panicked and disconnected the call, dropping the phone. Unfortunately she'd gone too close to the edge. Brushing against the pillow one last time finished her off. Her arms flexed, her toes curled, and she arched her back as she pressed herself down against the pillow, riding it through to the end of her orgasm.

She rolled onto her side, one arm crossed protectively over her chest, and retrieved her phone. She looked at the unknown number and tried not to think of who it might have been on the other end. What if it had been someone from NASA or a private agency? What if someone had decided to take a chance on her, had been offering up her last chance of going to space, and she'd ruined it because she was jilling off?

"Idiot," she said. "Fucking idiot."

She tossed the pillow toward the hamper, sat up, and blocked the number. Even if it was someone calling with a job offer, she couldn't imagine ever working with the stranger who had been on the other end of that call. Blocking any future calls and living in blissful ignorance was much better than being forced to say no if the woman called back.

A week after Nina's visit, after Margot's inadvertent phone sex had been all but forgotten, all flights were grounded due to a chain of thunderstorms. The National Weather Service was reporting that the storms would cycle all day, leaving her no choice but to cancel and postpone everything until they had clear skies. Weather was one of the worst parts about doing business in this part of the country. Adding insult to injury was the fact that she thought flying in a thunderstorm would be absolutely gorgeous and thrilling as hell. But she couldn't risk the planes.

Margot gave Linnie and Rosie the day off, and they elected to use it to drive to Denver. Margot felt a little abandoned, but it was nice the airport to herself for a chance. The dark sky and the lack of passengers gave the place an eerie, otherworldly feel. Her footsteps echoed, and her voice sounded much louder than usual in the cavernous space.

Even the food truck wasn't risking the weather, so she had to venture out into the rain to pick up lunch. The city seemed deserted as she drove to the closest restaurant and picked up a chicken sandwich. The clouds hung low over the buildings, obscuring the mountains and keeping the sky and its temptations safely out of view.

She was gone for less than twenty minutes but, when she returned, a car was parked in front of the main entrance. She cursed herself for not locking the doors as she entered the still-empty terminal. The office door *was* locked, so she doubted anyone could have gotten in there. She left her food at the ticket counter and went down the corridor to the hangar with a growing sense of dread. If someone was messing with the planes...

A woman was standing next to Hawkeye, running one hand over the fuselage like someone might stroke the flank of a horse. The plane's starboard wing was between them, a barrier that Margot was grateful for as she crossed the room.

"Excuse me, you can't be back here." She tried to sound intimidating. The hangar helped the illusion by echoing her voice and making her sound bigger than she really was.

The intruder wasn't shaken. She turned and smiled, pulled off her sunglasses, and ducked under the wing rather than taking the long way around.

"Are you Margot Sullivan?"

"I am." She came closer, wary. The woman's voice sounded familiar. "Can I help you with something?"

The woman smiled. The woman had spectacular eyes; storm blue and shadowed by thick black eyebrows. Her hair was parted on the left and swept across her forehead to frame the right side of her face in such a perfect arch that Margot wondered how she had gotten from the parking lot without the wind making a mess of it. Her red blouse and the slacks it was tacked into were damp with the rain but her skin was dry, implying she'd been inside for a while. Maybe she'd spent the time fixing her hair for some reason.

"I certainly hope so. I'm J. Colleen Eckles." She held out her hand. "It's nice to meet you."

Margot instinctively took the offered hand. "You really can't be back here. We can talk in the~" She suddenly realized where she'd heard the voice before. "Did... you call my cell phone last week?"

Colleen chuckled and averted her gaze. "Uh yeah. Yes, I did."

"Oh, shit." Margot dropped her hand. "You need to leave."

"Wait, wait," Colleen held up her hands. "I'm sorry for just dropping in like this, but I think you must have blocked my number. I tried calling back the... the next day to apologize, but you didn't answer. Honestly, I don't really blame you. I took advantage of the situation. I apologize."

Margot shifted her weight. "It's fine. It's whatever. I don't know." She rolled her shoulders and looked around for some kind of escape. "What are you doing here?"

"I didn't just randomly call you that night. I really did have something to discuss with you. And after what happened, and then you blocked my number, I decided it was better to have the conversation in person. So here I am. I have a proposition for you."

"You want to hire me?"

"Sort of. Probably not in the way you're thinking. I don't want you to fly me anywhere. I need you to pilot something for me."

Margot's heart thudded against her ribs, but fear closed her throat, making her feel choked and beaten at the same time.

"Who do you work for? NASA? Astraea?"

Colleen pressed her lips together and furrowed her brow. In a moment her whole expression twisted and then relaxed. "Neither. Not anymore. Do you know anything about ion engines?"

"Some. It wasn't really my area of expertise."

"No. No, you were a pilot. You were trained to fly." She stepped closer, her excitement building. She put her arms behind her back, inadvertently striking the pose of a lecturing professor. "Ion engines are the key to interstellar travel. They have the ability to get us past Mars, past Pluto and the Kuiper Belt, far enough to really start exploring the universe. We can kick down our neighbor's fence and wander around their backyard."

Margot said, "Sure. Even I know ion engines are the goal, but they're still theoretical. They're too impractical."

"They *were* impractical, because they lacked the thrust to get a ship off the ground." Her eyes were shining and her voice had become more measured. "Generally people believe that even if you had an ion engine, you'd need a second, traditional engine just to break atmosphere, and the added weight and fuel negates the benefits. But an ion engine that can get a ship off the ground by itself exists. And it will *work*. I know it can."

"There's a catch." Margot had to keep her voice steady. She could feel the old excitement building, all the same traps she always found herself drawn to. "There has to be some kind of a catch."

Colleen wet her lips and looked around the hangar. "Are we alone here?"

"Just tell me."

"The engine exists," Colleen said. "I know it exists, because I designed it. I helped build it."

"But..."

"If we want to use it, we're going to have to steal it."

CHAPTER FOUR

IT WOULD be easy to pretend this moment wasn't really happening. The windows were almost pitch black, the airport was empty, silent, and still, and the beautiful woman in front of her had the voice of a Mysterious Sexy Stranger Margot had heard on the phone while masturbating. And this succubus was here now offering Margot everything she'd ever wanted but with an enormous catch. It had to be a dream or a hallucination.

But if it wasn't real, why could she feel her hands shaking as she fed quarters into the vending machine? Why could she hear the drum of rain on the ceiling, feel the humidity, and why could she hear Colleen moving a chair behind her? In a dream, they would just be sitting somewhere else. She wouldn't hear the thudding inside the machine as a bottle of soda tumbled out.

But it couldn't be real.

She carried the sodas over to the table where Colleen was seated. Her visitor, real or not, seemed content to wait until Margot was ready. She popped the top, took a sip of her drink, and they sat silently and listened to the rain. She watched Colleen, who examined the label on her bottle. Eventually Margot leaned forward and rested her elbows on the edge of the table.

"Okay," she said. "Go."

Colleen sat up straighter, as if a switch had been flipped. "I'm an aerospace engineer. I've spent my entire career working out how to make engines that run better, faster, and more efficiently than what we have now. I was working as a researcher when I had an idea. I figured out a way to gain power in an ion engine without also adding weight or sacrificing reliability.

But I didn't have any resources. So I reached out to people who did."

"NASA?"

"Air Force."

Margot raised an eyebrow. "You went to the military?"

Colleen shrugged. "Stupid idea in retrospect, but it seemed brilliant at the time. The sciences are constantly getting their budgets slashed. Meanwhile if the military says they have a shiny new plane, Congress falls all over themselves to throw money on the pile. And it worked. I was given a lab, I had assistants, a whole team dedicated to help make my idea a reality. We spent years working on a prototype, even after the ISS happened, we knew that eventually we'd need a way to get back up there. We saw the disaster as a sort of... pause button to give us time to iron out any tweaks so we'd really be ready for today, now, when we're finally going back up."

"Something tells me things didn't work out the way you imagined."

Colleen wrinkled her nose. "When the new missions were announced, I contacted the guy in charge of the project. Colonel Boshears. I thought our time had finally come, you know? The new age of space travel. The perfect time to reveal a new, more efficient way to explore the universe. But it turns out they had other things in mind."

Margot said, "They're sticking with what they already have, despite all the money they put into your research?"

Colleen grunted and finished her soda. She stood up, tossed the empty bottle in the recycling, and drifted to the windows. She looked out, hands in her pockets, framed by the washed-out pane. Margot remained seated but turned to keep an eye on the other woman. She looked like the picture of calm, cool, and collected, but there was clearly fire boiling under that deceptive surface.

"Do you know why it took so long for people to start coming around on electric cars?"

Margot shook her head even though Colleen was looking outside. "Cost? Lack of charging stations. Uh..."

"The cost was too great, they said. To build more of my engines, which they said were still officially unproven, would be too much. And then they would have to refit every shuttle they already have, which would cost even more money and would also be an added delay on the first launch. We're talking about actual travel between Earth and Mars, we're talking about making laps around Jupiter, and these guys are worried about cash flow."

"If the engine really is unproven—"

"It's not going to prove itself sitting in a damn supply closet." She walked back to the table but didn't sit down. "That's where we come in."

Margot said, "I don't even know if there's a 'we' yet. I was skeptical even before you mentioned the Air Force. Wouldn't stealing something from them be... sort of... treason?"

"It's only treason if we plan to sell it to another country. And it's not even really stealing if our intention is to test it, then give it back."

"I don't think the law works that way."

Colleen slapped her hand on the table. "It's *my engine*, damn it!" She slowed her breathing and lowered her voice. "It's been over a decade of my life. I put everything into that project, and it's just going to rot in some closet until the military can figure out how to use it as a weapon. I need to prove to them it's viable. I know you understand what it's like to have your dream thrown away. If you help me with my dream, I can help with yours."

"You have a space-worthy shuttle?"

"I will. I have the elements but I need to build it to very precise specifications. I need to know the height and weight of my pilot." She held Margot's stare. "I know you know that I don't have many options. The amount of people who are capable of flying this ship who aren't currently attached to one program or another could be written on a gas station receipt. I admit you are my only choice. But even if you weren't, you're who I would want. I know your career, I know how close you came. You're a space pilot who never got the opportunity to go up. Helping me with this can right both our wrongs."

Margot stood up and walked away. "And send us both to prison when they catch us."

Colleen followed. "I'll take full responsibility."

"That's not how aiding and abetting works!"

She went behind the ticket counter. Colleen stopped on the customer side of the desk.

"Do you think we're the only ones out here planning something like this? We have all the official agencies, sure, but there are probably just as many people in their barns or in makeshift garages thinking they can go to the stars now. That's how Enver Crane got his start, remember? The only difference is that *we* are the ones who can do it. I have the brains to build a ship and you have the skills to fly it and get back in one piece. Separately, we're just two people with shitty luck who will never get to see their dreams come true. Together, we can actually make it happen."

Margot kept her eyes lowered, drummed her fingers on the desk.

"You don't have to make your decision today. It's a really huge ask." She took a card out of her pocket and slid it across the counter with two fingers. "Think it over. Come out to where I'm working and take a look at the set-up. I'll even show you the schematics for the engine."

"Not that they would mean anything to me."

Colleen shrugged. "It might help you believe I know what I'm talking about. I would say there's no deadline, but to be honest, we have to do it sooner rather than later. I know where the engine is right now, and I'm confident we can get to it, but the military likes to shuffle its deck from time to time. And who knows how long the sky will be open. But you do have time. A little time."

Margot picked up the card and examined the information on it. "This is insane. A homemade ship with a prototype engine? You're basically asking me to risk blowing myself up with a science project made by someone I've never met."

Colleen shrugged. "I figure the odds are the same as what you had with NASA or what the Astraea people are working with."

Margot sighed and thumped the card with her finger. "I'll think it over."

"Fantastic," Colleen said, sighing with relief. "That's all I ask."

"Yeah, sure. Death by misadventure or life in prison."

Colleen smiled. And damn it, Margot had to admit it was a great smile. She was a sucker for a beautiful brunette with a great smile.

"What's life without a little risk?" Colleen asked.

Margot sat silently with her elbows on her desk, hands folded together in front of her face. Across from her, Linnie sat at her own desk reading the same article Margot had spent the previous afternoon scrutinizing. There wasn't much literature about Joan Colleen Eckles, but she had expected that. There was never a tremendous amount of coverage on the scientists who did the hard mathematic work to enable space flight. The astronauts were the athletes, the sexy pin-ups who got all the glory.

But Colleen was apparently important enough that a small niche website had done a whole in-depth interview with her while she was working on the ion engine. There was a picture and everything, proving the slightly manic woman she'd met yesterday really was a rocket scientist.

Linnie finished reading the article and looked across the office at her. "You met this woman?"

"Yep."

"Do you think she's the real deal?"

Margot started to answer, then sighed and shook her head. "I don't know. It's really her, I can believe that. But as for what she's claiming...? I have no idea."

"You could go to prison."

"Only if I actually survive the launch." She leaned back in her chair. "It's crazy! It's literally an insane thought, right? This woman worked for years on a project and had it taken away from her, and that made her snap."

Linnie said, "You didn't snap when your dream was taken away."

Margot shrugged. "Not noticeably, anyway..." She looked toward the window that looked out onto the hangar. The bay doors were open and the morning sun reflected off Hawkeye's windscreen.

"What are you thinking?"

"I'm thinking..." She pushed her hair out of her face. She'd worn it down today, after spending the entire night tossing and turning as she thought about the offer. "I'm thinking what if she's crazy, which she obviously is. A person would have to be a little insane just to come up with this plan. But what if she's just crazy enough to make it work?"

Linnie said, "I'm not going to argue with that."

"Every person who's gone to space had to be a little crazy just to climb on the shuttle."

"But that's with an entire billion-dollar agency backing you up every step of the way. And things still go horribly wrong! And when they just go a little bit wrong, you have a whole crew of super-geniuses on the ground looking for a solution. What's your backup here, a criminal who is already borderline reliable?"

"What if it's my last chance?"

Linnie hung her head. "Margot..."

"No. You don't know what it's like to work your whole life for something and then have it taken away. I was meant to be on that shuttle and it's just damn bad luck and stupid decisions keeping me from it now. Don't I owe it to myself to follow every potential route to finally get what I worked so hard for?"

"Of course you do. But you're talking about taking a huge risk with practically no real reward. Even if everything goes perfectly, you're going to come back to Earth as a criminal. It'll be the end of your life, right? You'd go to prison, and even if it was for a couple of years, then you'd be an ex-con. And what about this place?" She gestured at the office around them. "What happens to Magpie when you become an infamous rogue astronaut? What happens to Rosie and me?"

Margot sagged again. "You're right. Of course you're right. I have to think about something beyond myself. I can't risk your livelihood just because of some stupid fantasy."

Linnie winced. She got up and crossed the office, rounding Margot's desk. "If I thought there really was a chance," she said, "if I thought there was any possibility you might actually be able to hitch a ride on this crazy lady's ship and go to outer space, you know I'd be cheering you on. But I don't think it's a real opportunity. If I'm honest, I think it's just another chance to get your hopes crushed. I really don't want you to go through that again."

"I don't want that, either." She took Linnie's hand. "Thank you, Linnie."

"Sure. I'm sorry." She looked at the clock. "Do you want me to take up the first tour?"

Margot shook her head. "Flying will do me good. It'll clear out the cobwebs." She pushed herself out of the chair and kissed the top of Linnie's head. "Thanks for playing devil's advocate."

"Any time. Rosie and I are going out tonight. Drinks, dancing, general merriment. Come with us. See how great life on the ground can be."

Margot considered refusing, but a night out actually sounded like a great distraction. "I think I'll take you up on that. Thanks."

She left the office and went out to the hangar. Hawkeye, tried and true, waited. He was her Old Faithful, the only way she was ever going to beat gravity and touch the sky.

She could make her peace with that. She had to.

Rosie was elated when she found out Margot was coming out with them, and her inclusion caused an immediate change of plans. Instead of the normal downtown bar they usually went to, she decided they would drive into Pueblo to visit a proper establishment. Margot protested but it seemed as if the decision had been made without giving her a vote. She resigned herself to being their project and went home to change into what she hoped would be an acceptable outfit for wherever they ended up: black button-down blouse and tuxedo pants. If nothing else, the dark colors would help her blend in.

When they arrived, Rosie elected herself the designated driver. Margot chose a stool at the bar and watched her colleagues head out onto the dance floor. They immediately grabbed hold of each other and, within two verses, completely forgot Margot existed. That was fine by her. She could keep refilling her glass, kill time watching everyone else have fun, and then go home to sleep. Tomorrow would be another day. It didn't matter if it looked exactly like the day before. An endless trail of lookalike days were all she had to look forward to, so why not steer into the curve.

"Which one?"

The question came from her left, from a stool she could have sworn was empty but was now occupied by an Amazon in a blue plaid shirt. Her hair was cut short at the sides but long on top, and she had a knowing smile on her lips.

"Sorry?" Margot said.

The Amazon gestured at Rosie and Linnie. "The ladies you came in with. You haven't stopped staring at them, so I assume there's an unrequited, third wheel thing going on. I just can't figure out which one you're jealous of."

"Oh." She looked at them again. "Neither. Both. I mean, I don't... they're my friends. I'm not interested in either of them. But that?" She watched them laugh as they pressed their hips together. "I'm jealous of what they have. Not just the dance. The everything."

"Well, what's stopping you?"

Margot shook her head, tucking her bottom lip into her mouth. "I don't know anymore."

The Amazon leaned closer. "I'm Amanda."

"Hi, Amanda. I'm Margot."

"Nice to meet you, Margot." She turned on the stool and leaned in even closer. "I can't offer you everything, but maybe I can give you a reasonable facsimile for a little while."

Margot finished off her latest refill in one swallow, dropped the glass back on the bar, and stood up. She motioned for Amanda to follow her.

"Show me what you got."

Five minutes later she was straddling Amanda in the backseat of her car. Her blouse and slacks were both unbuttoned but she still had her bra, and Amanda was still fully dressed. Margot liked the way the rough material of the other woman's shirt felt against her skin. She rocked her hips, and Amanda's strong hands gripped the seat of her jeans to encourage a faster rhythm.

"This is fine," Margot gasped into a kiss.

"I'm aiming for more than fine, sweetness."

"No, I mean, this... specifically is very good." She punctuated that review with a lingering kiss, her tongue flicking against Amanda's parted lips. It felt wonderful to kiss someone again, even if it was a stranger. "I mean... in general... my life... it's fine. My life is fine."

Amanda said, "Okay," and moved her mouth to Margot's neck.

"I'm a pilot."

"That's hot."

Margot ran her fingers through the shock of hair on top of Amanda's head. "I'm about to get fucked by a spectacular woman."

"Yes, ma'am, you certainly are."

Margot closed her eyes and leaned back. Amanda took the hint and kissed lower, licking Margot's chest before she kissed her bra. Margot took off her shirt and reached back to unhook her bra. As soon as it was out of the way, Amanda's lips were on her nipples, licking and sucking. Margot arched her back.

"I haven't been fucked in ten fucking years."

"Damn, baby," Amanda said. "What a waste of these beautiful little tits." She resumed her kissing, circling her tongue over one pink nipple before she pulled one arm back and started reaching into Margot's pants. "You want to fuck or be fucked? After ten years, should be lady's choice."

"I don't care, just make me come." She kissed the stubble on the side of Amanda's head, brow furrowed with desperation. "Please."

Amanda laughed. "Yes, ma'am." Her hand found its way into Margot's underwear and she gasped at the touch. "Should've known you were a pilot."

"Yeah?" She managed to open her eyes and looked down at Amanda.

"Why's that?"

"Swagger. You got that sharp jawline, long and lean body... like a fuckin' bird." She grunted. "All you Air Force girls have it."

Margot's shoulders jerked. "What?"

"Slip away from the base in Colorado Springs, come down to get a little fun in the suburbs. I fuckin' love it."

"I'm not... I'm not Air Force..."

Amanda said, "You're not? But you said you were a pilot..."

Margot pushed away from her. "I have to go."

"Baby, wait..."

"I can't do this. I'm sorry."

"Don't be sorry, but you've... ten years. At least let me help you out."

Margot fell onto the side of the backseat, grabbing for her clothes. She kept repeating, "Sorry, shit, I'm sorry" as she tried to cover up with one hand while seeking the door handle with the other. She practically fell out of the car and stumbled to her feet. When she turned around, Amanda had slid over and was holding out her shirt. Margot grabbed it, quickly pulled it on, head down and too embarrassed to look around for witnesses.

"I don't know what I said, but I'm sorry," Amanda said. "Are you okay?"

"Yeah. I'm...." She pushed her hair back away from her face. "Fuck. I don't know. Thank you for trying. I hope you don't feel like... you know. It's not your fault. It's absolutely my stupid issues. I'm sorry."

"Hey, I'm fine. I got laid last week. You gonna be okay?"

Margot nodded. "Yeah. Yeah. I have my friends. Thank you. I'm sorry."

Amanda smiled sadly. "Take care of yourself, fly girl."

"Yeah, I... thanks. Sorry."

She buttoned up her shirt as she fled across the parking lot. It didn't make sense why being mistaken for Air Force had triggered her that way, but it had broken something in her. Suddenly she felt like an imposter, a poseur. She wasn't the pilot she dreamed of being. She was just a cabbie with a fancier ride. If she was going to live a life of anything but regret, she had to take a risk. She had to be willing to risk everything, actually.

She hoped she could convince Rosie and Linnie to cut their night short so they could drive her home. She had a long night of thinking ahead of her.

The dirt road was blocked by long wooden fence and a gate with a keypad and speaker. A rusted metal mailbox on a slanted metal pole told her she was at the right place, but it looked like an abandoned parcel of land. Still, she had come this far, and she wasn't going to let a stupid gate stand in her way. She'd waited for her day off to give herself time to rethink this, but the idea refused to let her go. Turning back now would only deepen her regret and second-guessing. Either way, she was going to take care of this dangling carrot right now.

Margot didn't feel like calling ahead, so she left her car blocking the gate and climbed over the fence. The dirt road stretched out through a field of sparse brown grass and hard-pack dirt before it curved out of sight behind a stand of trees. She doubted there was anything as extreme as landmines to worry about, but she stuck to the middle of the road when she started walking, just in case.

Ten minutes and two wide turns later, she found a small house that was dwarfed by the barn behind it. The house was modest and unassuming; the barn was two stories tall and seemed to be just as wide, with a door wide enough to parallel park three cars on the threshold. Margot could hear the sounds of metalwork being done in the barn, so she bypassed the house and walked across the yard.

"Hello?"

The noises stopped. Margot stopped as well, standing just inside the massive shadow thrown by the barn as she waited.

J. Colleen Eckles came out of the darkness in a pair of grease-stained overalls. At first Margot thought she was topless underneath it, but then she spotted the straps of a tank top. She was wearing welding glasses, which she pushed up onto her forehead when she saw who her visitor was. A smile slowly spread across her face.

"You changed your mind."

"I considered my options enough to require further conversation."

Colleen nodded slowly. "Okay. I can work with that for now." She took a rag from her pocket and wiped her hands with it. "Want to see what I'm working on?"

Margot took a deep breath. She wondered if it was too late to change her mind.

Fuck it. She was here. She'd come this far.

"Show me," she said.

Chapter Five

FROM THE daily journal of J. Colleen Eckles:

Sometimes the secret to getting exactly what you want is to give up hope. I thought I'd shot for the moon and missed. I came back to home base feeling like I was adrift among the stars. What good was the ship I'm building with no one to fly it? What was the point of risking my safety and that of my friends - okay, accomplices - if there was no possibility of getting it off the ground. Tracy suggested taking a crash course in flying, but that plan had no chance of success. We needed a real pilot, someone who had received the precise training required for breaking atmosphere. And we needed someone who wasn't in any way involved in the current space race.

M was custom-made for our plan. She was a pilot, she was chosen for a mission, and going by everyone's 'young, fresh, new' initiatives, she was unlikely to ever get another chance to go into space. On top of that, she ended up settling less than a hundred miles away from our current base of operations. It was perfect. It seemed like destiny when I drove up to St. Elmo with my pitch all loaded up. I was half expecting her to hop right in the car and come back with me.

But she said no.

Oh, she said she'd think it over, but I'd been in enough funding meetings to know what a polite dismissal sounded like. It was a crushing blow. I spent the day after that disastrous trip wondering what the hell the next step would be. We didn't have a backup pilot, and I wasn't prepared to risk Tracy on what would definitely be a suicide mission. But was I really going to just give up?

I was in the barn taking out my frustration on a piece of scrap metal when I heard her shout. I recognized her voice but didn't want to believe it. I tried to think of who it might really be, but there she was. She wasn't just perfect on paper, she looked the damn part. Denim jacket, V-neck white t-shirt tucked into jeans. Tall and reed-

thin, eyes behind aviators, blonde hair just long enough to be picked up by the wind. She looked like she could be Iceman in a gender-swapped version of Top Gun.

She claimed she still wasn't ready to agree, and I forced myself to remain as neutral as I could, but she came all this way. That has to be worth something.

Margot stood on the runner and leaned into the cavity that would become her cockpit, if she agreed. Colleen remained on the ground a respectful distance away, arms crossed, silent except to answer direct questions. Margot appreciated the opportunity to look on her own without a saleswoman chattering in her ear the whole time.

The ship was about the size of her Cessna, narrow at the front and widening out to a pair of flat wings at the back. It was still mostly a skeleton and, while she wasn't an engineer, she could at least extrapolate the finished product from what she was looking at. The wings would just barely pass through the barn doors, but there was enough wiggle room that any pilot worth their salt wouldn't have any issues. Her main concern was the lack of storage space.

"There's no way this is the long-term design."

Colleen said, "Oh hell no, are you kidding me? I don't have that kind of money. No, this is proof of concept. This is, uh, the *Spirit of St Louis,* Lindbergh crossing the Atlantic to show the big boys it can be done if they're willing to shell out for a full, official mission. This is entirely safe, I guarantee, but I'm not trying to send you to Pluto. You're just going to go up, orbit once, and come home."

To a prison cell, Margot added silently. "Where does the engine go?"

Colleen walked to the back of the ship, motioning for Margot to follow her. When they were behind it, Colleen indicated a gap between the wings. Margot was stunned.

"That's too small and way too big."

"Explain?" Colleen said.

"There's no way an engine that size will have enough thrust to break out of Earth's gravity well. That's what you're aiming for, right?"

Colleen nodded but seemed unconcerned. "It'll work. Trust me. What did you mean about being too big?"

"You want to steal this engine from somewhere, right? Something this size would be like walking into Target and walking out with a sofa. It's the sort of thing that would be noticed."

"I have that all figured out."

Margot put her hands on her hips. "Okay. Then explain it to be, Doctor. Walk me through this brilliant heist of yours."

Colleen smiled. She lowered her chin and looked up through her eyelashes like she suspected Margot was trying to trick her. "No."

"What do you mean no? You claim to have a plan, but you're not going to tell me what it is?"

"Damn right I'm not. The other day, you were absolutely adamant that you weren't going to do this. You swore up and down you wouldn't change your mind. And now here you are, out of the blue, claiming you had a change of heart. If you're in my place, you wouldn't find that a little suspicious? You could be wearing a wire."

Margot held her arms out to either side. "You want to pat me down?"

Colleen raised an eyebrow. "Tempting. But these people aren't going to just tape a microphone to your bra. They have all kinds of listening devices." Her eyes dipped down to the V of Margot's shirt, where she'd hooked her sunglasses. "There could be a tiny bug in the screw of your glasses."

"You really are paranoid."

"Planning what I'm planning, that's how you stay safe. Boshears may have gotten to you, or you might have had a crisis of conscience. You're lucky I'm letting you see this much."

Margot sighed and rolled her eyes. "Okay. What *am* I allowed to know?"

"You can see the ship. You can be aware of how far along I am with it. You're not allowed to know the timetable or any of the other people involved with the recovery."

"Recovery?"

Colleen shrugged. "Sounds better than the other word."

"Theft."

"That's your word, not mine."

Margot rolled her eyes. "I'm not wearing a wire. I don't even have my phone on me."

"I'd really love to believe you."

"Oh, for crying out loud..."

She remembered something she'd seen outside the barn and got an incredibly stupid idea. But her frustration with Colleen's paranoia was great enough that she didn't give herself time to think before she marched back around the ship and out of the barn. She went to the hose coiled up under a faucet, found the end, and angrily twisted the spigot until she felt the hose buck to life in her hand. She turned around to see Colleen had followed her out.

"You think I'm wearing a wire?" She held her arm out to the side and turned the hose on herself. The water was hot, then shockingly cold, but she clenched her teeth and kept dousing herself. She hit her chest, jeans, even sprayed both her boots just for good measure before lifting her arm and letting the water course down over her face. She spluttered and squinted through the wall of water.

"How waterproof do you think their shit is?"

Colleen's eyes were wide with shock, but she was holding back laughter.

"I'd say another two or three minutes would really put my mind at ease."

Margot spit water and bent down to turn off the faucet. "Fuck you. You either trust me or I walk right now. You can't have it both ways."

Colleen's eyes dipped down, then quickly away, and Margot remembered she was wearing a white shirt. She refused to close her jacket; if Colleen could be distracted by the sight of someone's bra, she wasn't a scientist worth trusting.

"Well?"

"Let's go inside," Colleen said, already walking. "I'll get you a towel."

Margot pushed her hair out of her face. "Sounds good to me."

She flicked the excess water from her fingers as she followed Colleen across the lawn.

The interior of the house was a miniature city with buildings constructed of books, binders, and cardboard boxes filled with loose papers. Margot felt like Godzilla as she carefully navigated the single aisle between the stacks, which grew from the floor, chairs, and tables to the point where she wondered how anyone could actually live in this space. Colleen didn't seem to notice the cramped quarters as she moved without thought and quickly left Margot behind.

By the time Margot reached the relatively open clearing of the living room, Colleen had returned with a pair of large fluffy towels.

"If nothing else, you get points for the dramatics."

"Thanks," Margot muttered.

She draped the larger towel around her shoulders like a shawl and dried her hair with the other. Colleen moved some technical manuals and notebooks off the couch, either adding to existing stacks or starting new ones in a precious square of free carpeting.

"Hopefully you understand why I have to be a little bit insane about security. I only know you from what I've read on the internet. I don't know if you're the kind of person who would go running to the authorities or say 'fuck the man' and do the vigilante thing."

"Yeah. I'm not exactly feeling too generous toward the authorities at the moment. At least the authorities who are making the decisions about who gets to go to space."

She moved to sit on the part of the couch Colleen had cleared off. Colleen took the armchair which was already empty; most likely her chosen seat. Margot still felt like a drowned rat and she dabbed at her neck with the towel as she sat down.

"If you're planning any kind of violent theft, I can't be part of that."

"No violence." She raised two fingers, then drew an X over her heart.

Colleen sat with her knees apart, slightly hunched forward. Margot was acutely aware of her bare arms, mostly exposed shoulders, the cleavage revealed by the tank top under her overalls. She was lanky, long arms and neck, and it left a lot of skin on display.

"I know someone stationed at the base where my engine is being stored. She's sympathetic to our cause, and she's kept an eye on the inventory while I've been working on the ship. For the past few years, it's just been gathering dust, but a few weeks ago she saw a notification that the entire department was being moved to an off-site facility in Utah. It took some doing but she found a work order so she knows when it's being moved. We'll have a very small window where it isn't at a government facility or the bowels of a heavily-secured base surrounded by twitchy men with guns."

"But the truck or whatever they have the engine in will still be driven by, and most likely guarded by, those same twitchy men with their own guns."

"They'll be much easier to handle out in the world, trust me. Knowing where they'll start and where they're going gives us the upper hand. They'll be traveling north to Denver, and then it's straight over the Rockies into Utah. I have someone driving the route twice a week until she knows it like the back of her hand."

"Another her. Is everyone in your little gang a woman?"

Colleen looked confused by the question. "Yes...?"

Margot shrugged. "No, nothing. Just confirming." She didn't have a follow-up, and she wasn't even sure why she'd asked. It was good to know at any rate. "So the plan is to ambush the truck that's carrying your engine at some point along I-70."

"Hopefully closer to Denver than to Salt Lake City, but I admit we'll have to ad-lib a little on the actual day. There are two options. Either our boys go across the Rockies, which is a straight shot, or they'll go up to I-80 to get around the mountains by going through Wyoming. It seems like a roundabout trip, but it's marginally quicker to go that way. We have two plans depending on what they decide. One if our driver turns west and another if he goes straight."

"Which is the better plan?"

Colleen shrugged. "They're both good. It doesn't matter which route they choose, we'll be ready. It's basically like a train shifting tracks." She narrowed her eyes. "You do know you're not involved with this part, right? I'm not going to ask you to be involved in the actual heist."

Margot said, "No, you want me to be the getaway driver. It definitely benefits me to make sure your plan is solid so we get to that point." She chewed her bottom lip. "There's one huge glaring flaw in this whole endeavor. As soon as your engine gets stolen, this Bursar guy—"

"Boshears."

"Whatever. He's going to know exactly who to blame."

Colleen nodded. "I've considered that. I have wheels in motion. Nothing locked in yet, but you'll know when we're set. For now, if it sets your mind at ease, he doesn't even know this place exists. It's not tied to me at all. It belonged to the grandma of an ex, so there's no paper trail that would lead him here even if he knew to look for me."

Margot took in that information. It did make her feel a bit more secure. "The other women on the team. How many of them know that I'm involved?"

"Two," Colleen said. "Three if you count me."

"How many women are there total?"

"Counting the two of us sitting here," Margot said, "seven."

Margot considered that. That was a lot of people, a lot of potential cooperating witnesses who could point fingers at her if things went south. Going to prison after achieving her dream was one thing, but to be caught at the early stages before they even got the engine would be devastating. If Colleen and her crew failed, she wanted the chance to slip away into the shadows where she could get back to her life. At the same time, five other people wasn't a whole lot of hands. If something went wrong, if a member of the team was incapacitated, could the others pick up the slack without sacrificing elsewhere?

Colleen was watching her think. It was unsettling but, at the same time, she liked that there was no pressure in the observation. Colleen seemed content to wait as long as it took for the gears in Margot's head to grind out a response.

"I don't want anyone else to know my name, if you can avoid it."

"Deal."

"And I don't want to meet any of them."

Colleen hesitated. "That might be harder to promise, but I'll do my best." She rubbed her hands together.

"Damn it," Margot whispered. "For now, and subject to change if *any* new information comes to light between now and when this ball actually starts rolling..."

"Yeah...?"

Colleen leaned closer, eager. Margot sighed, the practical part of her brain already regretting what she was about to say.

"I'm in. But I have a catch."

Margot stood in the open hangar bay and watched a glint over the mountains slowly grow into Hawkeye. The plane gleamed like silver, like a sunbeam brought to life, and she couldn't help but smile as Linnie dipped the wings in a brief hello. Margot raised her hand to return the greeting and kept watching the landing. There was a time when she thought she would never trust anyone with her plane. She'd known Linnie for years, trusted her implicitly in every aspect of their business, but she still got sweaty palms the first few times she took out Hawkeye, the airline's only plane at the time.

The trepidation hadn't lasted long, and soon she trusted Linnie as much as she trusted herself. It had been a big step for her, putting that much faith in someone else, but it had paid off time and again. Now she was hoping it would pay off more than it ever had before.

Margot had gotten back from Colleen's fifteen minutes earlier. She'd spent the entire drive preparing for the speech she had to make and, as she watched the plane coast to a stop, she wished she'd just gone straight home to delay the conversation until morning.

Linnie opened the plane door and helped her passengers off. It was a young couple - him, tall and dark-haired; her, blonde and wearing glasses, laughing loudly at something he had said before the door was open. When she reached the bottom of the stairs, the wife took out her phone and snapped a quick picture of the plane, Linnie, and the hangar. The husband shook Linnie's hand when they were back on the ground and followed his wife away from the plane.

Margot smiled and nodded to the couple as they passed. The wife's eyes widened and she grinned brightly, nodding enthusiastically.

"Fantastic, it was so cool!" she said.

The husband was slightly more sedate and nodded as he passed. "It was great, thank you."

"Thank you for choosing Magpie," Margot said to their retreating backs.

Linnie stopped at Margot's side. "Great couple. Visiting from Chicago."

"Sunset over the Rockies package. Newlyweds?"

"No, I don't think so."

Margot was impressed. "Keeping the romance alive. Kudos to them."

As they walked into the office, Linnie finally noticed Margot's outfit. "What the hell are you wearing?"

She plucked uncomfortably at the cuffs of the sweatshirt. Colleen had loaned her an old sweatshirt and a pair of slightly too-big jeans so she wouldn't have to drive home in soaked clothes. It was another reason she should have just gone home for the night.

"That's a long story."

"Does it involve the lady you went to see? Engineer lady?"

"Yeah. Come on." She held open the door to the office for Linnie and followed her in. She shut the door, closed the blinds, and also closed the blinds that looked out onto the hangar.

Linnie slowly lowered herself into her desk chair. "Whoa, big time business talk. Is everything okay?"

"I don't know." Margot sat behind her own desk. "I talked to Eckles. I saw the ship she's building, or at least the skeleton of it. I got an idea of what she's trying to do."

"And?" Linnie leaned forward, intrigued.

Margot spoke slowly. "I think she has something solid. It's tough to say at this stage, but based on what I've seen and the talk we had, I think she might actually pull it off."

"That's fantastic!" Linnie said. "So did you sign on to be her pilot?"

"That's the thing I wanted to talk to you about." She stood up and started pacing. "You know that I don't put my faith in anything blindly. I have to double-check, I have to supervise, I have to be part of the process as much as possible. I can't just sit back and wait for someone to ring a bell for me to perform like a trained seal."

Linnie shrugged. "Sure. We've all decided it's part of your charm." She realized what Margot was building to and sat up straighter. "Oh..."

Margot cleared her throat. "Yeah. I need to be there while she's building the ship. And it's just far enough away that I can't exactly just pop back and forth between flights. I thought about letting her move into one of the hangars..."

"You can't do that because if she was caught, Magpie would be implicated."

"Right. We need to stay as clean as we can."

Linnie said, "Wait, if you're thinking about staying at the house where she's building this thing, you're going to be implicated anyway."

"Right. I will be, but you'll have plausible deniability."

"Me?"

Margot stopped pacing and looked at her. "I want you to take over Magpie. At least for a little while. But... with this plan, the odds are good I won't come back. I'll either blow up on the runway or get arrested, so you'll be on your own eventually anyway. We might as well hammer out the details while we can before everything goes to shit."

"Wow." Linnie picked up a pen and began twirling it with her fingers, a nervous habit that would eventually turn into drumming it on the arm of her chair. "I always kind of thought I'd advance somehow. Maybe start my own airline or something. I wasn't going to leave you in the lurch or anything like that, but I thought it was a natural... you know...? Growth?"

"I get it."

Linnie stared at the wall. She chewed her bottom lip and began drumming the pen on her chair. Margot resisted a smile at her prediction coming true.

"Obviously I'm honored. I don't know if I'm ready."

"You're ready. You're a good pilot, and a good businesswoman, and I wouldn't trust anyone else with this business or with Hawkeye and Hunnicutt. If I go through with this insane scheme, the only options for

Magpie are to let it go under or hand it over to you. If I do it early enough hopefully you won't be swept along in the aftermath."

"The place won't be the same without you. It'll be a lot more work, for one."

Margot smiled. "We can hire a new pilot before I go. You'll finally get to be the person making the schedules and yell at your subordinates for being late."

Linnie snapped her fingers. "At last, the tables have turned!" She tossed the pencil onto the desk. "Seriously, though. You really think this is the end?"

"We're talking about..." She lowered her voice. "We're talking about stealing military property. I don't think anyone will get hurt, but I also don't think that matters in terms of legality. Colleen is definitely going to jail when this is all over. I'll go with her if I actually survive the mission."

"You mentioned that before. How likely is the possibility you die doing this?"

Margot shrugged. "I don't know the exact odds, obviously, but they're pretty high with any kind of experimental craft. Part of the reason I'm relocating to Eckles' place is to improve those odds. If I'm there I can help her troubleshoot anything that might come up. Regardless, I'm trying to be realistic here. The ship could fail at any point of the mission. The engine could fail, her soapbox derby spaceship could be destroyed on launch, breaking atmosphere, or reentry. Or I could just crash the damn thing." She shrugged. "It's all possible."

Linnie said, "I don't want to think about that. So I'll focus on you getting life in prison. You know, what I like to call the optimistic outcome."

"Oh, not life," Margot said. "Probably just thirty years, twenty with good behavior."

"At your age, that might as well be life, right...?"

Margot gasped. "Rude."

Linnie got up and came around the desk. Margot saw the hug coming and thought it would be more awkward to refuse, so she allowed it to happen. She patted Linnie on the back and smiled as she calculated how long she needed to wait before she could extricate herself from it.

"I'm sorry," Linnie said, "I know you're not big on hugging. But I wanted to get it out of the way early just in case you stopped me."

"I can handle a hug for the big moments."

"Well, you can expect another one when the end finally comes for real." She stepped back and wiped at her eyes. "Okay. Well, what sort of timeline are we looking at? Weeks? Probably not months."

"I don't know exactly, but it might be days."

Linnie blew air out past her lips and nodded. "Well, okay then. I guess we better get to work finding your replacement. Clock's ticking."

Margot didn't have to be told. She'd been hearing the ticking ever since she left Colleen's barn. She just hoped there wasn't a bomb waiting when the ticking hit zero.

CHAPTER SIX

FROM THE daily journal of J. Colleen Eckles:

A coup!!!!! We got our pilot! She's not an enthusiastic yes, not yet, but I would be suspicious of enthusiasm at this point. What I'm asking is c r a z y, I know it's crazy, otherwise I'd have to be crazy. We're taking baby steps here, but I woke up today thinking about our conversation and I can see it in my head as clear as day. I can see her sitting in that cockpit in her jumpsuit and I know it's going to happen. Besides, that hose thing proves that she's got a little bit of crazy in her, too. Just the way I like 'em!!

I realized yesterday that I redacted our pilot's name but then put more than enough information for people to know exactly who I was talking about. That's less than ideal. But I assume if it gets to the point where anyone is reading this, the jig will be up anyway, so I'm leaving it for now. I may go back and Sharpie it out.

And that brings me to a bit of a downer: Boshears has apparently been asking about me. I.B. let me know my name was floating around the base like a ghost, but she doesn't know the full story yet. She'll keep me updated. Not gonna lie, that almost put a damper on my mood. But no one other than I.B. and J even knows where to find me, and I feel every day there are fewer people who even remember I ever worked there, so I'm not going to let it weigh on me very heavily.

M surprised me when she insisted on actually staying here at the Garage to observe the work as it happens. I'm absolutely thrilled to have her, of course! It'll be good to have some pressure and for someone looking over my shoulder to make sure I don't get tunnel vision. Plus it's been pretty lonely, if I'm honest, so it'll be great to have company.

I can't wait to tell all the other Sitting Ducks that we got our Holy Grail!!

Looking back, I wonder if I should have told her that's what we're calling ourselves. Well, too late now. She'll find out soon enough.

Margot and Linnie spent three days looking for pilots, and two more days vetting their top choices before they started making calls. They planned to gauge interest and bring the best candidates up for test flights while Margot was away. She would come back as often as she could to check in, and for interviews, and then she and Linnie would make the decision.

"Don't you want to fly with them?" Linnie asked.

"They'll be your copilot," Margot said. "You'll be the one sharing an office and a business with them. My opinion on this is secondary to yours. I just want to be sure I'm comfortable with whoever ends up with my planes, and I'm sure I'll agree with anyone who passes muster with you."

Linnie smiled, touched by the show of trust. "Thanks, boss."

Margot packed a bag, trying hard not to think about the fact she wasn't coming home when all this was over. There really wasn't going to be an "over" for her. She sat on the foot of her bed and looked around at the things she'd gathered over the years. Framed photos of her father, Linnie and Rosie outside of Magpie with the planes in the background, self-portraits in the pilot's seat of Hawkeye with Pikes Peak framed in the window behind her.

This was the life she planned to leave behind. The people she loved, the business she built. She should have felt more, should be emotional about walking away. It should have felt hard, but she had a harder time packing for a family trip to Sacramento when she was a teenager.

She took her phone out of her pocket and dialed her father's number. She hadn't planned to tell him what was going on until they were much closer to the endgame, but she had a sudden urge to hear his voice.

"Hey, look who it is. I've been leaving a saucer of milk on the back porch every night just in case you snuck back."

Margot smiled. "Hey, Dad. Can you talk?"

"Sure, you're more interesting than the person I'm talking to now. Ow!" He laughed and she heard him close a door. "Everything okay?"

"Yeah, everything's fine." She stared at a spot high on the wall. She chewed her lip.

"Oh, this is definitely an 'everything's fine' silence. What's going on? Hit me with it."

She rubbed her forehead with her free hand. "So. I'm thinking about doing something kind of crazy. It's a no-going-back sort of thing, you know? I can take a few more steps and still run away but soon there's going to be a point of no return."

"That sounds ominous." The laughter was out of his voice now. "Does this have to do with your dream of going into space?"

"Yeah," she said.

"You found a way. And it's... well, of course it's dangerous. When you say no going back, do you mean that literally?"

She nodded. The tears were starting to prick her eyes now. "Yeah."

Silence on the other end of the line. Eventually he said, "Okay," and then there was more silence. Margot chewed her lip and waited. Finally, he spoke again.

"Do you remember what you said in the hospital after you tried to launch yourself over Duchalk Gorge?"

She remembered the concern on her face, and the pretty nurse who told her she was very brave, but she didn't remember having a conversation with him. "No."

"You said 'I know what I did wrong.' You could have died in a couple of different ways that afternoon, and you were hurt badly enough that I got a visit from Child Protective Services~"

"What?" That was news to her.

"~but your main concern was your next attempt. I'm sure you remember the next few weeks you spent as a prisoner in our house. I didn't even want you to have access to scissors because I was terrified you'd try to make another flying machine. Then one day I came home from work and found you had tried turning your sheets into wings."

Margot covered her eyes. "God, what an absolute pain in the ass I must have been."

Her father sighed with relief. "Ah, vindication. I've waited years to hear you acknowledge that! Yes, Margot Kathleen, you were a curse on my house. But the day I found you with those wings, I knew that you were never going to pay attention to the word 'no.' Once you had an idea in your head, you were going to chase it down no matter who or what was in your way. That was the day I realized that I could do everything in my power to keep you safe, but I couldn't stop you. And I decided I wasn't going to be the one anchoring you to the ground."

She smiled and brushed her cheek with the back of her hand. "That's probably why I got as far as I did in the space program."

"Well, I won't take *all* the credit. Sixty-forty sounds fair enough."

Margot laughed. "Fair enough."

"Whatever you're going to do, dangerous or whatever, I trust you've thought it through and you know yourself well enough to make the decision. Just promise me you'll be as safe as possible while you're doing the dangerous stuff."

"Helmets and pads always," she said, remembering the rule he'd instituted after her crash.

"Good girl. And keep in touch, if you can."

She nodded. "Will do. Thanks for the pep talk."

"I'm here whenever you need it. Love you, kid."

"Love you."

She disconnected the call and rested the phone against her chin. She felt monumentally better about her decision. She was effectively walking away from her whole life to commit suicide in a spectacular manner. But there was a chance she'd survive... and there was a chance that the ship would work and she'd finally, finally, *finally* make it to space. When all was said and done, she was comfortable absolving herself for anything she had to do in achieving that goal.

Margot got up and went to the closet to finish packing.

Colleen called her property The Garage, which seemed like as good a name for it as any. Two weeks later, when Margot returned, Colleen was waiting for her outside the barn. Today she was dressed more conservatively in a polo shirt and jeans, although the whole outfit was still marked by grease and dirt. Her hair was also a tangled mess, although she'd made some effort to smooth it out and pulled into a ponytail. Margot couldn't help but feel like she was picking up a date. No. Ridiculous. Colleen was just used to this being her own private island, and she was responding to the fact she'd be sharing the property with another person. It had nothing to do with her personally.

Not that she wanted it to. Definitely... not.

She parked near the house and had one bag out of the car by the time Colleen reached her. "Welcome back," she said. "Need a hand with anything?"

"No, thanks. I travel light." She pulled the larger suitcase out of the trunk and dropped it to the ground with a heavy thud. "Relatively speaking. I figure I'll be running up to St. Elmo enough that I can just pick up anything I left behind instead of carting it all up here."

"Sounds smart," Colleen said. "I'll show you where you're staying."

Margot followed Colleen inside. The towering stacks were still present, but the amount of flat surfaces had almost doubled. She could actually imagine someone sitting down for a meal at the dining room table. Colleen noticed her noticing.

"Yeah, after you were here last time, I got kind of a shock about how I'd been living. I figured if someone else was going to be living here, I should try to make amends."

"I appreciate it."

"Dining room, kitchen." She pointed down the hall. "There's a laundry room on the other side of the pantry through there. You saw the living room. And as for where you'll be sleeping..."

They went upstairs which a quick glance revealed was only made up by three rooms: two beds and a bath. Colleen paused in the hallway.

"I took the bigger bedroom because... well, why not? But if you'd prefer..."

"No, I'm fine with whatever."

Colleen nodded and opened the other door. It was technically a bedroom, as the door bumped the foot of a bed, but she could see it had been adapted into a room for sewing supplies. Thick bolts of fabric leaned against the wall and were piled haphazardly on the bed, and various kits filled cubbyholes on either side of the room that took up most of the remaining space. They remained in the hall because there was barely enough room for one person to stand inside, let alone two.

"Like I said... there *is* a bigger room." Colleen smiled sheepishly.

"It's fine. I've slept in worse." She went into the room and found a place in the corner where she could put her bags.

Colleen said, "I'll help you move all this stuff to..." She scratched the back of her neck and wrinkled her nose. "Well, we'll find a place for it. I'll let you get settled in."

"Thanks."

Margot waited until Colleen was on the stairs before she closed the bedroom door. She really had slept in places worse than this, but at the moment she was hard-pressed to think of any. At least there was a window, at the head of the bed. She side-stepped the standing rolls and leaned over the mattress, opened the curtains, letting some light in. The glass was covered with dust and cobwebs, so she found the end on one of the bolts and used it as a rag. She would have to get some actual water involved at some point, but for now she was happy to just send some spiders packing.

Once the window was passably clean, Margot realized she had a view of the barn. Colleen was crossing the grass, head down, thumbs hooked in the pockets of her jeans so that her elbows stuck out. Margot took a moment to fully appreciate the fact she was putting her life in this woman's hands. She was trusting her with an incredibly criminal plot which would lead to something unbelievably dangerous. They'd had two conversations, for crying out loud.

Colleen stopped at the barn door and turned around, looking up at the window. Margot tensed but didn't retreat, instead raising her hand in greeting. The corner of Colleen's mouth twitched and she returned the wave. They looked at each other for a beat. Margot was grateful for the glass and the distance because it made the silence between them necessary instead of awkward. Finally Colleen's shoulders hitched in what might have been a laugh, then she raked her fingers through her hair and pivoted on one foot to go back into the barn.

Margot stepped back as well and sat on the bed. She sniffed the air, looked down at the blanket, and wished she'd brought her own bedding from home. Hopefully Colleen had some extra stuff laying around. Worst case scenario, she would have to sleep on the couch. It still wouldn't be the worst place she'd ever spent the night.

She looked around the room. It was cramped and it smelled strange, and she was all but positive there were spiders nesting all over the place, but it was her new home. Maybe her last home. This would most likely be the last bed she slept in before she went into space. Or before she died.

She shivered at the thought, put it out of her mind. She had plenty to distract herself with to keep those morbid thoughts at bay. She got up and began to strip the ancient linens from the bed. If nothing else, doing a load of laundry would help her feel like this was a home rather than a coffin.

Margot came out to the barn to see Colleen standing on the ship. She was astride the cockpit with her back to the door, bent forward at the waist to wrestle something out of the guts. Margot took a moment to admire the seat of Colleen's jeans. Then she shook her head and wondered if she should have just finished fucking Amanda to get it out of the way before she set out on this mission. She cleared her throat and Colleen turned and straightened up.

"I started some laundry. Those blankets and sheets..."

"Oh, yeah." Colleen wiped some sweat from her brow, leaving her hair sticking up at the front. "I think some of that stuff is older than we are." She walked to the wing, crouched, and hopped down to the ground. "I have some extra if you want to swap it out."

"I was going to ask," Margot said. "Thanks. I was also going to make a grocery run, if you could possibly tell me where the closest store is. Do you realize you don't have any food?"

"What? I have food."

"Six boxes of Cheerios and a cupboard full of preserved chemicals doesn't count as food."

Colleen waved her off and went to retrieve a water bottle that was sweating on her tool kit. "What do you know? You were an astronaut. You ate paste."

Margot smirked and looked at the ship. Before, she'd examined it with a critical eye of someone faced with a decision. Now that she had crossed the Rubicon, she looked at it like a pilot who would be asking this ship to keep her alive in an environment no human was ever supposed to be in. She also had to look at it as an accomplice, and a thought had been nagging at her.

"I know how you plan to get the engine, so I assume fuel won't be an issue. But how the hell did you get enough material to make an entire space-worthy vessel?"

Colleen smiled and swallowed a mouthful of water before she answered. "It's a trash ship. Cast-offs from wreckages, botched missions, scuttled prototypes. One of my people has access to the scrapyard.

Technically they keep everything to cut down on overhead, cannibalizing past ships to suit up the new ones, but Erica skimmed a little off the top. Aluminum sheets are sturdy and lightweight, and it's strengthened with titanium alloy plates, all of it molded to these." She moved closer and tapped an exposed panel with two fingers. "Thermal tiles to keep you from bursting into flames."

"I appreciate that."

"Yeah, I'm looking out for you." She patted the side of the ship like a rancher showing off a prize stallion. "The woman in charge of getting me these things is also going to get you a spacesuit. But we're going for a real one rather than something that's been tossed out, so there's a greater chance they'll notice it missing. We also had to wait to confirm we'd get the right size. You're more petite than our backup."

Margot said, "You had a backup? You said I was your only choice."

"You were. We had a backup the same way that if you miss your flight from Los Angeles to New York, your backup plan is to walk there instead. But that's a moot point now. You're here and now the ball is really rolling."

"Let me know if there's anything I can do to help. I'm not an engineer, but an extra pair of hands is always useful. And I can run errands. Like buying groceries."

"Oh, right, the store." She turned and pointed south. "There's a co-op about eight miles that way, in Halcyon. Don't expect a whole lot of selection, but you can get the staples."

"A co-op? Don't you have to, like, join...?"

Colleen chuckled. "No, you just shop. I can give you some cash."

"And let me know anything you might want me to pick up."

"Well, you just said I'm good on Cheerios, so..." She took out her wallet and passed Margot some money. "It's been a long time since I had a woman offer to shop for me. And are you going to cook, too?"

"I might as well. I have a mental image of you trying to microwave a whole frozen turkey and..."

Colleen laughed. "Damn. Laundry, shopping, and cooking. If you also do windows, I might have to propose before all this is over."

Margot rolled her eyes. "Yeah, well, I did always dream of having a prison wedding, so." She pocketed the money. "The town is called Halcyon, you said?"

"Yeah, eight miles, straight shot on the highway. You can't miss it. The co-op is on the close side of town so you'll go right by it when you arrive."

"Got it." She gestured at the ship. "Good luck while I'm gone."

Colleen hoisted her water bottle in a toast and took another drink, turning to examine her work. The woman looked like she was posing for a magazine cover, and Margot was glad she didn't have a camera or she'd have risked sneaking a picture. She snapped herself out of her ogling and left before she could get caught gawking.

As she backed out of the driveway, she wondered if Colleen being so objectively attractive was part of her willingness to sign on to this mission. It had been a really long time since she'd gotten laid, not counting the aborted parking lot encounter, and she was a sucker for dark-haired women with blue eyes. And she had a great body, the way she filled out her jeans and her polo shirt...

Margot realized her non-driving hand was resting on her thigh and creeping higher. She shook her head, put both hands on the wheel, and cleared her throat. She definitely should have fucked Amanda.

She had gone almost a mile when she spotted a car parked on the shoulder. At first she thought it was a typical stranded motorist and slowed down to see if she could offer any assistance. When she got closer, she saw the driver was behind the wheel in a dark blue baseball cap and sunglasses, one gloved hand resting on the brim of her hat in a "casual" pose that served to conceal her face.

Margot sped up and quickly left the car in her rearview. She spent the rest of the drive wondering if she should pull over and warn Colleen that she was being surveilled. Maybe she knew. Maybe it was to be expected, but she still couldn't shake the feeling of dread that settled over her. If she had come this far and taken this many risks just to have it taken from her now, she'd go insane.

She decided she would warn Colleen when she got back to the house.

If Colleen was still there when she got back.

CHAPTER SEVEN

MARGOT TOOK her time driving around Halcyon a bit to acquaint herself with the closest sign of civilization, just in case she needed anything in the future. She saw all the usual places: bank, laundromat, library, gas station. When she felt familiar with its layout, she retraced her steps and parked at the co-op. It didn't take her long to pick up the essentials, and she headed back to the Garage with plenty of time left to start cooking dinner. She wasn't going to try anything fancy; Hamburger Helper would be enough for the inaugural meal.

The mysterious car had disappeared by the time she passed the same spot. She honestly didn't know how to feel about its absence but, since it didn't coincide with a swarm of government officials descending on Colleen's barn, she decided to take it as a good sign. She parked in the same place she had before, in a patch of dead grass next to the house, and carried the groceries in.

She was looking for places to put everything when Colleen came in from the barn. "I thought I'd see if you needed a hand with anything."

"You can help me find places for this stuff."

Colleen examined the contents of one bag. "You're really going to cook all this stuff?"

"Yeah. You put them together, add water, apply heat, and voila. You've got real food. It's magical."

"Not in my experience, but I trust you." She scanned the other bags. "Did you get any, um... anything sweet?"

Margot revealed a bag of cookies and passed them to Colleen. "Only if you agree to share."

"But of course." She tore open the bag and took out a couple.

"So," Margot said, trying for casual, "on the way into town, I saw something kind of odd. There was a car parked on the shoulder about a mile down the road. The driver was in the car, but she was blocking her face. I don't know if she's spying on you or what, but either way, I thought if should be mentioned."

Colleen chewed the cookie slowly. "Did you get a license plate number?"

"No. I didn't think it was suspicious until I was already past her."

"Damn. Well, we have to track her down somehow. We can't leave her out there, she's a threat."

"But if she is the government, we can't just ask her to please go away."

Colleen nodded her agreement. "No. We're going to have to kill her."

Margot felt the blood rush from her face. The room suddenly felt frigid. "What..."

Colleen held her stare for an eternity before she finally cracked. "God, the look on your face! We're not going to kill anyone, relax." She put the cookies back where Margot had gotten them. "I know exactly who you saw, it's fine."

"Who was it? How do you know who it was?"

"Her name is Jessie. She's working with us. She drove by the place, saw your car, and decided to keep her distance until it was safe. She came by after you left."

Margot relaxed. "Is she still here?"

"No, she left before you got back."

"I still don't appreciate the joke. I'm not entirely sure how far you're willing to go with this, and I thought you might have really crossed a line."

"Sorry." Colleen sounded sincere. "I couldn't resist."

"It's okay. Try to keep jokes about homicide to a minimum, if you can."

Colleen nodded. "I promise. I feel like I should observe, learn your ways. It doesn't seem fair for you to always be cooking for us."

"I don't mind it. I'm used to cooking for myself, and this is just double portions. You just focus on building our spaceship and I'll keep you fed. Deal?"

"Works for me, sister."

She held her hand up. Margot stared at it.

"What," Colleen said, "you don't high-five? I thought all astronauts and pilots did that shit."

Margot reluctantly slapped her palm against Colleen's.

"There we go!" Colleen grinned and snapped her fingers. "How long until the food is ready?"

"Considering I haven't even started, it'll be a little while."

"Okay. I'll be out in the barn. Call me when there's about fifteen minutes left and I'll go clean up. And if I haven't said it before, I really appreciate you doing this. It'll be nice to have a home-cooked meal for a change."

"Well, from a box. At least tonight."

"It's still a step up from what I'm used to. Thanks."

"You're welcome."

Colleen brushed past her and left the house. Margot drifted closer to the door and once again watched Colleen walk away through a window. She had a sexy strut, which Margot noted without shame this time because she decided to stop wasting time fighting it. J. Colleen Eckles was a damn sexy woman and it was only proper to acknowledge that fact.

And now Colleen was going to cook her dinner. It wasn't the sort of set-up she'd expected to find in this place, and it was far more domestic than she'd ever anticipated for herself, but she was surprised to find she didn't necessarily hate it.

She let that realization settle and began looking for cooking implements.

Colleen came in earlier than she said and spent the extra time clearing off the dinner table. She also found bowls and set them out before she went to wash up. A few minutes later she sat down across from Margot in a clean shirt, her hair clearly brushed down with wet fingers.

"This looks amazing. Thanks."

"No problem." Margot held her hand out across the table, palm up. Colleen stared at it. Margot made a 'come on' gesture. "Grace."

"What...?"

"We have to say grace before we eat the meal. I'll let you do it this time and then we can alternate."

Colleen's lips twisted like she wanted to smile, but her eyes were terrified. "Are... a-are you serious?"

Margot withdrew her hand. "Maybe next time you'll think twice about that 'kill her' crack."

Colleen sighed with relief. "Geez. You almost gave me a heart attack. Not that I have a problem with religious people... per se. But seeing as I'm bisexual and I also believe in science, I don't really have much to talk about with church-going people."

"Same here. I mean not about the~" She cleared her throat. "I'm gay, not bisexual."

"Well, I won't bring any boys around if it'll make things weird." She raised her glass and took a drink, then dug into her food.

Margot shifted in her chair, uncertain if the plan was to eat in silence. That sounded tremendously awkward, but she'd done it before. Still, it was her first night in the house, and she wanted to promote at least some minor kind of civility between them.

"So, um." She cleared her throat. "Where are you from?"

Colleen looked up from her bowl. "Pardon?"

Margot shrugged. "I assume your team has done all kinds of research on me. You probably know things about me that I've forgotten. Fair play. Tell me about yourself."

"I suppose you have a point." Colleen cleared her throat and rested her elbows on the table. "I'm from a place no one has ever heard of in Tennessee called Centertown. We had about twelve students in my graduating class. I had a saintly angel of a teacher who saw that I was interested in building shit and figuring out how things worked, so he found scholarships and talked my parents into letting me leave the state for a technical school. That's where my engine was born, and the rest is history."

"Your parents didn't want you to go to college?"

"*God* no," Colleen said. "Paying money for school was ridiculous, and moving away from home to attend it was stupid. Dad said if I wanted to take things apart, I could just go down to the shop where his buddy Dwayne worked and apprentice as a mechanic. 'Actually *make* money instead of just throwin' it away up north.' But Mr. Keegan convinced him a real education was worth it."

"What did they think when you started working with NASA?"

Colleen twisted her lips and looked down at her food. "Cynical. But to their credit, they told me exactly what was going to happen. The powers that be would pay for everything I did and then steal it right out from under me." She flipped her free hand, smiling tightly. "I haven't had the nerve to confess what happened, so we haven't talked in years. Luckily our relationship is shitty enough that staying silent for half a decade isn't really suspicious."

"Still, I'm sorry."

"Are you close to your parents?"

Margot said, "My dad. Mom died when I was little."

"He must be thrilled you chose such a safe profession."

Margot laughed. "He learned when I was a kid that he had two options: either he could find safe ways to raise a thrill-seeker, or he could wait for a cop to show up on his front porch to tell him his daughter had done something stupid. Support meant safety."

Colleen nodded. "That sounds reasonable."

"We're supposed to be talking about you."

"We did!" Colleen said. "Small town nobody, college, special government lab, and now here. Fill in the blanks with various garages, windowless labs, workshops, and you get the gist. I haven't led a very exciting life."

"Stealing from the military will probably raise your cool factor a little."

Colleen smirked.

"I know we're trying to keep me as separate as we can from the other, you know, conspirators. But can you at least tell me where you met all these women who are helping you with the... project?"

"We met all over the place, over the past couple of years. Some of them worked at the lab where I designed the ship. It was a melding of the science world and the military world, neither of which is particularly brimming with women, so we gravitated toward each other. Iris and Tracy reached out when they heard what happened. They told me if I ever needed anything, give them a call. I trusted them enough to follow through when I came up with the plan. Erica and Jessie are exes."

"That's four. I thought you said there were five besides us."

Colleen raised an eyebrow. "Pushing for information? Don't make me pour a bucket of water over you."

"You're the one who started naming names."

"True. The last one is Laura. We met when I was researching the engine, basically trying to see if anyone had ever tried to build one before. She floated the idea back in the 2010s, but never actually tried to make it a reality. I got in touch and we became friends. She's the first person I told about the engine, and the one who encouraged me to share it with the world."

"So you wouldn't be in this mess if it wasn't for her."

Colleen shrugged. "That's one way to look at it, I guess. But it's not her fault the government is a bunch of thieves and liars. If it wasn't for her, my designs would never have gotten out of a notebook and I might've ended up at Dwayne's shop anyway. She's as pissed off about this as I am, so she's willing to do whatever it takes to make sure we put it right."

"Sounds like a solid team."

"We're nothing without someone to take the damn thing up." She toasted Margot with her drink. "You really came through for me. I kept insisting that it would work out, and I think a couple of them were starting to have their doubts."

Margot said, "You told me you had a backup plan."

"Yeah, I also told you it was a terrible plan. I would take the ship up myself. Better than no one."

"Guaranteed to fail."

Colleen shrugged. "But if it worked, just long enough to prove the engine was viable, that would be worth it."

"I admire your insanity."

"I admire yours," Colleen said. "Taking a cardboard box down the steepest hill in the state and using a washed-out bridge as a ramp? That takes some ovaries, girl."

Margot said, "So you did do research on me."

"Of course I did. I know all your dirt."

Margot's first reaction was to laugh, but Colleen held her gaze with such a steady, unwavering stare that she started to wonder just what kind of dirt they'd come up with.

She was sure it would come up in due time.

From the daily journal of J. Colleen Eckles:

Big day, but equal parts boring and infuriating. I'm not even going to talk about that damn ship. I can see what needs to be done, and I know I can do it and I have the materials I need, but it's such a fucking slow headache that I feel like it's a race to complete it before I lose my damn mind. It helps that M is here now. She finally came through and she's burned a lot of bridges behind her, so I can't quit now without blowing up her whole life. That will keep me motivated.

Also J stopped by. The woman is a whiz when it comes to finding intel, but what a tiresome person. She's suspicious of EVERYONE. If a bank teller greeted her by name, I bet she'd switch banks. She still doesn't trust M, despite my vouching for her. I told her about the dousing incident, but she insists there are bugs that could have survived it. At that point, how do you even live your life? If everyone is out to get you, how do you exist in the world?

M staying here is an adjustment. But I think it'll be a good thing once we're both settled in. She cooked me dinner, which was a really nice surprise. I can't say she's a great chef, but she's better than me and Stouffer's, so that's all that really matters. I don't know how our personalities will mesh. Dinner went well, but that could just be n~

Margot was aware of the music playing well before it woke her up. She finally realized it wasn't part of her dream and opened her eyes, staring into the dark until she remembered where she was, and rolled onto her back. The music was definitely coming from inside the house, downstairs. Her watch said it was just past four o'clock in the morning.

She didn't mind the music. And normally she could sleep through anything, but her mouth was dry and she hadn't gotten a glass of water for her bedside. There wasn't really anywhere for her to put it, to be honest, except for one of the shelves, and she wasn't convinced she'd gotten all the spiders out.

She kicked away the blankets, found a way out of bed - it was more difficult than she anticipated without much room on either side - and headed downstairs.

Colleen was in the living room, tucked cozily into an armchair with her legs drawn up close to her chest. She had a small notebook open against her thighs, which were bare, and she was writing quickly across the page. She was dressed in a white button-down shirt and what appeared to be a pair of briefs, which exposed her from hip to her feet.

Margot couldn't stop staring at those legs, so entranced by them that it took her a second to realize Colleen had stopped writing and was now staring at her.

"Did I wake you up," Colleen asked at the same time Margot said, "Sorry."

Colleen picked up a remote control and aimed it at the bookshelf. A radio Margot hadn't noticed earlier quickly became silent.

"No, I was just coming to get something to drink. What are you writing?"

"Oh." She looked down at the notebook. "Just a journal. You know, keeping track of the day to day of what's going on."

Margot came into the living room. "Are you sure that's wise? It could be evidence."

"Well…" Colleen kept her voice measured. "If they do arrest me, it'll be really hard for me to claim I'm not doing this. If they get me, they get the ship. If they get the ship, I have a big engine-shaped hole in the back that anyone with half a brain cell will be able to identify. So yeah, this journal is a big red flag, but I figure I don't have much of a defense anyway." She shrugged. "I keep everyone else's name out of it."

"That's something, I guess." Margot reached under her hair and scratched her neck. "I'll just get my water and head back to bed. Your music was fine, by the way. I don't mind a little noise."

"No, it was rude of me. I can be more considerate. I'm used to being by myself out here, and it gets kind of spooky at night."

"I imagine."

She went into the kitchen, leaving the light off since she could see by the living room's light. She filled a glass at the sink and turned to see Colleen had followed her. Fortunately she was focused on the fridge and apparently didn't see Margot jump in surprise. Colleen opened the fridge door and bent forward to look inside, and Margot was again distracted by long, exposed legs, now draped by the wrinkled tail of her dress shirt. Her feet were also bare, impossibly small.

Margot took a long swallow of her water and averted her eyes to the ceiling. The ceiling was safe. There were no legs on the ceiling.

"I don't sleep much," Colleen explained as she popped the top of a V8. "I find micro-naps are much more satisfying."

"That's the thing where you sleep for five or six minutes throughout the day?"

Colleen nodded, finishing the can in three long gulps. "It doesn't work for everyone. But I started when I was a teenager and I don't think I could do it the normal way even if I tried. That's one of the reasons I offered you the big bedroom. I'm not exactly using it."

"Now that I know the truth, I might take you up on it. That sewing room is, uh, really tiny."

"Yeah." Colleen chuckled. "I don't think it was actually intended as a bedroom despite the bed being in there."

She leaned against the counter and the kitchen fell silent. Margot considered saying goodnight and taking her glass upstairs, but would that be rude? Or was it more rude to keep Colleen from getting back to her journal? She sipped her water.

Colleen broke the silence. "I like your pajamas."

Margot looked down at herself. She was wearing a NASA T-shirt and blue plaid pajama pants. She curled her toes inside her socks.

"Thanks." She was conditioned to respond to compliments in kind, so her sleep-deprived brain produced the worst two words she could possibly say in that moment. "Nice legs."

Colleen laughed softly. "Thanks. Not bad for a computer nerd, huh?"

"Mm." She flinched and looked away. She finished her water and refilled the glass. "Well, I'll go on back to bed. Sorry again for disturbing you."

"No, it's fine. Like I said, it gets creepy at night. Any time you can't sleep, feel free to come on down." She gestured at herself. "I'll try to wear pants more often."

"Don't do it on my account," Margot said before she could stop herself. "Good night."

"Night."

Margot fled back upstairs and sat on the foot of her bed with the full glass of water, which she didn't really want now. She put it on one of the shelves, spiders be damned, and slid back until she felt the pillows against her hips. She pulled the blanket up over her, rolled onto her side, and tried to get to sleep fast enough to pretend the entire interlude had been a dream.

From the daily journal of J. Colleen Eckles:
Well FUCK.

Chapter Eight

THEY DIDN'T talk about their late-night talk the next morning, or at the next dinner they shared. The only acknowledgement that it actually happened was a bag of Colleen's things had appeared in the hallway by the time Margot woke up. Margot accepted the silent offer and moved her bag into the bigger bedroom. After sleeping in the linen closet, it felt like a suite at the Ritz. She opened the shade and opened the window, which looked out at the front of the house instead of the barn, to let in some fresh air. The room didn't smell bad, per se, but Colleen's scent did linger, and she felt that might be distracting if it was still around at bedtime.

The shower was also cramped, a tiny tub shrouded in a transparent curtain that she couldn't see the point of. At least there wasn't any mildew or mold that she could see. Honestly, the house was in much better condition than she'd feared. A little peeling wallpaper, some cracks in the drywall, and there was the ever-present threat of bugs, rodents, and other wildlife sneaking in, but it was decent enough considering the circumstances.

The following week was a comfortable adjustment. They learned each other's habits, figured out when and how to stay out of each other's way, and managed to coexist in the house without getting on each other's nerves. Margot spent time in the barn observing the ship's construction, and Colleen was good about taking the time to explain what she was doing and what she'd already done. They also set up a workstation where Margot could familiarize herself with the console that would be installed in the ship. The buttons weren't hooked up to anything yet, but it was a big help to know where everything was.

At one point she'd looked up to see Colleen watching her with a smile. She curled her fingers away from the buttons, self-conscious.

"What?"

"Nothing." Colleen pushed her hair out of her face and looked away. "It's just... I don't know. Watching you mime the controls while I'm working on the ship. It's like a little kid who wants to be near daddy, so he gives the kid a fake hammer to bang on a piece of wood."

Margot smirked. "Well, I'm not calling you 'daddy'."

"Don't knock it," Colleen teased.

Margot cleared her throat and averted her eyes. Colleen also fell silent, obviously worried she'd gone too far.

Finally, Colleen cleared her throat. "So... um, not today, but we need to get you measured so I can get to work on the cockpit," she said. "Weight is going to be an issue, so leave your vanity at the door."

"I'm a pilot, you don't have to tell me that. I'm definitely going to be skipping dessert for a while, though."

Colleen smiled and said, "Ah, you're fine," so softly that Margot wasn't entirely sure how or if she should read into it. She decided not to.

"So, I noticed the washing machine in the house doesn't really work..."

"It works."

"It causes a seismic event every time you put in more than half a load."

Colleen shrugged. "It still *works*. The next closest machine is in Halcyon, and I'm not lugging bags of my dirty clothes all that way just to sit in a laundromat for an hour."

Margot said, "Well, that's what I'm here for. Leave a bag outside your bedroom and I'll take it tomorrow."

"Really?"

"Hey, I cook, I clean, I might as well do laundry, too."

Colleen nodded as she considered the offer. "Yeah, okay. I'll even leave you some quarters."

"Much obliged."

The next day, the bag of clothes was sitting outside of Colleen's bedroom. Margot took it and her own bag down to the car after breakfast. When she got to the head of the driveway she almost turned toward Halcyon but took a moment to consider it. She knew Halcyon had a laundromat, and it was the middle of a weekday so it probably wouldn't be terribly crowded. But, on the other hand, there was a washer and dryer in the opposite direction that she could use for free. As a bonus, it would give her a chance to check in with Linnie and her new probationary pilot.

She turned toward St. Elmo.

Hawkeye was coming in for a landing as she approached the airport. She smiled and waved even though she knew it wouldn't be seen, and she had no guarantee it was even Linnie flying. She wasn't waving at the pilot;

she was saying hello to her old friend. The plane looked glorious, gleaming and perfect as it sank out of the sky. A good pilot could make a plane act like a living creature, and whoever was at the controls definitely had a knack for it.

Margot parked a few minutes after Hawkeye touched down. By the time she got into the terminal, Linnie was behind the ticket counter entering something onto the computer. She glanced up with her professional face on as Margot approached, then did a double-take with her normal, gleeful expression when she recognized who it was.

"You should know we don't take pity on unemployed pilots, no matter how much they beg us to take a plane for a spin."

"Oh come on. I'll bring it back with a full tank of gas, I promise."

Linnie held out her arms as Margot came into the pass-through behind the counter and they hugged tightly.

"God, I miss seeing you every day!" Linnie said. "I can't believe it's only been a week. Rosie is sick of hearing me complain." She stepped back and squeezed Margot's shoulders. "She's going to be so pissed. She's in Denver picking up a part."

"Is—"

"Everything is fine," Linnie cut her off. "She just used all her backup of some backup and needs to get more before it becomes a necessity." She shrugged. "Always overprepared and we love her for it."

"We do, we do."

Linnie raised her eyebrows and lowered her voice. "So? How's the, um, all the stuff going...?"

"The 'stuff'?"

Linnie looked around and motioned for Margot to follow her into the office. "Yeah, well, you know. It's... sub-legal, right? Like spies. We have to be careful what we say."

Margot laughed. "The bird flies at midnight."

"Exactly!" She shut the door and shrugged. "So it's going well?"

"Yeah. Yeah. I mean, I only get the surface stuff of the actual build. It looks solid. Trustworthy. She seems to know what she's doing."

Linnie narrowed her eyes. "I sense a 'but' coming."

Margot sighed dreamily. "And it's a great one..."

"What?"

Margot went to what used to be her desk and sat down on the edge of it. "Colleen. Her ass. Her... well, her whole damn body, really. She does not look like what an engineer should look like." She worked her teeth over her bottom lip. "I'm stuck in a house out in the middle of nowhere with this spectacular, brilliant, hot as hell woman, and it's not fair that I can't do anything."

"Is she straight?"

"No."

"Married?"

"No."

Linnie held her hands out questioningly. "So...?"

"Because this is a mission! This is..." She ran her hands over her hair, tugged on her ponytail, and looked at her feet. "We're supposed to be working together."

"Rosie and I were just supposed to be working together, too. Then one night, I found her in the hangar, fast asleep in her chair with a smudge of grease on her cheek and that red baseball cap of hers on backward." She chuckled at the memory. "And I knew that I had to do something about her, about how I felt, or it would become an issue. It would hurt the work if I didn't explore those feelings."

Margot said, "I'm not talking about *feelings*. Sure, she seems like a great person and we get along well, but this is just..." She gestured vaguely. "She has a great butt."

Linnie laughed. "You two are planning something insane. You're both basically planning to end up in jail, right? Best case scenario?"

"Yeah."

"So." She crossed the room and cupped Margot's face with both hands. "You're out there in the middle of nowhere building an illegal spaceship in a big house all by yourself with a woman you find hot. Don't be an idiot. At least gauge her interest. Who knows where it might go."

Margot twisted her lips. "Okay. Well. I'll think about it. The real reason I'm here is because I want to borrow your laundry room."

"Sure, mi casa," she said. "Do you still have your emergency key?"

"Yep."

"Come here." She pulled Margot into another hug. "Are you going to stick around long enough to have dinner?"

"Probably not. I need to get back as soon as the laundry is done or she'll probably panic and think I'm calling NASA or Russia or something."

Linnie nodded. "Okay. Well, go see Rosie before you leave. She misses you as much as I do."

"Yeah. Oh! I almost forgot to ask you how the new pilot is working out."

"So far so good! I think she's too worried about impressing us to actually be herself yet. But she's smart, capable, friendly. I think I saw a TARDIS baseball cap in the backseat of her car the other day, so that gives me hope that she's worth the trouble."

"Fingers crossed." She'd met the new pilot, Casey, at her interview, but there was a whole world between someone's interview skills and how they performed in reality. She was relieved to hear her instincts had been right. "Okay. I'm heading out. I'll try not to mess up your house too much."

Linnie said, "And no snooping."

"No promises. See you later, Linnie."

"You'd better, or Rosie will skin me alive."

Margot left, internally telling herself that she could stick around until Rosie got back from Denver, but she was already pushing things by going to St. Elmo instead of Halcyon. She would confess when she got back to the Garage but, if Colleen was feeling antsy and noticed she'd been gone longer than necessary... But no. Colleen would be too busy in the barn to even notice the time going by. As long as she got back before dark she would be fine.

Linnie's house was quiet and still, and she paused on the threshold with her bags of clothes. She felt like a thief, despite the fact she'd used a key and had been an invited guest dozens of times. There was nothing she found comfortable about being in someone's house when they weren't there. She pushed through the awkwardness and went through the kitchen to the laundry room.

She started with Colleen's clothes. She tried to ignore looking as she loaded handfuls of clothes into the washer, terrified of catching a glimpse of something lacy or frilly. But the only underwear she saw was normal, utilitarian, boring. She let down her guard and spotted a pair of green briefs decorated with tiny daisies. Not sexual at all, absolutely not arousing. They were cute.

But somehow, damn it, cute was worse.

She slammed the lid of the washer and fled the room.

Margot distracted herself by vacuuming the living room, tidying the bookshelf, and putting away the dishes. When she finished with Colleen's clothes, she folded them and returned them to the bag, hoping they would survive the trip back to the Garage without getting too wrinkled. She also ignored the delicates then, too, as much as she could.

Her last load was almost finished when she heard the front door open. "Margot, you still here?"

"Laundry room!" Margot called.

Linnie and Rosie came in through the kitchen. Rosie made a shrill, happy noise and ran to Margot, hugging her so tightly it was almost an assault. Linnie grinned and slipped out of the room.

"I hate the new pilot so much!"

Margot laughed. "Linnie already told me she's working out well."

"She's dumb and she can't sing and I hate her guts." She stepped back. "Can you please stay for dinner? Please? Lin texted to tell me you were here and I hot-footed it all the way from Denver."

"I'm sorry, I've got to get back." Although if pressed about *why* she had to go back, she wouldn't be able to come up with much of a reason. She couldn't even really explain it to herself. But the longer she was away, the more anxious she was to get back. "But I'm so glad to see you. I'm going to come back when I really have time to hang out and gossip."

Rosie sighed. "Okay. As long as you promise a real visit. Soon."

"Promise."

The dryer buzzed and Margot went to get her last load of clothes. When she came back, Linnie had reappeared and was standing next to the bags on the table.

"Hey, I just folded all that. Don't mess it up."

Linnie held her hands up and retreated. "Rosie says you promised us dinner."

"I will, scout's honor. On a day when I don't have to rush through it. You two deserve more than a rushed meal."

Rosie helped her fold the clothes, and Linnie carried the bags out to the car. Rosie said, "Are you really doing okay out there with the sexy mechanic?"

Margot rolled her eyes. "Linnie told you?"

"Linnie tells me everything."

"I'm doing great. It's a crush caused by going too long without a girlfriend. I'll get over it."

Rosie shrugged. "Well, don't overthink it." She glanced over her shoulder to make sure Linnie was still outside. "Did she tell you she realized how she felt about me when she saw me sleeping?"

"Yeah." Margot couldn't help smiling. "It's a great story."

"I spent *six months* flirting my ass off with that woman, and she finally gets the picture when I'm unconscious." She shook her head and chuckled. "I'm just saying, you never know what will work. Take the risk, all right?"

"I'll... take the advice."

"Fair enough."

Linnie came back inside and they said their goodbyes. Margot repeated her promise to spend an entire day with them at some point in the near future before she headed out. The sun was low in the sky when she left St. Elmo, and it had started painting the landscape with long shadows by the time she keyed in the code for the Garage's front gate. She drove to her normal parking spot and practically stood on the brakes when she saw a car was already parked in it. The car lurched to a stop and she scanned the yard for the owner.

The whole property seemed abandoned. She cautiously pulled up and parked, then got out of the car and approached the barn as quietly as she could. She heard voices inside, two women. Colleen sounded angry, but the other was calm. When she got close enough to make out what they were saying, both voices fell quiet.

"We might as well just ask her at this point," the stranger said.

Colleen sounded pissed. "Margot? Come on in."

Margot considered running. Instead she came around the door and stopped in her tracks for the second time in ten minutes. The woman standing with Colleen wasn't a stranger. She was shockingly tall, with her hair shaved at the sides. She was the kind of woman that might be described as an Amazon by someone who met her at a bar in Pueblo and then tried to fuck her. Her arms were crossed over her chest, and she looked much angrier than she had when Margot fled her car.

"I... guess your name isn't Amanda."

Colleen looked confused. "You know each... Who is Amanda?"

"I told her that was my name when I met her at a bar." She rolled her eyes at Colleen's horrified expression. "I told *you* I was going to check up on her."

"I didn't think that would include *stalking*," Colleen said. "What the hell, Jessie?"

Margot's cheeks burned, and she struggled to keep her eyes from watering. She felt humiliated, violated, and she was starting to rethink the whole thing. She glared at Colleen. "So you didn't know about this?"

"Absolutely not. I wouldn't have agreed to it. And if I'd known about it after the fact, I would have apologized to you."

Jessie shook her head. "We're missing the point here."

"No, we're not," Colleen said. "You crossed the line."

Jessie ignored her and pointed a finger at Margot. "*You* lied."

"What? When did I lie?"

"Today. You claimed you went to Halcyon for laundry. I was watching the laundromat and you never showed up."

Margot rolled her eyes. "Oh my God, I went to St. Elmo instead. I thought I would take the opportunity to check in on my friends. Which was free, by the way, so I still have Colleen's quarters." She pulled the rolled coins out of her pocket and held them out. "Just in case you were going to accuse me of theft next."

Colleen took the roll. "For the record, I'm not accusing you of anything."

Margot looked at Jessie. "So have you been following me?"

Jessie scoffed. "Yeah, like I could follow anybody out here. Real conspicuous when we'd be the only two cars on the road."

"Then how..." She fixed a glare on Colleen. "Not accusing me of anything, huh? Just telling her where I'll be and when."

Colleen held her hands up in defense. "All I did was text her when you wouldn't be around so she can come by and give me updates without the two of you crossing paths. I didn't know she was using it for this reason, I swear. And after this little debacle, the updates stop. They're kind of pointless now that we're all standing here looking at each other anyway, I guess."

Margot took a series of slow breaths, hands on her hips. "I don't like being spied on, and I don't like being accused of spying. I went to St. Elmo. I saw Linnie and Rosie, and that's it. I did laundry. It's out in the car. And so help me, if you start stalking them to see if they're working for the CIA or NASA or the Illuminati or whoever you're afraid of~"

"She won't," Colleen said. "You have my word."

Jessie looked enormously angry. She uncrossed her arms and moved closer to Colleen. "You wanted this thing shored up. You wanted it completely impenetrable. That's what I've been giving you. And if you want to drop those walls now, I hope you enjoy the consequences."

Colleen didn't blink. "I trust Margot. You can back off, and back up."

Jessie did her one better and left. On her way out, she glanced at Margot and puckered her lips in a snide, sarcastic kiss. Margot curled her lip in disgust.

They listened to Jessie slam her car door, then the revved engine, and the sound of her departure up the road. They stood together in the silence, looking at the floor or the barn walls to avoid eye contact.

"Since she didn't say it, I will. I'm sorry, Margot. I swear to you, it won't happen again."

"Okay." Margot ran her hands through her hair. "I don't have to forgive you because it wasn't your fault, but I appreciate the sentiment." She dropped her arms. "I'm going to take the clothes inside. I'll leave yours by your bedroom."

"Thank you."

"Sure." Margot turned to leave.

"They're not all that bad," Colleen said.

Margot didn't feel like smiling, but she did relax her posture a little. She shrugged. "I guess we'll have to wait and see, hm?"

Later that night, Margot was reading in bed when there was a knock on the door. "Come in." She was in her pajamas but still resisted the urge to pull the blanket up over her. If Colleen could hang out in the living room without pants, she could be equally immodest. The door opened and Colleen poked her head in, leaving her right arm outside and out of sight.

"Hey." She looked around the room. "I like what you've done to the place."

"Oh, yeah, I really made it my own," Margot joked. "Is everything okay?"

Colleen nodded. "Yeah. Yeah. Um... you said you went to your friend's house to do the laundry?"

"Yeah. Linnie Payton. Your spy probably told you everything you need to know about her."

Colleen flinched and looked away. "Yeah. Have you... did you tell her about me?"

"She knows I'm down here with an engineer, the person building the ship. I didn't give her any firm details. I haven't even told her your name." She ran through her memory, wondering if that was a lie. "Why, what's up?"

"No, it's nothing, it's just..." She was smiling weirdly and, after a moment, came into the room. She was holding two boxes, which she held out to Margot. "I think she probably meant to put this in your laundry, not mine."

Margot frowned, put her book down, and took the boxes. The blood drained from her face when she saw the first one - Boxer Brief Strap-On Harness - and she had a fair guess what the other box was, but she looked anyway. Six inches. There was a Post-It stuck to the front of the second box with Linnie's unmistakable handwriting. "JUST IN CASE!"

She forced herself to look up. Fortunately, Colleen seemed equally embarrassed, although there was a touch of true amusement in her smile as well.

"I di-didn't... I-I..."

Colleen finally laughed and waved off her stammering. "Don't worry about it. I have friends who would have done the same thing. Thank you for doing my laundry for me. It all smells a hundred times better than when I use the machines here."

"Yeah, because these machines probably have mold in them or something." She was very aware she was still holding a box with a dildo on the front. She tucked it out of sight. "I'll be happy to do it again the next time you need another load done."

"I appreciate it. And no one will be stalking you when you do. Promise."

"Thanks."

Colleen backed out into the hall. "Goodnight."

"Night."

When the door was closed, Margot sagged against the pillows and exhaled sharply. She looked at the ceiling, shook her head, and stowed both boxes in the gap between the mattress and the night stand. She would bury them with Linnie after she got done torturing her to death.

CHAPTER NINE

THE SCOOPED back of Colleen's tank top. A bead of sweat on tanned skin, trickling along the curve her shoulder blade. One arm flexed as she raises a bottle of water and pours it onto her face. The water splashing, cascading, dripping. Wetting her tank top. She turns. She sees Margot watching. And Margot—

Margot woke up, snorting into her pillow and then pushing it up against her face. She grunted but didn't know if it was from frustration or the lack of closure from the dream. She rolled onto her back and pushed her pajama pants down under the blanket. She thought about retrieving the dildo but she really wanted to wash it before she used it. Besides, she didn't think this would take very long.

She put her free hand behind her head, closed her eyes, and wet her lips. She thought about kissing Amanda - or apparently *Jessie* - the way it felt to press against her in the backseat, hands on her bare skin, tongue on her breast. At some point during the fantasy, the woman under her transformed into Colleen.

Margot touched herself as she imagined the sunbaked taste of Colleen's skin. Two fingers, pursing her lips and imagining Colleen's pressing against them. Stroking and teasing as she pictured Colleen putting her arms up to allow her tank top to be peeled off. That damn tank top... she'd only seen it once, but it was all she could think about. If it had been in the bag of laundry, Margot hadn't seen it. She dragged her free hand around to her face, stroked her cheek, and let her fingers slide over her lips as she pushed her middle finger against her folds.

Something in the wall clunked, and there was a gurgle, and then the already-familiar hush of water running through the pipes. Margot opened her eyes and held her breath. The shower. Colleen was just a few feet away at that very moment, standing in the shower, naked, wet, scrubbing away the sweat and the dirt of the day.

"Oh, fuck," Margot groaned, moving her hand faster. Scenarios popped across her mind's eye: the silhouette through the fogged curtain, soapy hands moving over a toned thigh, suds concealing those magnificent breasts. Hair flattened by the water. Margot was gasping now, lifting her hips to meet her hand as she sucked two fingers of her other hand.

She teased herself, holding back until she heard the water stop. She held her breath and closed her thighs around her hand, trembling as she pictured what Colleen was doing.

Toweling off. "Fuck..."

Dripping from every flexed muscle and curve. "Oh fuck..."

Maybe she had masturbated in the shower.

That finally did it. She bit down on her finger as she came, hard enough that there were teeth marks in the skin and probably would be for a while. She was aware that the bed was creaking under her, knew that Colleen could hear it, and if she came to check on her...

"Come in here," she whispered, "come in here, come in here..."

She heard the bathroom door open and risked a look at the closed bedroom door. She wanted Colleen to appear, she was terrified of what would happen if she did, but the door remained stubbornly closed. When she heard the other bedroom door close, she gave in and finished herself off, choking back the noisier reactions and trying to keep as still as possible so the bed wouldn't give her away.

Afterward she lay with one hand between her legs and the other on her breast. She stared at the ceiling as she listened to Colleen moving around elsewhere in the house. Living in this house was going to be absolute hell if she didn't figure out some way to keep her hormones under control. She glanced at the nightstand, sensing the toys hidden in the shadows beside it, and cursed Linnie one more time before she rolled over and tried to force herself to sleep, praying she'd taken care of any more dreams her subconscious intended to inflict on her.

Colleen was already at the table when Margot came down for breakfast the next morning. She was in a button-down shirt with the top few buttons undone, her chin resting in one cupped hand. Margot prided herself in not looking down into the wide gap as she passed. She went to the cupboard and found the box of Pop-Tarts she'd gotten the last time she got groceries. Only two left.

"I need to do another supply run," she said. "Is this flavor okay or do you want to mix it up?"

She waited for an answer and, when none came, looked over her shoulder. Colleen's lips were slack, her eyes closed.

"Colleen...?" She moved closer to the table and bent down. She looked frozen, almost like wax. The hand which wasn't holding up her head was curled loosely around the handle of a coffee mug. Margot furrowed her brow and stared in confusion.

Colleen opened her eyes. Blinked. Inhaled through her nose and sat up straighter. "Oh hey."

"Were you asleep?"

"Yeah." She laced her fingers and stretched her arms over her head. "Micro-naps, like I told you. I fall asleep for a couple of minutes throughout the day and I end up more rested than if I was in bed for six hours at night."

"And it just happens randomly?"

Colleen laughed. "No, I can control when it happens, obviously. It would be a serious problem if I just passed out from time to time. But you weren't up yet, so I thought it was a good time to get in some rest. Have you been here long?"

"No." Margot sat across from her and opened the pastry package. "I was just asking about Pop-Tarts. Do you want a different flavor when I get more?"

"No, that's fine." She made a face. "You're just going to eat them cold like that?"

Margot stopped. "They taste perfectly fine cold."

"Yeah, but they taste *great* hot."

"They taste different. Sometimes I don't want anything piping hot in the morning."

Colleen shook her head. "You're weird, Margot Sullivan. But that's what I like about you." She got up and went to the counter. "I'm just going to have some toast and head out to start work."

Margot turned in her seat. "Here's a question. When's the last time you left this place?"

"I don't know. It was before you got here and started running all my errands for me."

"You're not feeling a little cabin fever?"

Colleen shook her head. "I have my work. If I left, the work wouldn't be getting done, and that would make me anxious. I'm happy staying here."

"That's a quick way to losing your mind," Margot said. "You need to step away from the work sometimes. Rest your brain and your body. You're smart enough to know that."

"What if I take a day off, and then I'm one day late? They move the engine but I'm not ready to install it yet? What if we get the engine but by the time we're ready to test it, the government has already tracked us down?" She shook her head. "I need to finish the ship. I need to have it ready when

Iris gives the go signal."

"You're already working around the clock. Burn-out is a real thing. I don't want to go up in a shuttle built by someone who burned the candle at both ends for months. If anyone can get the ship ready in time, it's you, and if taking a day off from time to time makes you miss the deadline, then... then the deadline was impossible to hit anyway."

Colleen considered the argument. "Okay. I'll let you take me to Halcyon for an afternoon, two or three hours *at most* if you let me measure you for the cockpit today."

Margot said, "Really? You're ready for that?"

"I can rearrange the schedule a little, but yes. It's a vital part of the design and I'd rather not put it off any longer than I have to. Once we have that locked down, we can rush other parts if we have to."

"Deal," Margot said.

Colleen seemed to relax a little. "Okay, then. We'll go out after breakfast."

Margot was so thrilled she'd won the day-off argument that it took her a moment to realize what 'measuring' would entail. Colleen touching her, examining her, maybe even asking her to undress down to her underwear to get a proper baseline. She looked down at the remaining Pop-Tart and pushed it away.

The ship in the center of the barn tended to absorb all the attention and awe, but the entire building was an impressive place, once Margot took a second to actually examine it. A few horse stalls had been removed to accommodate the ship and give Colleen room to work, but the ones at the back were still intact. Most of them were filled with clutter, farm tools combined with things Colleen had obviously brought in to build the ship. Spare parts, large machines that Margot couldn't begin to guess at their function, and stacks of paneling.

Colleen pointed her toward the stall at the back, which turned out to be empty except for a padded seat and what looked like an old-time switchboard leaning against the wall.

"We can do the measurements back here," Colleen said. "Have a seat, make sure the chair is comfortable."

Margot settled into the chair and wiggled a bit, testing how it held her weight. It was a little stiff, but that would be a good thing. Too comfortable would be a flaw, might make her relax too much. Spaceflight required full alertness. This chair would serve their purposes well.

"How'd you get your hands on all of this?"

"I told you, my people are good. Most of the stuff is technically salvage, but you know these space agencies. They throw things out the first time something new and shiny crosses in front of them. Some of it has flaws, but

I can compensate so they don't affect the overall integrity. It's a junk ship, but it's still solid. The only thing that matters is the engine, and I guarantee that's pristine."

Margot stood up. "I guess that's comforting to know." She glanced at the measuring tape in Colleen's hand. "Well. Okay, I guess..." She reached for the top button of her blouse.

"I could leave..."

"You're going to see me anyway when you take the measurements," Margot said. "It's fine."

Colleen nodded, but still averted her gaze as Margot unbuttoned her shirt and pulled it off. She was wearing a normal black bra with matching briefs. Nothing overtly sexy, but given Colleen's aesthetic, it might be exactly what she found appealing. She took off her shoes and quickly doffed her jeans, mentally demanding that she stop thinking about what Colleen might find appealing.

"All right," she said, draping her clothes over the chair and standing awkwardly in the middle of the stall. "Doing this in a barn makes me feel a little bit like cattle."

"This was a horse barn."

"The point remains."

"Be good and I'll make sure you get a nice shiny apple after we're done."

Margot smirked.

Colleen approached, rested the fingers of one hand on Margot's right shoulder, and stretched across her collarbones. She dropped her hands and typed a number into her phone.

"You know that doing it this way will make the cockpit a little snug."

"I understand," Margot said. "It's all about optimizing space, weight, and material. I don't mind being squeezed in a little bit."

"I'll try to make you as comfortable as possible." She pulled the tape from Margot's left shoulder down to her wrist, muttered the number, and made another note.

Margot said, "Do you want me to type in the numbers for you?"

"Would you mind?"

"It'll give me something to do other than just standing here like a mannequin." It would also help distract her from the feel of Colleen's fingers sliding over her bare skin.

Colleen handed her the phone. "Thanks. It might speed things up a little. Okay. Right arm."

Margot used her left hand to enter the number into the phone. Colleen stretched the tape from below Margot's arm, down to her hip.

"Okay, um..." Colleen hesitated, then slipped her arms under Margot's and stepped in. Margot held her breath and was forced to look into

Colleen's eyes. "Sorry..."

"S'okay."

Colleen pulled the tape around and pinched it in front of Margot's chest. Margot was aware of the skin on her arms erupting in goosepimples, and she desperately hoped Colleen didn't notice. Colleen seemed to be incredibly focused on getting the numbers right. She dropped the tape and stepped back, and they both breathed a sigh of relief.

Until Colleen crouched down in front of her and rested the tape against her upper thigh. Margot inhaled sharply, her whole body going tense.

"Sorry~"

"Nope..."

"We can..."

"It's fine," Margot said. "Inseam. Necessess..." She flinched and shook her head. "Necessary measurement."

Colleen got the numbers for Margot's legs as quickly as she could, then stood up and took a step back in the same motion.

"Next we need to, um, weigh you, get a proper weight. But we can do that closer to the actual launch so it's more accurate."

Margot nodded and handed back the phone. "Uh-huh. Sure." She stared at Colleen, who returned the stare for a moment before she started looking for somewhere else to rest her eyes. She settled on the phone screen.

"So you-you can get dressed now."

"Oh right."

Margot grabbed her clothes and stepped into her jeans. Colleen looked torn between leaving and standing there for no reason, which resulted in her swaying a little as Margot buttoned, zipped, and straightened. The awkwardness hung in the silence between them.

"Sorry about... you know, gasping." Margot winced. "It's just... you know."

"Yeah, hey. No. Sensitive area, someone touching you there without warning. I should have said something before just putting my hands on your thigh."

"No, that was fine, you can touch me." She flinched. "When... you're... you were measuring me. So I was expecting... touching."

Colleen chuckled and scratched her head. "Okay. So this went about as well as expected, so I'll just go get to work on designing that cockpit."

"Great."

Colleen fled. Margot took a second to compose herself, smoothing down her hair and checking her clothes, then followed. Colleen was already at her worktable, making marks on the blueprint with a pencil that looked like it had been smashed flat. She wasn't sitting, but rather bent at the waist with her weight resting on her elbow so that her ass stuck out. Margot rolled her eyes at the temptation but then looked anyway as she passed.

She was almost to the door when she stopped and turned around. "I'm always fine with you touching me. Just for the record."

Colleen stared at her, utterly confused. "Okay," she said.

"I just wanted to say that. In case you thought maybe I gasped because I didn't want you to, or had some issue with being touched." She shrugged. "Now I've said it. So."

"Noted."

"I'll be in the house if you need anything."

Colleen nodded and went back to her scribbling. Margot watched her, then left her to the work.

That night, while Margot was cooking chicken and rice for their dinner, the sky blacked out and soon broke open with rain. Colleen turned on some hanging lights to continue her work, and Margot watched her from the kitchen window. It was like she was on a stage, performing a one-woman show with the most impressive prop ever seen in theater. Eventually she turned off the lights and ran through the rain to come inside, and Margot busied herself so she wouldn't have to explain her ogling.

The door slapped shut, and Colleen shook the rain out of her hair as she came into the kitchen. "Hey. I'm going to go change before we eat."

"Okay."

"Smells great."

Margot batted her eyelashes and curtsied. "Well, thank you so much, honey, I have to keep my man happy."

Colleen chuckled nervously. She wasn't standing up straight, like she was still ducking down to avoid the rain. "What?"

"You know. Like you're a husband from the fifties coming home from work, and I spent all day slaving over a hot stove..."

"You said you didn't mind cooking."

"I don't!"

"I can cook from time to time if you're~"

Margot laughed and waved her hands for a time-out. "I'm not complaining. It was a bit. I was doing a bit. Trying to be funny."

"Oh." Most of the tension faded from Colleen's posture, but her shoulders remained hunched. "Sorry. I do feel kind of guilty about you doing all the chores around here. You know, the... so-called woman's work."

"I really don't mind. We each have our jobs. I'm just killing time until my real job is ready." She gestured out the window. "Flying that thing. That's the real woman's work in this house."

Colleen smiled. "Hell yeah, it is." She turned to go upstairs, reaching up to squeeze her neck as she did.

"Hey, hold on. What's up with that?" She gestured at her own neck.

"I tweaked my neck reaching for a tool. It was stupid. The shower usually unkinks it."

Margot put down the spoon she was stirring with. "Don't be silly. Come here. Turn around."

"It's really okay. I do it all the time."

"There's no point in suffering if you don't have to. I do this for Linnie all the time."

Colleen reluctantly turned around. Margot put her hands on Colleen's shoulders and pressed down with all her fingers. She extended her thumbs and worked them in wide circles on either side of Colleen's neck. The muscles were unbelievably tight, but she could already feel them becoming looser. Colleen must have felt it too, because her head lolled forward as if her spine had been snapped. Margot noted that she was taller than Colleen. Not by much, but enough that it seemed very noticeable at this particular moment. She felt powerful, dominant, and she squeezed harder.

"Oh-h, wow," Colleen moaned.

Margot grinned. "Good?"

"Mm-hmm. Wow."

"I've gotten my fair share of compliments on my backrubs," Margot bragged. "How's that pressure?"

"Good..." Colleen sounded hypnotized.

Margot continued to massage even after she felt the tension fade. She was also a little hypnotized by the way Colleen's head rocked side to side with each squeeze and stroke. Her hair was just short enough to leave a gap above her shirt where the bare skin of her neck was visible. Margot stared at the skin, tanned and damp, and licked her lips. She wanted to lean in, kiss away that wetness, but she wouldn't.

"That's good," Colleen whispered.

"Yeah?" Margot asked, squeezing again.

"No, I mean... that's good." She eased away from Margot's touch. "I-I'm... it's all good."

Margot snapped out of her trance. "Oh right. Yeah. Okay." She snapped her fingers and aimed finger guns at Colleen, hating herself throughout. "Let me know if you ever need another rubdown."

Colleen smiled tightly at her. "Will do. Thanks. You're a miracle worker."

"No problem."

Colleen left the kitchen, taking the stairs two at a time, while Margot fled back to the stove to stir the food like her life depended on it.

When Colleen came back down, they both silently decided to act like the massage hadn't happened. Margot served up their food and suggested they eat on the porch so they could watch the rain. Colleen agreed and they went out.

Colleen had changed into clean jeans and a T-shirt, and she put her bare feet up on the railing so they could get splashed by the rain. Margot sat beside her, a perfectly normal and platonic distance between their chairs. Thunder rumbled from the mountains, but neither of them saw any lightning to go along with it.

"It was raining the day we met," Colleen said.

"Yeah." Margot didn't know if it was an idle comment or an invitation to start a conversation. She had nothing to add either way, so she just stayed silent.

"I'm really glad you came around."

Margot shrugged. "There are plenty of pilots out there who could do what I can do. I'm not special, just nearby."

"I already told you why you were chosen," Colleen said. "We started with a whole list of pilots who could pull this off. And yes, I suppose there are other pilots who would've worked. You're the only one who not only had the qualifications but also didn't drive me insane. I liked you when we met. You were tough. You took that airline and made it your own. I knew that whoever flew my ship couldn't just be a hired gun. It had to be someone I felt a connection with."

Maybe it was the rain, or the dream, or the vulnerability she'd shown while she was half-naked in the barn with Colleen's hands on her, but she felt emboldened to say what she said next.

"That's not actually how we met."

"What? Of course it was."

Margot looked at her and raised her eyebrows. "Okay, it wasn't the first time we *spoke*. You called and caught me..."

Colleen's eyes widened slightly and she nodded her head slowly. "Oh. Okay. So we're going to talk about that? I kind of thought you wanted me to forget it happened."

"Well, you were a stranger then, and now you've seen me in my underpants. Why let it be awkward? You called and listened to me masturbate."

Colleen laughed nervously, her pale cheeks flushing pink as she avoided her gaze. "Did I ever apologize for that?"

"What's to apologize for? You didn't make me answer the phone when I was in that condition."

"I guess." She put her feet down and sat up straighter in her seat. "Still, I didn't hang up when it became clear what was happening."

Margot sipped her water. "What *did* you do?"

Colleen let the question hang. The rain pattered on the awning over their heads. Margot looked at Colleen, examining her face as she considered her answer. Finally Colleen wet her lips, turned away from the yard, and locked eyes with her.

"Are we really doing this?"

Margot raised her shoulder in a 'why not?' gesture.

Colleen's lips curved. "I touched myself. It was a turn-on. I knew what you looked like and I had just heard you in the throes of passion. It was hot, and I rubbed one out."

Margot smiled, feeling triumphant for some reason.

"It seemed weird to bring it up once you became... once we were, you know..."

"I get it. And you don't have to feel weird." Her ears burned, and she almost stopped the next words before she said them. "I've masturbated about you, too."

Colleen quietly exhaled, a sound Margot couldn't quantify.

"Is that okay?"

"Yeah," Colleen said. "Sure, I'm... yeah."

More rain sounds. Margot liked being out in the open like this to watch storms. With such a big platform, it was easy to see how the waves came, how it could be heavy in one spot and just a light sprinkle just a few yards away. Cool breezes wafted up onto the porch and brought with them the smell of sharp ozone. She breathed it in and closed her eyes. It was her favorite smell. After a couple of seconds that felt like much longer, she realized that Colleen wasn't going to be the one to break the silence.

"I didn't want to make you uncomfortable. I just thought, since we're out here alone, asking each other for trust, it would help to have all the cards on the table."

She thought she saw Colleen's tension fade a little. "Makes sense. And are they? The cards? All on the table?"

"Yeah. All the ones that matter."

Colleen nodded slowly, thoughtfully. "In the spirit of that, I think the time has come for you to meet the rest of the group."

"I—"

"They're putting as much at risk as we are. Some of them are risking more. If Iris gets caught, she could be court-martialed. They deserve to know the woman who will be taking us over the finish line. And if there's another landmine like Jessie waiting to be activated, I'd like to know before the last minute so we have time to adjust whatever needs adjusting."

"I guess that makes sense."

Colleen nodded. "I'll reach out, see when they can drop in for a visit. I don't know if we can get them all at once, or if we'd even want to gather everyone in one place at the same time, but I'll see what we can do."

"I look forward to it."

This time when silence fell, the awkwardness didn't fill in the gaps. Margot went back to her rice, and Colleen put her feet back up on the railing, and they watched the rain. It was nice, it was comfortable. It was almost domestic. Margot thought maybe this was enough. Maybe this was exactly what she'd always wanted. Romance was fine, but really all she wanted was someone she liked sitting next to her to while she ate dinner. It was enough.

Then Colleen said, "And if you ever decide you want to fuck me, just let me know."

Margot choked on her water.

Chapter Ten

RAIN PATTERED on the ground just beyond the porch, accompanied by an increasingly rare growl of thunder. Other than clearing throats and the occasional squeak of wood when one of them changed positions, the porch was silent as Margot and Colleen finished their dinners. When her bowl was finally clean, Margot stood up.

"I think I'm going to turn in."

"I'm sorry if I crossed a line," Colleen said.

Margot said, "Hey, no, it's, you were just, hey," and then decided to give up on speech. She shook her head and gave Colleen a thumbs up. "No problem. It's, it was, you're fine."

Colleen smiled, her eyes pained. "Still. Sorry."

"Okay," Margot said, then escaped into the safety of the house. She rinsed out her bowl and then moved on to the pan she'd used to cook their meal. She scrubbed hard, focusing on the water and bubbles swirling down the drain. Her skin felt electrified. She wondered if that was a byproduct of the storm. She'd heard that sometimes these storms could cause physical reactions. Goosebumps, hair standing on end, things like that. She wondered if her fingers would spark on the faucet and tried it. Nope, apparently not.

Who the hell just randomly made an offer like that? What kind of person casually suggested...

She blew out a lungful of air as if that would push the thoughts out of her head. She was blushing. She was anxious. She felt like she could run at the wall and go straight up, not stopping until she was on the ceiling like a cartoon character. She put her hands on the edge of the counter and tilted her head back. Eyes closed, she counted to ten under her breath. She inhaled and counted again. Exhaled, counted again.

After a full minute of counting, Margot pushed away from the counter and went back outside. She couldn't go to bed and pretend that conversation hadn't happened. She needed closure on it, or she anticipated an entire night of tossing and turning and reenacting potential replies rolling around in her mind. She stepped out onto the porch and went straight to the railing.

"I don't want you to think that~" The words died on her tongue as she saw Colleen was fast asleep in the chair. Her arms were crossed over her chest, head on her chin, body relaxed. She still had her feet up on the railing. Her shoulders rose and fell with slow, rhythmic breathing. Margot closed her mouth and stared. She mentally ticked off seconds.

After three minutes, Colleen's eyelids fluttered and she lifted her head. She looked at Margot and her confusion faded into understanding.

"Hi."

"That's *really* how you sleep."

"We talked about this," Colleen said, putting her feet down.

Margot frowned. "I know, but... is that it for the night? No more sleeping for you?"

"No, I'll probably get another three or four by morning."

"That's-that's... that isn't..." She gestured wildly. "That's not right! After a whole day of climbing around that ship, hammering and welding and whatever else it is you're doing, you need more than a tiny little snooze. You need to actually do the ritual, you know? Take a shower, brush your teeth, climb into a nice soft bed, wrap yourself up in a cozy blanket... Sleep is about more than just the mechanics of sleeping. It's about going to bed!"

"Lying still for six hours does not sound like my idea of a good time. It sounds like a medical condition. I've never needed that."

Margot scoffed. "The metal bars I felt in your shoulder beg otherwise. How often does that sort of thing happen?"

Colleen shrugged. "Once in a while."

"You need to take breaks."

"This again?"

"Yes, this again. You need to step away. Recharge. Get away from here so your brain can process things and move forward."

Colleen looked out at the rain, which was starting to diminish. "I don't want to leave. My project is here, the ship is here."

"You're acting like you're already a prisoner. What if we get away with this?"

Colleen smirked. "We won't."

"But if we *did* somehow, you would crash and burn so spectacularly the flames could be seen from space. I'm worried about you."

"It's how I've lived my whole life."

Margot pointed at the barn. "This is different. This is do-or-die, and it's the culmination of your life's work. You cannot keep going like this without some kind of–" She dropped her hand. "Oh."

"What?"

Margot relaxed as the pieces fell into place in her mind. "Oh," she said again.

Colleen narrowed her eyes. "What just happened?"

"Stand up."

"Why?"

Margot motioned for her to stand, so Colleen did. Margot walked to her, cupped her face in both hands, and leaned in. Colleen frowned but didn't withdraw.

"You need some kind of outlet. If you won't go for a long drive or take a ten hour nap, then there's something else you can do to reset."

"What–"

Margot kissed her.

The first kiss was tender and soft, touching her lips to Colleen's like dipping her toe in the water. She leaned back, ran her tongue over her lips, and leaned in again. This time Colleen moved to meet her, and their second kiss was passionate and hungry. Margot squeezed her eyes shut, and Colleen pressed into her body, all lean muscle and wonderful curves. Colleen's hands went to Margot's hips and pulled her forward. Their hips met and Margot bent one knee, her thigh between Colleen's legs.

When Colleen breathed in, Margot ended the kiss but didn't withdraw. She opened her eyes to see Colleen impossibly close, staring at her.

"What was that?"

"Woman's work," Margot said.

Colleen laughed and kissed her again. Margot would be happy if they stayed there, making out on the porch while a rainstorm passed by, but eventually Colleen shifted her weight and moved toward the door. She broke the kiss, took Margot's hand, and led her back into the house. Margot closed the door behind her and let Colleen take her upstairs, but stopped her at the landing.

"Wait..."

Colleen stopped and looked back. "Is everything okay?"

"Can..." She glanced at the closed door of Colleen's room. "Can I make a stupid request?"

"Sure." Colleen came back, closer to her, and Margot smelled the storm on her skin and hair. "What is it?"

Margot lowered her voice. "Can you put on that tank top?"

"What tank top?"

"The one you were wearing the first time I came out here. You had on a tank top and overalls."

Colleen grinned. "Oh. You like that?"

Margot wet her lips. "Your tits looked great in it."

"Yeah, they do, don't they?" Colleen kissed Margot's lips. "Yeah, I'll go change. You go in your room and get ready."

Margot blushed. She nodded, because her voice couldn't shake if she didn't speak. Colleen stepped around her to go into her room, and Margot hurried into her own room. She practically dived onto the bed, crawled up toward the nightstand, and retrieved the boxes Linnie had snuck to her in the laundry bags. She'd thought they were new, but her trembling fingers discovered that they had already been open. She found a second Post-It inside: "Don't worry, all cleaned and ready to go!" with a winking face.

"Oh, I should be so pissed about this," she whispered, but she couldn't make herself care. She dropped the boxes and got off the bed. Shoes went off, and she held her breath as she unbuttoned her pants and pushed them down. She traded her normal underwear for the boxer brief harness, then sat on the foot of the bed to see how the dildo part worked.

She had just gotten it in place when the bedroom door opened. She looked up and almost choked on her tongue.

Colleen, in her tank top and overalls, the bib lowered and hanging at her waist. It looked even better in the dark, and her arms were even more impressive. She stood on the threshold for such a long time that Margot thought she was waiting for an official invitation. Then she realized Colleen's eyes were locked on her lap, where the toy was currently rising as if in response to the sight in front of her. Margot shifted awkwardly, unsure what to do with her hands, so she rested them on the mattress next to her hips.

"Do you want me to give you a blowjob?" Colleen asked.

Margot swallowed hard. "Sure."

Colleen came into the room and knelt in front of her. Margot moved her legs apart and watched as Colleen gripped the toy and brought it to her mouth. She circled the tip with her tongue and then, in one swift move, took it into her mouth.

Margot cough-choked at the sight. She'd never really seen the appeal of a blowjob with a toy, since there was no actual contact happening, but she was in the midst of an epiphany on the subject. Seeing a gorgeous, sexy woman on her knees, playing with a sex toy, while said toy was attached to her lap, was incredibly arousing. She bit her lip and put one hand on Colleen's shoulder.

Colleen looked up at her and kissed the tip of the toy. "Is this okay?"

"This is... a lot more okay than I thought it would be."

"Good." Colleen smiled and went back to what she had been doing. Margot sighed and rolled her head back on her shoulders, then looked back down to enjoy the show.

She honestly wouldn't have minded if the whole encounter had ended there, it was definitely more than she'd gotten in ages, but then Colleen sat up and kissed her. Margot gasped in surprise and fell back, and Colleen climbed on top of her, straddling her. Margot felt the toy awkwardly pressing against the thick material of Colleen's overalls and suddenly regretted her fantasy not including a skirt.

But Colleen was on top of her, kissing her, and she was free to run her hands over those amazing breasts, and she took full advantage of the situation. Colleen arched her back and pressed herself into Margot's caress, and once again Margot thought if this was as far as it went, she would consider the whole night a victory. She didn't need anything else.

But then Colleen moved her lips to Margot's ear and whispered, "I want you behind me when you're fucking me."

Margot could only grunt an affirmative response as she squeezed Colleen's breasts. She rolled onto her side to dump Colleen off of her. They pulled away from each other and Margot stood next to the bed and watched as Colleen shed the overalls, kicking them off her legs as she scooted higher toward the headboard. Margot felt lightheaded as she got back on the bed and walked on her knees until she was in position. Colleen, also on her knees, put one hand on the headboard and looked over her shoulder.

"Tank top on for this?"

"Tank top absolutely fucking on," Margot said.

Colleen smiled. "Then fuck me, Sullivan."

Margot licked her fingers and put her hand between Colleen's legs. They both moaned at the contact, and Margot used her fingers to part the folds before guiding the toy forward with her other hand. She held her breath, then let it out slowly as she pushed inside. Colleen whispered, "Fuck," stretching the word out as long as it could go, dropping her head and moving her hands higher on the headboard.

"I've never used one of these before," Margot admitted.

"You're doing fantastic, babe... just do what feels natural... please."

Margot grabbed the bottom of Colleen's tank top and wrapped the material around her fist, then she started to thrust. Sweat beaded on her forehead and her lips were salty when she licked them, but she didn't dare waste a hand to wipe it away.

"Keep talking," Margot said. Her hair had fallen forward and was covering her face, sticking to her sweat.

Colleen said, "Feels so good... you feel so good inside me, Margot. Don't stop..."

Margot moved her free hand down, bit her lip, pressed her fingers between Colleen's legs. Colleen cried out and then nodded.

"Yes, right there..."

"Yeah?" Margot said.

"Yeah, yes, fuck, Margot."

"You gonna come for me?"

"I'm so close."

Margot thrust harder, pulling Colleen to her by the shirt, tightening her arm around Colleen's hip. Colleen pushed herself up, twisting, reaching to pull Margot to her. Margot kissed her hard, feeling the tremor in Colleen's lips as she neared orgasm. She moved her hand up under the tank top, stroking and then squeezing when she found a handful of warm skin. Her fingers found the nipple and teased it as she changed the angle of her thrusting.

Colleen cried out, then turned her head to break the kiss as she cried out her orgasm, dropping back onto her hands to push back against Margot's hips. Margot put her hands in the small of Colleen's back and stared down at her, breathless, the emotion of the moment faded to leave behind the reality of what had just happened. Colleen folded her arms under her head and wiped her mouth over her forearm.

"You okay?"

"Mm-hmm," Colleen said dreamily. "I need a second..."

Margot said, "Okay," and pulled out, shifting to one side and dropping onto the mattress. She lay on her back and looked at the ceiling. She was aware of the toy still attached to her hips, still unnaturally pointing straight up, but she lacked the energy required to take it off at that exact moment. She put her hands on her stomach and counted the steady rise and fall as she breathed. It was still raining outside; she could hear it now, and thunder made the window shake.

After twenty breaths, she turned her head to see Colleen was also staring blankly, but her eyes were on the headboard. She sensed Margot looking at her and turned to meet her gaze.

"You sure you're okay?"

Colleen nodded. "I'm great." She pushed herself up onto her elbows. "That was probably better than a nap, honestly."

Margot couldn't help smiling at that. "Nice to know where I rank."

Colleen scooted closer and stroked her hand over Margot's jaw. "This face. God, this is a great face. Handsome."

"Handsome," Margot repeated, arching an eyebrow. "I've gotten that once or twice before..."

"It's not an insult."

"No, I don't take it as one. I like it."

Colleen relaxed. She brushed her thumb over Margot's bottom lip. "Thank you for fucking me."

"My pleasure. I actually don't mind having a cock. As long as it's removable."

"You certainly know how to use it."

Her hand skimmed over Margot's chest. Margot resisted the urge to arch her back to give herself more curves there; it was an exercise in futility and she hoped Colleen would see the truth soon anyway. Colleen's hand hesitated at Margot's waist where her shirt had been pushed up. Margot remained very still to see what might happen next. Colleen cleared her throat and bent her wrist so that her palm was hovering just above the exposed strip of skin between the shirt and her harness.

"You said this was about my mental health, taking a break. Does that mean I can't~"

"I really hope you will."

"Yeah?"

"Please," Margot said breathlessly. "Tell me what you want."

Colleen looked at her. "I want to go down on you."

Margot nodded. "Yeah. Yes, please."

Together they got her harness off, letting it and the toy drop off the side of the bed to the floor. Colleen moved fluidly, rising up and repositioning herself between Margot's legs without seeming to move at all. Margot braced herself, using her elbows to push herself higher as Colleen kissed the inside of her thigh. Her lips were soft, gentle, and Margot sighed, trembling at the effort of keeping her eyes open.

"It's been a long time," she said.

"Do you want me to be gentle, sweetie?" Colleen asked.

Margot shook her head, her skin tingling from the 'sweetie'. "I don't know. Do whatever you want to me."

Colleen made a sound almost like a purr, and then pulled Margot to her.

The sounds Margot made after that weren't words. They were mostly strings of vowels, gasped and groaned as Colleen did things with her tongue that shouldn't have been possible. She wanted to whisper instructions, encouragement, even just say Colleen's name to goad her on, but when she opened her mouth, the only thing that came out was "Fuck fuck fuck." She grabbed the blankets with both hands and decided to just give in to what was happening.

"You can pull my hair," Colleen said between using her mouth for other things.

Margot didn't even question it. She moved one hand to the top of Colleen's head and grabbed a handful. Colleen made a noise of approval and it made everything in Margot's body tense with pleasure.

"Fuck fuck fuck," she said again. "Colleen..."

"Call me Joan when I'm inside you."

Margot couldn't process that so she just moaned the name, making it three syllables, "Jo-o-an," and bit off the last letter with her orgasm. She went limp, releasing her grip on Colleen's hair, collapsing against the pillow. She was breathing hard and her thighs were twitching and she felt like she was on the verge of a seizure, but then Colleen's weight settled on top of her and she was grounded with a series of small kisses that slowly brought her back to coherency. She parted her lips and Colleen's tongue teased her, and she shivered hard again.

"Are you okay?" Colleen whispered.

Margot nodded. "I forgot your real first name was Joan. I thought we were roleplaying or something."

Colleen chuckled and brushed her nose against Margot's cheek. "Not this time. I don't really like my first name, but people so rarely use it that it has... I don't know, power. In the right situation. With the right person saying it."

"I get that." Margot kept her eyes closed. "I want to do it again."

"I think you need a break, babe."

Margot smiled and patted Colleen's cheek. "Oh, now look who is the expert on taking a break." Colleen chuckled and turned her head to kiss Margot's palm.

"I meant... just... in general."

"Oh. Oh, yeah." She turned her head and kissed Margot's palm. "We're going to do that again. I've still got all kinds of stuff I want to do to you."

"Mm. Make a list." Margot let her hand drift from Colleen's face to her chest. "I never even got to see your boobs."

"Well, we can fix that," Colleen said.

Margot smiled, but her brain chose that moment to finally fall asleep.

It was still raining when she woke up, terrified that some or all of what she remembered had been a dream. But there was a body next to her in bed and someone else's hand was on her stomach, a leg resting on top of hers, and she knew it had been real. She opened her eyes and slowly rolled her head to the right, hoping to catch Colleen sleeping. But her eyes were open, and she smiled when she saw that Margot was awake. She reached out and brushed the hair away from Margot's face, and Margot smiled at being tended to so sweetly.

"Hey," Colleen whispered.

"Hi." Margot blinked and repositioned herself on the mattress so she didn't have to turn her head so far. "Were you just watching me sleep like a psycho?"

"I was making sure you didn't have nightmares."

"Oh. In that case your ogling is sweet." She stretched as much as she could without moving much. "So even after that, you don't sleep?"

"I've slept twice."

Margot rolled her eyes. "That's... you don't get the same benefits. You don't get dreams!"

"What's so good about dreams?"

"Sometimes they come true."

Colleen smiled and leaned in to kiss Margot's lips. Margot brought a hand up, curled her fingers on Colleen's neck to keep her from pulling away, turned the kiss into something deeper. Her other hand went to her stomach, taking Colleen's and guiding it lower. Colleen allowed herself to be repositioned and, when she was cupping Margot between the legs, she took over. The kiss continued as Colleen slipped two fingers inside her.

Colleen slid closer, hooked her leg over Margot's and pulled it, opening her legs wider. Margot moved her hips to guide Colleen's touch and, faster than she would have liked, she came again. She sighed with release and kissed the corner of Colleen's mouth.

"Sorry. I went with the moment."

"It was a good moment," Colleen said, pecking Margot's cheek, then her chin and her nose. "How long as it been since you were with anyone?"

"Ten years. Not counting the time with Jessie."

Colleen tensed. "You fucked Jessie...?"

"Not... all the way. We didn't actually..." She gestured with her hand. "There was kissing, some light nudity, but we didn't..." She furrowed her brow. "What is it? Are you okay?"

"Yeah." Colleen looked stunned. "Yeah."

Margot pushed herself up on her elbows. "I'm sorry. I probably should have mentioned it before we went this far, but there wasn't a whole lot of planning in this."

Colleen pushed her hand through her hair a few times, leaving it sticking up in spikes as she stared toward the window. Margot put a hand on her shoulder.

"Hey. What's going on? You mentioned Jessie was an ex..."

"She wasn't just an ex," Colleen said. "She was my fiancée."

Margot's eyes widened. "Oh."

Colleen shook her head and turned to face Margot again. "I'm sorry. I don't even know what I'm feeling. It's just weird to find out the woman I just slept with also came close to sleeping with a woman who broke my heart." She reached out and squeezed Margot's thigh. "It's not your issue to deal with. You were being lied to at the time, so there's no way I could blame you even if I wanted to."

"It's still weird for you. I get it." She kissed Colleen's shoulder. "Do you want to take me to the shower and wash off the places she touched?"

Colleen chuckled. "I don't actually think that's... oh, well, why not. Worth a try."

Margot grinned and threw back the blankets.

CHAPTER ELEVEN

MARGOT LINGERED in bed the next morning, tangled in the sheets and listening to the sounds of Colleen moving around downstairs. It had been easy to get swept up in the moment, but now there were very practical things to consider. Would anything change? Had everything changed? Would she go downstairs and have breakfast with Colleen like it was any other day? Would they kiss good morning or act like the relationship was the same it had been yesterday?

She finally extracted her legs from the blanket and sat up. She saw the dildo and harness on the floor and looked around for her phone. She snapped a picture and sent it to Linnie with the caption: "Very funny, asshole. Works great, btw." She silenced the phone and put it in her pocket, then retrieved the toy and took it into the bathroom. She would clean it later when she showered. She dressed, jeans and a button-down shirt, and braced herself before she finally went to face the music.

Colleen was in the kitchen working on breakfast. She was in a tight T-shirt over baggy, ripped jeans. Her hair was a mess, and her feet were bare.

"Taking the day off?"

Colleen smiled without looking up from the pan. "No. But I'm allowing myself a late start. I hope you're not upset that I left. You wouldn't have been able to sleep very well with me just sitting up..."

"No, I get it. It's fine." She was at one end of the counter, as far from Colleen as she could be without leaving the room. "Are we going to talk about~"

Colleen finally looked up. "Is there anything else to talk about? Sorry, I don't mean to be rude. I just thought it was fairly self-explanatory."

"Was it?"

"For me. But if we need to lay it all out... Last night was a lot of fun. I liked being touched by you, whether it was the massage or the shower, or anything in between. You're great in bed. I really hope we can do it again. And I'd like to do it a lot, actually." She raised her eyebrows. "Was that... a- are we on the same page?"

Margot said, "Yeah. Yes, absolutely, the same goes for you. You were..." She exhaled a laugh and shook her head. "You were amazing. I was just thinking more about..." She moved a hand between them. "This. Us. Normal times, when we're clothed and interacting without the nakedness and the touching. How are we going to go about that?"

"Oh. Oh, I see." She chewed her bottom lip. "I don't know. Does it have to change?"

"No! Nope," Margot shook her head. "I don't think it does."

Colleen said, "I'm fine with change if that's something you need. I don't want you to think I'm just using you for sex."

Margot laughed. "I don't think I'd be necessarily opposed to that, in all honesty. But really, what we're doing here isn't conducive to a long-term romantic entanglement. We're not going to go on dates or anything. We'll just be professional, like we've always been."

"Right. But now at night, I'll go to bed with you."

Margot felt her ears burning. "Right."

"And touch you. And put my mouth on you."

"Okay, pervert, shut up. None of that shit before I've had my breakfast."

Colleen laughed and poured a cup. Margot came closer to take it, and looked out the window as she took her first sip. Colleen went back to the stove where the eggs were almost done.

"So." The way Colleen said it indicated something big was coming next, so Margot turned away from the window to offer her full attention. Colleen carefully put the spatula back on the counter and faced Margot. "We should probably talk about Jessie. Or, uh, Andrea? You thought her name was Andrea?"

"Amanda. That's the name she gave me at the bar. We almost hooked up, but then I freaked out and ran before things could get very far."

"How far did it get?"

Margot shrugged. "Second base, I guess? My shirt was off. There was some kissing. But that's as far as it went."

Colleen relaxed. "Okay. I can handle that. It's weird, but it's not horrifyingly weird. Now it's your turn." She gestured at the open space between them. "Whatever you want to know."

"Okay. Fiancée? Like you were going to get married?"

"That's what the title usually suggests, yep." Colleen looked like she wanted to crawl out of her skin and disappear. "We met when I was working on the engine. She was this hot, cool bitch with a truck who got away with breaking the dress code because she was so fucking brilliant. She made me feel smarter because she would take my ideas and polish away the rough edges until it was actually feasible. This whole project is happening because she filtered my random insanity into a workable framework."

She went back to the stove and began serving up eggs. "We started sleeping together after about a month. I was head over heels for her, even though I could tell I was basically just a distraction for her. We'd been together for about six months when I asked her to marry me. She said 'sure'."

Margot raised her eyebrows as she sat at the table. "*Sure?*"

Colleen smiled ruefully, serving up their breakfast. "Yep. I've gotten more enthusiastic reactions to asking if someone wants the last French fry. So nothing really changed except I could tell my friends we were engaged instead of just dating. I thought once we had the engine all set up and ready to go, we'd shift our focus to wedding prep. It was logical. Finish this project, then take on the next one. Then one morning I casually mentioned where it would happen."

"Hold on, let me brace for this," Margot said.

Colleen cleared her throat and deepened her voice. "Venues? Oh. Are we really going through with that?"

Margot cringed. "Oh my god."

"So I told her, yeah, I thought we were, unless she'd changed her mind. She said 'I'd rather not'. And went back to looking at her phone."

"How is she not buried under the barn right now?"

Colleen laughed. "It was a horrible thing to say, but after a few fights and a few long nights of crying and beating myself up, I realized that I'd been trying to force the relationship into being something it wasn't. We would never have survived as a married couple. And now when I think about being *married* to her? Married to *Jessie?*" She shivered. "I mean, okay, the sex was great, but that's all it was. I know I freaked out a little when I found out you'd been with her, but that was mainly because I was worried you might end up in the same gravity well I almost fell into."

Margot said, "No. No, as hot as she might be, I'm very glad I didn't end my dry spell with her."

Colleen smiled. "I'm glad, too. Are you always that, um... enthusiastic?"

"Oh, that was nothing. Wait until I'm chill enough to take my time."

"Mm. Can't wait."

When Colleen finished eating, she put her dishes in the sink. "I'm going to be out in the barn all day. Are you going to be observing?"

"I think I'll make a grocery run."

"Okay." Colleen stopped next to Margot's chair and surprised her by leaning down and lightly kissing her lips. She hesitated before she pulled away. "Is that all right?"

Margot nodded. "Yu-hum, uh huh." She smiled and brushed her fingers over Colleen's cheek. "I was wondering about that."

Colleen smiled. "See you in a little while. I put a grocery list on the fridge. Feel free to ignore as much of it as you want."

"I'll take a glance, at least. And one of these days you're going to have to come with me. I meant what I said about you getting away from this place now and again."

"What are you talking about, last night I went all the way to the Moon."

"Flirting won't get you out of this!"

"Can't hurt," Colleen said as she pushed through the back door. From the porch she called over her shoulder, "Come out to the barn when you get back! I'll try to have a surprise for you!"

Margot rolled her eyes but chuckled softly. "The Moon, huh...?"

"So," Colleen said, "there won't be quite as much room once the console and all the control systems have been put in."

"Of course," Margot said.

"I'm missing a lot of the interior shielding which will go down here."

"Where your knees are?"

"Yes, around there."

"So fascinating, J. Colleen Eckles."

"Thank you, Captain Sullivan."

Margot was seated in the pilot's chair with her hands on Colleen's hips. The chair had been set into place, the gaps between it and the hull padded by blue quilted blankets. Colleen was seated on top of her, pants-less, shirt unbuttoned and lacking a bra. Margot was more dressed, in a Magpie Air T-shirt, her underwear, and her socks which were out of sight inside the body of the ship.

She'd gotten home from groceries, put everything away, then showered and changed into more comfortable clothes before she went out to the barn as instructed. Colleen showed off how the chair fit into the overall design before she dropped her bombshell question.

"You ever fucked in a spaceship before?"

Now, twenty-two minutes later, they could both answer that question in the affirmative. As christenings went, it beat the hell out of smashing a bottle against its nose.

Margot slid her hands back to Colleen's ass and pulled her closer. Colleen grunted and bit her bottom lip as she resettled her weight. Margot leaned forward and kissed Colleen's cleavage, tracing the hard bone with her tongue before turning her head to gently brush her lips over the soft flesh of one breast. Colleen chuckled and rested her hands in Margot's hair.

"You're terrible for my work ethic," Colleen said.

"This is a stress test," Margot said, her voice muffled. "We're making sure the chair can handle the pressure of re-entry."

Colleen pushed down. "So I'm heavy enough to equal escape velocity? I think I'm insulted."

Margot looked up and batted her eyelashes. "How can I ever make it up to you?"

"You really went ten years without getting laid? You're the horniest woman I've ever met."

"I'm making up for lost time." She pressed her face between Colleen's breasts again, making her laugh and squirm. She looked up again and settled back against her seat. "I have a serious question."

"Shoot."

"Will there be a radio onboard? I assume we'll have some kind of communication, but I mean an actual radio. If I want to broadcast."

Colleen frowned. "Who do you want to broadcast to?"

"No one in particular. But like I said, I know I'll be in communication with you and home base. But at some point you're going to be swarmed with people who want to take you into custody. If I'm up there looking for a place to land, I want to be able to talk with people before I just invade their airspace."

"I suppose that makes sense."

"Are you still worried I'm a spy?"

Colleen said, "I never thought you were a spy. Not once, not for real."

"I could be a Russian honey pot, here to lure you with my feminine wiles."

"I think the Russians would send someone with bigger tits."

Margot gasped. "I vill haff you know that I am biggest-titted voman in my eeen-tire village!"

"What a sad little village."

Margot growled. "Stupid American." She grabbed Colleen's collar and pulled her down, kissing her hard.

They were well into another spirited round when Colleen suddenly sat up and twisted at the waist, looking toward the door. Margot went still.

"What is it?"

"Car."

Colleen rose up off Margot's lap and vaulted out of the cockpit. She moved so quickly that Margot barely had time to appreciate the sight of her bare legs and ass when she dropped to the barn floor and recovered her clothes. She tossed Margot's pants up to her, and Margot squirmed into them. Colleen did the same, tugging the pants over her ass at the same time she moved toward the barn door and peered out.

"Are you expecting anyone?" Margot asked, a stupid question given her reaction, but she couldn't help but hope.

"No." She looked around the edge, still buttoning her shirt. "It's Iris."

"Which one is Iris?"

Colleen said, "One who isn't supposed to come here, ever. Stay in the barn."

"I thought I was going to meet~"

"Stay in the barn!" Colleen said, probably harder than she intended. She tucked in her shirt and headed outside.

Margot climbed down using the stepladder leaning against the ship's side. She tried to keep out of sight from the driveway, moving furtively, and found a spot where she could peek out through gaps in the wood. She held her breath as though that would render her invisible.

Their unexpected visitor had arrived in a nondescript white van, the kind that usually ended up on Dateline or the local news. The driver was a tall Black woman, hair braided tight against her skull. She wore an olive drab T-shirt and khaki pants tucked into boots. She was every inch the soldier, and Margot remembered that Iris was the group's contact inside the military. The one who would give the go signal, and risked a court-martial for feeding Colleen information.

Colleen approached, hands out to either side. Iris even stood like a soldier. She wasn't exactly at attention or at ease, but found some rigid middle ground that made her look almost robotic. Margot watched her speak, her body language betraying nothing. Colleen listened, then put a hand on her forehead and began pacing. Iris tracked Colleen with her eyes but remained perfectly still. After a brief conversation, Colleen turned and walked back toward the barn. Iris followed.

Margot considered running, hiding in one of the back stalls, but it was too late. Colleen crossed the threshold and gestured vaguely at her, not slowing down.

"Margot Sullivan, our pilot. Margot, meet Iris Benham."

Iris stopped at the threshold and turned her head, Terminator-like, to lock onto Margot. She nodded once in greeting.

"Hi," Margot said, dumbly unable to think of anything else. Iris didn't respond. She simply looked forward again.

Colleen had gone to her workstation and was hunched over the blueprint. She grabbed her thin pencil and began making marks.

"What's going on?" Margot asked. "What happened?"

Iris said, "That's need-to-know infor~"

"Tell her everything," Colleen snapped. "Margot gets to know everything." She looked up and proved it by answering her question. "We found out why the engine is being moved. The government isn't just shuffling the deck, they have a purpose this time."

Iris said, "The engine is going to be disassembled."

"What?" Margot went to Colleen. "You said it was revolutionary. How can they just take it apart?"

"Because they're the fucking government and that's what the fucking government does. Because it was made using parts that can be recycled into other things, and they love to cut fucking corners."

Iris said, "They're moving the engine to allow Enver Crane to take the engine apart to see how it was built in the first place~"

"So he can *steal* our work." Colleen shouted and threw her pencil across the room. "*Enver fucking Crane!*"

Margot reached for her but stopped short of actually touching her. "So what does this mean?"

"It means we only have one shot," Iris said. "It means that if we aren't ready when the time comes, my engine will be lost forever."

"And the only proof it ever existed will be Enver Crane's bastardization of it." Colleen glared at the ship. "He's Teslaing me."

"Technically he's Edisoning you," Margot said, stumbling over the word.

Colleen didn't give any indication she'd heard. She was still staring at the ship, the wheels behind her eyes turning calendar pages and listing everything that still had to be done. After a full minute of silence, she nodded once. Her jaw was tight and flexed once.

"I'll be ready."

"How long do we have?" Margot asked.

Iris said, "The Utah site is currently being prepped, and work orders for the move are in the process of being finalized. There are no hard dates, but everything is being inventoried~"

"Weeks," Colleen interrupted. "We have weeks. At most."

Iris looked hard at Colleen. "That is a generous interpretation. Given the progress they've already made, we have twenty-five days before the engine leaves the base. Plus or minus three days."

"That's over three weeks, practically four."

"Three and a half weeks?" Margot looked at the ship. That morning it had seemed so complete, but now she could only see the gaps and unfinished areas. The control panel wasn't even installed yet, for crying out loud. "Is that going to be enough time?"

Iris said, "No," at the same time Colleen said, "It'll have to be." The two women glared at each other. Colleen picked up a tool and walked to the ship with determination. "I can make it work."

"Colleen..."

"Not now."

Margot backed up. She ended up standing next to Iris, and looked over at her. Iris was watching her with an unnerving steadiness.

"I've heard a lot about you," Iris said.

"Really? From Colleen?"

"From Jessie. Your record is impressive. I hope you get a chance to prove yourself."

Margot watched Colleen attack a segment of the ship with renewed fervor. It almost looked like she was attacking something on the underside of the wing.

"I hope so too," Margot muttered.

Iris left almost as quickly as she'd appeared, with a promise to return the following day. Colleen said she would get in touch with the others and they'd have an emergency meeting.

Once they were alone again, Margot felt adrift in the center of the barn, at a loss for how to shift from the energy of before to where they were now. She approached the worktable cautiously, unsure if Colleen even knew she was still there. She was making frantic marks on the blueprint with the pencil she'd retrieved.

"There are things we can cut," Colleen said, either to herself or to Margot. "I don't like to go without them, but we can if we have to. So I'll move them to the back burner and focus on the things that can't wait. The console. Can't have you going into space if you can't control the damn ship."

"Maybe we need to take a second—"

"A *second*," Colleen snapped. "We don't have a second, Margot. Twenty-five days. Does that look like a ship that can handle the vacuum of space in twenty-five days? Because I know I wouldn't want to go up in it, and I'm definitely not going to send you up in it."

Margot pressed her lips together. "I know. I know, but... if you start making rash decisions, it could do more harm than good. You're running full-speed down one road when you could be considering your options."

Colleen straightened and looked at her. "My options? I don't have options, Margot. It's this or failure. In a month, my engine won't exist anymore, and all the work I did on it will be cannibalized by that Astraea piece of shit." She scoffed and shook her head, bending down to start marking again. "Typical, right? A woman busts her ass for a decade to make something revolutionary, and some prick comes along and steals her toy, then says he invented it. Who do you think history is going to remember?"

"Do you want them to remember you as a mad scientist who stole from the military and then blew up a spaceship that looks like it's part of a soapbox derby?"

"I thought you liked the ship."

"I do. It's a gorgeous ship. But Colleen, it's a long way from being ready."

Colleen shook her head. "Not if I buckle down."

Margot said, "So I guess our little field trip is canceled."

"Well, do you want to go to the movies or do you want to go to space?" She sighed and pressed the heel of her hand against her eye. "I'm sorry, Margot. That was meaner than I intended."

"I just want you to think about it."

She was already marking the paper again. "I'm done thinking. I need to work."

Margot nodded. She watched Colleen edit the blueprint for a few more minutes and then, when it was clear the conversation was over, she turned and left the barn.

She didn't see Colleen for dinner, or at any other time during the night. At some point a lantern went on in the barn, and it was clear that she intended to work straight through until morning. Margot left a plate of food in the fridge and went upstairs to shower. She didn't expect to sleep much, but she must have drifted off at some point. She had no awareness of time passing before the blanket was lifted off of her and she opened her eyes to see Colleen crawling into bed next to her.

"Hey," she whispered, reaching out. Colleen was in her underwear and a T-shirt, and her skin was warm to the touch. "Are you okay?"

"I think I need you to hold me."

Margot rolled over and pulled Colleen to her. Colleen relaxed into the embrace, her head on Margot's shoulder.

"It was one thing when it was just my engine," Colleen said quietly, her voice muffled by Margot's shoulder. "If I failed at that, then I was failing at *my* dream. And that was okay. Lots of people have dreams that they fail to achieve, I could live with that. But now it's *your* dream, too. If I fail, it means your dream doesn't come true, and I don't think I'd be okay with it being my fault."

"Oh, hey." Margot leaned back so she could meet Colleen's eye. "Whatever happens, you got me closer to my dream than anyone else ever has. Win or lose, I'll always be grateful to you for that."

Colleen didn't look convinced, so Margot leaned in and kissed her. After a moment, Colleen began kissing her back.

"My head hurts," Colleen said when they parted.

"Do you want to lie down with me for a while?"

"Yes."

Margot guided Colleen's head down to her chest and stroked her hair. "Whatever happens," Margot said again, "I'm grateful to you. For everything."

She kissed the top of Colleen's head and listened to her breathing slow as, for the first time in probably a very long time, she fell into a deep sleep. Margot smiled and kept stroking Colleen's hair. She could be the one to stay up. Just this once.

CHAPTER TWELVE

THE FIRST car arrived just after eight the next morning. Margot had gotten Colleen to eat most of her breakfast at the table, but she carried the plate out to the barn so she could pick at it while she got to work. Margot was on her way to join her when she heard the tires on gravel behind her. She twisted to watch the car pull to a stop next to the house.

The woman who got out of the car was young and scowling, her curly hair bouncing as she strode across the lawn. "Who're you?" she asked when she was close enough to speak without raising her voice.

"Margot. Sullivan. I'm~"

"The pilot." The new arrival continued past her without slowing down. "Great. Nice to meet you. Tracy Wright."

"Okay..." Margot followed her into the barn.

Colleen was sitting in the cockpit. She glanced up when they came in, but immediately got back to work. Tracy stopped next to the ladder and put her hands on her hips.

"Give me a percentage."

"I don't report to you, Tracy."

"No, but my ass is equally on the line if we don't pull this off. I'm not going to put my ass on the line to steal an engine that you can't even use. Iris told me the clock just got cut way down, so I need to know what percentage you're at."

Colleen sighed. "I can get us to a hundred percent in time. I guarantee it."

"But where are you *right now?*"

"Eighty."

"Eighty?" Tracy twisted to look at Margot. "Are you comfortable with eighty?"

Margot said, "I'm comfortable with Colleen. If she says she can do it, I believe her."

Colleen sat up straighter. "How many deadlines did I miss when we were working on the damn thing, Trace? Tell me that. When they kept pushing us and pushing us, how many times did I not come through? Give me a percentage on that."

Tracy pursed her lips and didn't answer.

"That's what I thought. Now stop bothering me so I can actually work."

"Erica and Jessie are on their way. Is Professor Durand coming?"

"I don't know."

Tracy looked at Margot again. When she spoke, her voice was less confrontational. "The hotel where I'm staying didn't have breakfast. Is there anything to eat in the house?"

"Yeah, I can find you something. Come on."

It was strange to have someone else in the house, a place she was already thinking of as belonging to her and Colleen both. She went into the kitchen and searched the fridge while Tracy remained by the counter. Tracy spotted the box of Pop-Tarts.

"Oh, one of these would be perfect, actually."

"Are you sure?"

Tracy was already on her way to the toaster, opening a package. "Yeah, I'm a pretty cheap date." She put the pastries in and pushed down the button. She then looked at Margot and, for the first time since her arrival, seemed to actually see her. "So you're the pilot."

"That's me."

She looked Margot up and down. "Astronaut?"

"Sort of. All the training, none of the glory."

"That sucks. Good for us, though."

"Sure. If it's not rude for me to ask, who exactly are you? I know you're a part of all this, but I don't know any details."

Tracy said, "I'm the driver. I'm going to be the one behind the wheel when we get the engine. I worked in the lab when they were designing the engine."

"So you're a scientist?"

"God no. I was a liaison. I technically worked for a private company that–" She waved her hand. "I was a glorified go-between. The important thing is, I'm not anymore. But I was close enough to see the work J.C. was doing on that thing, and to be offended when it was mothballed." The Pop-Tart popped, and she hissed as she transferred it to a plate. "Damn, 'bout to burn off my fingerprints…"

"That might be a good thing, considering what we're about to do."

Tracy smiled at that. "Maybe so. You know, I should be thanking you. If you hadn't signed on, Plan B was for me to take flying lessons so I could be the one in the hot seat. That was a sure road to failure."

"Seems like Colleen had a lot of Plan Bs if I said no."

"Well, sure. Something like this, you have contingencies. But none of us were confident in any of them. I think the real Plan B would've been to just scrap the whole thing. So we appreciate you agreeing, if no one has said it yet."

"I'm happy I could be of use."

Tracy looked around the kitchen. "Last time I was here, there was like a whole library dumped all over the place. Papers and books everywhere. You have something to do with that?"

"No, that was all her. I think she got self-conscious about someone else sharing the house."

"Mm-hmm. And I'm willing to bet all the edible food around here is your doing. Erica and Iris were pretty convinced she was living out here eating salt and ketchup sandwiches. You kept our girl civilized, and that's no small feat. Did she tell you the thing about not sleeping?"

Margot said, "Yeah. Is it true?"

"It's about seventy-five percent true. She pulls all-nighters and randomly takes naps, but then sometimes she crashes *hard.* Erica said she once passed out for thirty-six hours. Me, I would consider that a coma, but Colleen refuses to admit it actually happened. She's convinced she gets by with two or three minute naps all day long, but she sleeps. I've seen her sleep."

So have I, Margot thought, but didn't say it out loud. "Do you really think she can pull it off?"

Tracy carefully chewed a piece of her Pop-Tart as she considered the question. Margot went to the fridge, retrieved the milk, and poured her a glass. Tracy nodded her thanks and took a sip, then finally answered.

"Yes. All the craziness we're dealing with, the uncertainty, the majority of it is centered on our part of the job. Or your part of the job. We're worried, but not about Colleen. She knows the deadline, and she's going to come through. And I feel a lot better about her mental health now that I've seen what you've done here. She's going to be ready, and you're going to keep her brain in one piece. That's your real job right now. Keep our mad scientist from really going mad."

"Big job. But I think I can handle it."

"You know what she calls us? This group?"

Margot shook her head. "I didn't realize there was a name, no."

"Sitting Ducks."

Margot laughed. "I guess it's apt in a lot of ways. She's the only one with motive to steal the engine, so it shouldn't be hard for the government to know where to look when it goes missing. The question is how long it'll take them to find this place."

Tracy shrugged. "Professor Durand has been working the numbers on that. It varies but, given that the house isn't connected to anyone in the heist, it shouldn't be a dead giveaway. They'll have to find us another way. The Professor gives us twenty-four to thirty-six hours after the heist before Colonel Boshears descends on this place."

"Is that enough time to mount the engine?"

"It'll have to be. She'll have the rest of us lending a hand for that, so it shouldn't take too long."

Margot nodded. "I don't like the fact I won't be able to do any test runs. I've been practicing with the console, but it isn't hooked up to anything. I have a good memory, but..."

"It's like practicing on a toy piano, then being asked to perform Beethoven at Carnegie Hall."

"That's exactly what it's like. Except the toy piano at least makes sounds. I have a pretty good imagination, but this..."

Tracy said, "You'll do great."

"You're just happy it isn't you."

"Damn straight. Sucks to be you, Sullivan." She smiled and winked.

Margot returned the smile and turned toward the door. "Sounds like we have more company."

"The rest of the Ducks." Tracy wiped the crumbs from her hands and pushed off the counter. "C'mon, I'll introduce you to everyone."

Iris nodded when Margot came into the barn, the only acknowledgement that they had met before, but it was still more than Jessie offered. She seemed unaware of anything other than the blueprint on Colleen's worktable. She was examining it so carefully that Margot was reminded of teachers who *wanted* to find errors in a student's paper. She shuddered at the thought of how close she'd been to having sex with the woman and thanked her brain for rescuing her from it.

The new arrivals were Erica Shearing, a Hispanic woman who seemed amused by the entire situation, and an older woman with short white hair and Buddy Holly glasses. The older woman stood separate from everyone else in a black-and-white outfit which looked more expensive than everyone else's entire wardrobe combined. She didn't introduce herself, so Margot had to assume this was "the Professor." She knew the woman's last name was Durand, but somehow the title seemed more fitting.

Colleen was sitting on the ship just behind the cockpit, legs splayed, working on something inside a panel she had lifted up. She didn't seem to be aware anyone else was present, too focused on what she was doing to pay them any attention.

Margot found it unsettling to have so many people in the barn. She'd always considered it Colleen's domain, and now there was a crowd of strangers with conflicting energies filling it up, and she wanted to fling open every door and window to let in some fresh air and sunlight. She settled for hugging herself and nodding a hello as Tracy introduced her to the group.

"Are you sure you're ready to fly this thing?" the Professor asked, her voice dry and husky. Her hand seemed empty without a glass of something old and brown for her to swirl.

"Yes," Margot said simply. This wasn't a woman who would be impressed with braggadocio or a cold listing her stats.

The Professor stared at her for a moment and then nodded. She looked up at the nose of the ship and shook her head. "This whole project has been madness from the beginning."

"Well, we all said that at the start," Erica said. "We told her it was absolutely insane, and now look at it! There's a damn spaceship sitting in the barn." She laughed and gestured at the ship like a game show hostess. "Is it really so crazy to think she can come through in the end?"

The Professor said, "I believe if anyone can do it, Miss Eckles is the best candidate. But I don't have faith that it's possible given the current guidelines."

Erica rolled her eyes. "You're fun."

Collen said, "All this talking is really helping the concentration, ladies."

Margot said, "Maybe we should have this conversation in the kitchen."

"I'll stay out here and keep going over the blueprints," Jessie said.

"No, you won't," Margot said. "You've all trusted Colleen this far, and now isn't the time to start panicking. Leave her alone and let her do the work."

Everyone, including Colleen, looked at her in surprise. Jessie seemed borderline impressed as she held her hands up in surrender and backed away from the worktable. Margot looked up at Colleen, who mouthed 'thank you.' Margot winked at her and ushered everyone out into the sunlight. Erica lingered and came over to her.

"Come to my car. There's something I want to give you."

They detoured to where everyone had parked. Erica opened the trunk and Margot looked inside to see what looked like an oversized dry-cleaning bag.

"You brought me laundry?" She realized what it was as soon as the words were out of her mouth. "Wait, is that the suit?"

Erica grinned. "That's the suit. Colleen sent me your measurements and I was able to find one without much problem. Getting it out was the hard part, but I got lucky. I thought you might want to try it on."

"Yes, very much. Thank you. Is there a helmet?"

"In the front seat. Let me grab it for you." She walked up to the front of the car and leaned in. The helmet she brought out looked more like a motorcycle helmet with a broad, clear visor than the typical fishbowls Margot was used to seeing in movies and film reels. "Brand-new model. Thrown out because the design is only feasible for smaller people."

"Meaning too small for men."

"Yep. So rather than mass-producing it and making an all-female team, they decided to go back to the drawing board."

Margot took the helmet. "Well, good for us, I guess." Erica took out the suit and closed the trunk. They started walking back to the house. "Sorry you got the job of rooting around in the trash."

"Are you kidding? When the trash is this advanced, it's like going to a Goodwill in Beverly Hills. If they have Goodwill there..."

"So how do you know Colleen?"

Erica smiled. "I'm an ex."

"Oh! You two..."

"For three years, off and on. You know how it is when you can tell the relationship is not going anywhere, but you still like the other person, and they're just so stupidly hot that you think, eh, might as well keep this going."

Margot laughed. "In principle."

Erica stopped on the porch and looked back at Margot. "Hey. Just between the two of us." She nodded at the barn. "You and Col? Have you...?"

Margot considered lying, but the way Erica was looking at her made her think she already knew the answer.

"Yeah."

Erica's smile widened. "That's awesome. You two look great together. I'm happy for you."

"Just between us, before we go in, do you think she can really do this?"

Erica looked at the barn, then into the distance. She came down off the porch to stand next to Margot and lowered her voice.

"Not long ago, that woman sat all of us down and said she was going to build a spaceship and steal an engine to power it, and she said she was going to get a real-life astronaut to fly the thing. Now look where we are." She patted the helmet. "I've never bet against Joan Colleen Eckles, and I'm not about to start now."

Margot nodded. "Thank you."

"Sure."

She wouldn't have said she had doubts, not out loud, but it was comforting to hear someone else so confident in Colleen's abilities. Margot looked back at the barn and then followed Erica inside.

The first official meeting of the Sitting Ducks happened in the living room. It was still overcrowded with books, manuals, binders, and loose papers, but everyone managed to find a place to sit. The Professor remained standing, automatically assuming the position of leader.

"I want to be utterly confident in this plan before anyone takes another step," she said. "Let's assume for the benefits of this exercise, that the ship is completely ready and done. I want us all to detail our parts of the plan."

Erica looked around the room and decided to risk going first. "Well, my job is essentially done. I provided the parts for the ship, the uniform. Right now I'm just backup for anyone who needs it. Happy to lend a hand, fill in any blanks that might pop up."

The Professor said, "It's those blanks I'm worried about. Miss Benham."

Iris was sitting ramrod straight, hands folded in her lap, and snapped her eyes to the Professor in response to her name. She dipped her chin as if accessing a memory file, and then spoke precisely, carefully.

"My job is eyes and ears. I will continue to provide information as it becomes available and, when the day comes to move, I will take responsibility for planning and executing our movements on the road."

Jessie raised her hand. "I'm Simpson, for those who don't know me. Intel. I dug up information on the pilot candidates." She looked at Margot before she continued. "I learned the names of the soldiers who will be in charge of transferring the engine and found the compromising information we're using to persuade them to help us. I also looked for dirt we could use on Boshears but I came up empty."

Margot said, "We're blackmailing people?"

"It's easier than eliminating them," the Professor said, too matter-of-factly for Margot's taste. She didn't like how much this group joked about murdering innocent people.

Tracy said, "I'll be the one at the wheel on the night in question. I've gotten my hands on the truck and it's in a secure place."

The Professor turned to look at Margot, who tensed. "Margot Sullivan. Pilot. NASA-trained. I'll be the one taking the ship up once everything is ready."

Jessie smirked. "Also providing stress relief to Colleen."

Margot's ears burned. "I don't... think that's... relevant."

The Professor said, "No, in a situation like this, it's absolutely vital. What sort of relief are you offering?"

Jessie raised an eyebrow. "Well, I don't think we need all the details."

Margot glared at her, and then something clicked. "Wait, Simpson? Is your name Jessica Simpson?"

Jessie's smile faded, but Erica covered her laugh by pretending it was a cough.

"I don't go by that name," Jessie said.

"Yeah, I don't blame you. And I can see why you said your name was Amanda when we met."

It was Jessie's turn to shift uncomfortably, and she dropped the subject.

Tracy cleared her throat. "So the plan?" When no one objected, she continued. "When Iris gives us the go-ahead that the move is happening, Jessie and I will take the truck out and move to intercept them. Erica and Iris will be in the back. The four of us will travel north toward Colorado Springs where we'll wait for confirmation on whether they plan to take I-70 through the mountains or go north to I-80."

The Professor said, "My bet is the mountain pass. It's a straight shot, so it seems shorter if you don't actually compare. I doubt they'll take the extra second to time it, so they'll go with that one. They'll feel like it's less wasteful."

Erica said, "It's also better for us. Less traffic, fewer eyes to see anything hinky. Lots of dead space in there."

The Professor added, "And lots of opportunity for them to realize we're tailing them just in case they happen to add extra guards at the last second. We have to be prepared for that."

Erica nodded.

Tracy continued, "We have a spot chosen on both routes, just in case. The soldiers driving the truck have been gently persuaded to pull over and take a break at one of those spots. They'll be stopped, and out of the truck, for half an hour to forty-five minutes. That will be our window to move in."

Margot was listening intently. This was the most information she'd heard about the actual heist. "Are we stealing their truck?" she asked.

"Too conspicuous," the Professor said. "Our hope is to create confusion. Maybe the engine was left behind in Colorado Springs, maybe the inventory was wrong. At any rate, we don't want anyone to realize anything is wrong until the truck has already arrived at its destination in Salt Lake City. They won't be able to say for certain when or where the engine went missing."

Iris said, "We break into the truck and transfer the engine from their cargo to ours."

"Wait," Margot said, "how heavy is this engine?"

"One hundred and thirteen pounds," the Professor said.

Margot said, "Even a car engine weights more than that."

Iris said, "This is not a typical internal combustion engine. It was designed to be lightweight. It will take four of us, but it's doable. We can transfer it from one vehicle to another without issue."

Erica said, "And then we bring it back here and we help Colleen bolt the thing onto the ship." She slapped Margot on the shoulder. "Then we send this one up into outer space. Easy as pie."

"We have another problem," Margot said. "This guy, Brochure..."

"Boshears," the Professor corrected.

"Whatever his name is. You said he's sniffing around. He suspects this is going to happen, right? So why does he even have to bother looking for you? It seems like his best bet is to either cancel the move until you've been neutralized or... hell, you have to be in a specific place at a specific time to steal the engine. He just has to wait and grab you when you show up."

"We've obviously considered that," the Professor said. "The engine *has* to be moved. Enver Crane is not overly patient, so delaying its arrival would make him angry. They don't like to irritate the man with the bottomless checkbook. As to lying in wait, we've seen to it that the Colonel will be otherwise engaged on the night in question."

Margot raised her eyebrows. "You've... how?"

"Never mind that. Boshears has arranged for two soldiers he believes he can trust to be in charge of the transport. But anyone can be bought with the right incentive."

"That's a lot to leave up to chance."

The Professor raised an eyebrow. "I only gamble on sure things, Miss Sullivan."

Margot muttered, "That's not how gambling works..."

"The point is," the Professor said, "we will have one opportunity to get this engine. Just one. Everything is in place to make that happen. Will you be ready?"

"Yes."

The Professor watched her carefully, then bobbed her head once in assent.

Margot's palms were sweaty, and she resisted the urge to blot them on her pants. It was hard to believe this was all really happening, but hearing the plan brought it out of the abstract. They had a spaceship, they had a team, and they had a plan. If everything went perfectly, if everyone in this room was as competent as they seemed to be, it was really going to happen.

In just over three weeks' time, she was going to be in outer space.

Chapter Thirteen

MARGOT STOOD in front of the full-length mirror and looked at her space suit. It was silver, with blue and white accents, not quite as bulky as the standard-issue NASA gear but with similar pockets and compartments for life-saving equipment. She felt a bit like a marshmallow in it but the flexibility was good. She flexed her fingers in the gloves and tried to get used to having fingers three times wider than usual. The ring around her neck where the helmet would lock in was small, but that only made it feel awkwardly like a stiff necklace.

"My, my, Ground Control to Major Tom," Colleen said from the door.

Margot stood arms akimbo, shoulders back and chin up. "What do you think? It's not exactly *Star Trek*, but I think it works for me."

Colleen stood behind Margot, chin on her shoulder and arms around her waist. "You look great."

"Where's everyone else?"

"Still downstairs. Tracy and Iris are going over the routes to double-check everything. I think you really won them over."

"Yeah? I didn't get that."

"They're impressed. You have to know them for a while to pick up on it, but trust me. If they didn't think you'd come through, they would be yelling bloody murder about replacing you."

Margot breathed out, relieved. "Erica seems cool."

"Erica is very cool." She squeezed Margot once more and let her go. "And thank you for not saying 'shouldn't you be working' yet."

"I figure if you're taking a break, you either need it or deserved it. Probably both." She started tugging at the catches on her suit. "How's it going out there?"

Colleen flopped down on the bed, arms out to either side. "That depends. How important is oxygen to you?"

"In space? Pretty important."

"Follow-up, unrelated, how long can you hold your breath?"

Margot got out of the space suit, leaving her in her underwear and undershirt. She stretched out on the bed next to Colleen.

"How's it really going?"

Colleen rubbed her eyes. "Fine. Okay, I think. I'm trying to be pessimistic, because that makes me work harder, but unbiased opinion... I think it's going to be okay."

"I have faith." Margot put her hand on Colleen's stomach. "Do you want me to go down on you?"

"There are people in the house. And two of them are my exes."

Margot said, "I don't mind if you don't." She leaned in and kissed Colleen's neck.

Colleen stiffened and pulled away. "Listen. About... about this..." She coughed quietly. "I'm really grateful we took this step before everything went crazy. But with the work I have to put in, I don't think it's going to be possible to keep... to keep doing..."

"You want to stop?"

"No," Colleen said. She put her hands on top of Margot's, pinning it to her stomach so she couldn't pull it away. "No, being with you has been like a drug. I hate the idea of not going to bed with you anymore. But given how much work I have to do on the ship, I can't dedicate the appropriate amount of time to you. It wouldn't be romance, it would just be sex."

Margot pushed herself up on her elbows. "I love being with you, too. Maybe it was just the drought, but I don't think so." She pulled her hand out from under Colleen's and moved it up to her face, stroking her cheek. "I really like you. I like being with you. I'm glad we were able to take the time to be together properly the first time. But things have changed. If you need a physical release, and you don't have time to snuggle afterward, I want to be there for you."

Colleen said, "It won't be like I'm using you?"

"Well. Sure. I don't think that has to be a bad thing, though." She moved her hand into Colleen's hair. "Do you have feelings for me? I'm not talking about love, I don't expect that yet, but something more than just liking me."

"Yes, Margot."

Margot shrugged. "Okay. Then use me. I'm happy to be used, and to use you in return. If we can make each other happy in the time we have left as free women, I don't need romance or sweet talk."

Colleen sat up and kissed Margot. "Is the oral offer still on the table?"

Margot grinned, pushed Colleen onto her back, and slid down her body.

Erica was in the kitchen when Margot and Colleen came back down. She looked over her shoulder at them, then leaned against the counter. "Ladies. Can I make you something?"

Colleen shook her head. "I need to get back to work. Is Iris outside?"

"Yep." Erica watched her go, then looked at Margot again. She whispered, "Hey," and tapped the corner of her mouth. Margot blanched and wiped a hand across her lower chin. She was about to ask if she'd gotten whatever evidence had been left behind, but Erica gave away her joke by laughing.

"You're my least favorite of everyone here."

"I love you, too." She pushed a bottle of water across the counter. "Everything good?"

Margot took the water. "Yeah. She had a little static in her head but I took care of it."

Erica raised an eyebrow but only said, "Good girl," as she took a drink from her own water. "Colleen really needs something like that when she gets into one of these projects. It keeps her tethered. Keeps her from running too wild."

Margot looked toward the living room, where the rest of the team was still gathered. "What about them? Do you know them well enough to be confident in their part of all this?"

"Oh hell yeah. The Professor, Laura, her job is to be the General of this whole thing. You saw the way she took charge in there. She keeps tabs on all of us and makes sure we're keeping straight and narrow. If anyone was slacking or got sloppy, she'd know, and she wouldn't hesitate to– uh oh, speak of the devil."

The Professor came into the kitchen and looked at them as if waiting to be invited into their conversation. Margot felt like a teacher had just walked in on her copying someone's homework.

"Miss Sullivan," she finally said, "may I speak with you outside?"

"Sure. Do you want a water?"

The Professor hesitated. "Yes, that would be lovely. Thank you."

Margot got her a bottle and followed her outside. She looked back before the door shut, and Erica pretended to nervously chew on her fingernails in fear. Margot stuck out her tongue and let the door slap shut behind her.

The Professor was already walking across the dry grass so quickly that Margot had to jog to catch up with her. They stopped next to the falling-down remains of a barbed-wire fence that was out of earshot from both the house and barn. The Professor put her hand on one of the rotted wooden posts and pushed it back and forth as if testing to see whether it would fall or remain upright. Finally she looked at Margot as if surprised to see she'd followed her.

"Margot Kathleen Sullivan. Daughter of Connor and Helen Sullivan."

"That's me," Margot said. "Birthday is May 22. Gemini."

The Professor stared at her. "Yes, I know. I obviously looked you up."

"I was making a joke."

"Oh." She looked across the landscape on the other side of the fence. Margot looked, too. Lots of dirt and rocks, with a few patches of brown grass. "This will make a good runway. Nice and flat."

Margot nodded. "Yeah. We'll have to flatten it out a bit to make sure there aren't any potholes or unexpected dips, but it should work fine."

"I know every woman in there. I've broken bread with them. Had conversations. I don't know you at all, Margot Sullivan, and you're arguably one of the most important pieces of this endeavor. I find that uncomfortable."

"Well, what do you want to know? You probably go all the pertinent information from the internet, but I'm an open book."

"Will you let Colleen die?"

Margot felt suddenly cold. "What?"

"If this mission begins to go south, if Colleen is in the crosshairs of the military police, will you allow her to die for the mission or will you try to save her?"

Margot wished she'd brought her water bottle.

"There is a chance for violence at every turn from this moment on," the Professor said. "If the soldiers decide they don't want to be blackmailed, Tracy and Jessica could be shot dead when they move to steal the engine. You might be forced to defend them. That would require returning fire. Would you be willing to kill for Colleen?"

"I wasn't aware we would have weapons."

"The question stands. There are at least a dozen ways you could cause the mission to fail. The bright side would be that if Colleen doesn't steal the engine, she's not a criminal anymore. Well, not as much of a criminal. She would be safe. You could make her safe by stopping the theft. Would you sacrifice the mission in an attempt to save Colleen?"

"No," Margot said at last. "She wouldn't want me to, no matter what we mean to each other. And I know she won't scrub the mission even if there's a chance I could die while piloting the ship. We both knew the risks when we started, and the fact we're sleeping together hasn't changed anything about our determination to see it through. Can I ask *you* a question?"

"I suppose that would be fair."

"What do you have to gain from this? You're risking real jail time for being involved with us. And no offense, but you don't really need to be here."

Finally a smile, small but unmistakable. "You know, out of all these women, you're the first one to ask me that. I guess everyone else just assumes my motives. I'm sick of women being ignored and passed over. I'm sick of our accomplishments being put in a closet, forgotten, and then pulled out so a man can turn it into a revolutionary invention. I didn't know Enver Crane would come along to cannibalize Miss Eckles' engine, but I knew someone like him was waiting in the wings. Colleen changed the future of space travel and as it stands now, nobody will ever know. If it requires breaking the law to make sure her contribution is recognized, I consider my sacrifice worthy."

"Even if it means death?"

"Even if it means death," the Professor said.

They stood silently by the post for a long time. Someone came out of the house and Margot turned at the sound, watched Jessie walk to her car and get behind the wheel. She was gone and the sound of the engine had faded by the time the Professor spoke again.

"Your mother..."

Margot tensed. "We don't have to talk about her, do we?"

The Professor shrugged. "She was a big influence on your life, consciously or not. Having a parent kill themselves~"

"I'd really rather not talk about it," Margot snapped.

"Her note said you were her greatest accomplishment. That's a lot to live up to."

Margot turned and walked away. The Professor followed, waiting until they were almost to the house before she risked speaking again.

"There's no shame in it, Miss Sullivan. It's quite noble, in fact, trying to live up to the expectations of a dead parent. I just need to be certain that you're aware of the emotions behind the motivation. If you have a realization at an inopportune moment~"

Margot spun on her. "You're a real piece of shit, you know that?"

Erica had just come outside and heard the outburst. "Whoa! Well, you're officially one of us now. We all think the Professor is all-around shitty. What did she do to you?"

The Professor grimaced. "We won't be prepared by coddling each other. This isn't some girls-bonding road trip. Lives are being risked, people with guns will be standing against us. Everyone's head needs to be in the right place."

"Weird justification for mentally torturing people," Erica said. "Have you satisfied your curiosity, you robot? Done poking at the fresh meat? Then get out of here."

The Professor smoothed down her blazer and walked away. Erica came down off the porch and squeezed Margot's shoulder in a show of support.

"You okay?"

"Yeah. As long as she and Jessie are kept as far away from me as possible."

Erica said, "A woman after my own heart. Don't worry. I don't think the Professor is going to be around much. But there's a bright side. When an asshole approves of you, it means they really think you're worthy. She's willing to let you stay, so she must like you. Hooray!"

Margot couldn't help but laugh. "Great. I'll be sure to get her address for my Christmas card list."

"Come on inside. Iris and Tracy have beers."

"Thank god. I knew someone in this group had to be fun."

Erica slung her arm across Margot's shoulders and led her back inside. "If you really have a Christmas card list, I better be on it."

"I'll probably be in prison by Christmas if everything goes according to plan."

"So trade cigarettes for stamps. Make it happen, Sullivan."

Margot smiled and, before she went back inside, checked to make sure the Professor was really gone. She understood the reasoning behind the Professor's attacks, but that didn't make it feel any better to be a victim of them. She hoped whatever secrets she'd been hoping to find had been exposed and there wouldn't be any further landmines to avoid.

Margot was in bed watching a video on her phone when she heard the water running in the shower. She tapped the screen to pause and looked at the door. Erica and Tracy were both camping out downstairs on the couch, so it might have been one of them, but something told her it was Colleen. She considered going to check on her, just in case the plan was to shower and then go back to work, but she decided to wait. She tapped the screen to start the video again.

"~approximately seventy percent, a huge improvement considering the numbers just a few short years ago," a reporter's voiceover said.

Enver Crane appeared on the screen, the newest villain in Margot's life. "Since the beginning of space travel, there's been some manner of junk up there for us to contend with. We learned to compensate and work around it. The ISS disaster pushed the situation to critical. That is why the ODIE mission was so vital, and why a seventy-percent success rate is so worthy of celebration. We are actually in better shape than we were before the space station was destroyed."

The image cut to footage of two women walking down a country road, holding hands, while a dog ran after something in a ditch.

"In the meantime, Colonel Noa Laurie isn't entertaining any thoughts about going up for a third time even though she was the one who opened the door."

It cut to a shot of Laurie, smiling into the camera. Her hair was down and she was wearing a blue Astraea polo shirt. "I'm enjoying my life on the ground far too much at the moment to go back up."

The bedroom door opened and Colleen came in wrapped in a towel, her hair still wet. "Hi. I saw the light was on. Do you want me to lay with you until you go to sleep?"

"Only if you lose the towel."

Colleen smiled, dropped the towel, and climbed into bed. She curled on her side and put her head on Margot's shoulder.

"I'm starting to see the appeal of this 'lay down on a soft bed for multiple hours' thing."

"It's good, right?" She stroked Colleen's hip. "Erica told me you actually do sleep."

A dramatic sigh heaved Colleen's shoulders. "No one believes me."

"Babe, I've caught you sleeping."

Colleen sighed. "I take—"

"Micro-naps," Margot said at the same time Colleen did. "Uh-huh. Sure. I'm just happy you're finally compromising."

"Mm-hmm." She looked at the phone. "What are you watching?"

"Interviews with Noa Laurie and Enver Crane. He doesn't seem like such a bad guy."

Colleen shrugged. "I don't think he is. Just blind to his privilege. He's a rich white guy who's never been told no. Or, if he has been told no, has always been able to buy his way to a yes. He knows there's an engine he can pick apart and it never occurred to him it might belong to someone else. He's a... an ignorant enemy, at the worst."

Margot poked around the phone, closing YouTube and eventually opening the camera. "We don't have any pictures of us together. Want one?"

Colleen pulled the pillow around to cover her chest and scooted closer. Margot rested her cheek on top of Colleen's head and snapped the picture.

"Nice," Margot said. "They'll probably use that on the news."

"Bonnie and Cly.. Cl..." Colleen narrowed her eyes. "What's the female version of Clyde?"

"Claudia," Margot said. "I'd rather be Thelma and Louise. At least they got to fly."

Colleen said, "Mm, good point."

Margot turned off the phone screen and put it down. She slid down and curled on her side, facing Colleen. They found each other's hands and linked fingers. Colleen's eyebrows were thick and black, and would be overwhelming if her eyes weren't so shockingly blue. She was stunning from a distance, but up close it was easy to get lost in the details. She felt almost hypnotized, so she wasn't surprised when the next thing she said came out of her mouth.

"My mom killed herself when I was three."

Colleen's expression changed. "God. I'm sorry, babe. I didn't know."

"The Professor brought it up today. She left a note that said I was her best accomplishment. She said now that she'd given me to the world, she didn't have anything else to contribute. I was *three*. How could she possibly have..." She pushed back that old anger and focused on what she really wanted to say. "My dad tried to keep it from me as long as possible, but at a certain point withholding information like that becomes cruel. And when exactly is a good time to tell a girl her mother said that in a suicide note? I really do think he did the best he could."

"Is that when you decided you wanted to be an astronaut?"

Margot shook her head. "No, I was a daredevil way before he told me about the note. But finding out what she said made every setback and failure hurt that much more. If I was her accomplishment, I had to amount to something. I couldn't just be a normal person living a normal life."

Colleen stroked a stray hair away from Margot's face. "I think you did pretty well for yourself."

Margot kissed the inside of Colleen's wrist. "Thank you. I ended up lying in bed next to a beautiful naked genius, I must have done something right. But whatever happens, even if that ship never gets off the ground, I want you to know I'm okay with that. I'm okay with this being as close to my dream as I ever get, because..." She squeezed Colleen's hand. "Because sometimes you get something so good, you never even thought to dream of it."

Colleen closed her eyes and took a second to control her breathing. "Thank you. That might be the nicest thing anyone has ever said about me."

Margot leaned in and kissed her.

Colleen smiled. "I can't wait to see you in my spaceship. Soaring through the sky. Standing on Mars. You're going to make history."

"Well, for right now... for tonight... I'd settle for you taking me to the Moon."

Colleen moved her free hand down to the waistband of Margot's pajamas. "The Moon?"

"Mm-hmm." Margot bit her lip and watched Colleen's face. "Can you get me there?"

"Let me see what I can do..."

CHAPTER FOURTEEN

MARGOT HAD grown fond of a particular restaurant on her handful of trips to Halcyon. A mom-and-pop home-cooking place that offered amazing burgers and the best fries she'd ever had. A few days after learning their new deadline, days which had been filled with the hard work of creating the runway, she decided the group had earned a treat. The work had been more grueling than any of them anticipated. The ground was flat and mostly featureless, but they had to clear away any scrub that might conceivably trip her up and fill in any ruts or rabbit holes that might spell disaster. Fortunately she had Tracy and Iris to help her out. They were fine workers, but hardly the best company.

So when she came into town to do laundry - now carrying five bags for all the women who had taken up residence in the house - she decided to stop and treat herself with a nice leisurely lunch. She had just received her food, admiring how the cheese melted perfectly on the patty, when a man pulled out the chair across from her and dropped down as if he was not only invited, but had been running late. He folded his hands in front of himself and smiled.

Margot stared at him. "Can I help you?"

"Boy, I sure hope so. I've been trying to talk to you for a long time, Margot. You're a hard lady to track down." He offered one hand, the narrowness of the table forcing him to keep his elbow awkwardly bent against his side. "Colonel George Boshears. It's a pleasure to finally meet you."

Margot sat up straighter and ignored his hand. He looked friendly enough. His silver hair was cut short, but not in an aggressive military style, and his smile seemed genuine. If she'd seen him in the store, she would have thought he was a grandpa or a former athlete, all smiles and charm. After a moment he dropped his hand with no apparent ill-will toward her for not accepting it. He twisted to sit sideways in his seat and looked around the restaurant.

"I like this place. I've eaten here a couple of times. The whole menu is good, but breakfast is where they really shine. You've got to try their biscuits and gravy. Homemade. Honest-to-goodness, homemade."

Margot remained silent.

Boshears tapped his fingers on the table. "I was in charge of a project, Miss Sullivan. It was a design project. We were going to create a new kind of engine for space shuttles and other orbital craft. We did a good job, we completed our mission, but in the end, decisions were made and the product we created was shelved. It happens all the time in this field. Research and development doesn't always lead to real-world applications. Is it frustrating?" He laughed. "Oh, it's frustrating as hell! But you move on to the next project."

Margot wondered if she should just get up and walk out. Would he follow her? It was almost certain.

"But there were some people on this particular project that refuse to move on. That can be very dangerous, for them and for us. If they do something rash, we'll be forced to respond."

"With violence," Margot said.

"If necessary," Boshears said, nodding his head slightly. "We obviously hope not. We want a peaceful outcome for everyone involved. That's where you come in."

Margot said, "The closest I've come to the government lately is paying my taxes."

He laughed again. "And we appreciate that, Miss Sullivan. But these people, the people who worked on my project, they're smart. We obviously hired geniuses to do our work for us. That becomes a problem when we can't actually *find* them to have a conversation. So how do you find people who are too smart to be found? You look for ripples. You try to find evidence of their presence."

Margot kept her breathing steady. This small town had once seemed quaint, but now everyone she'd seen the past few weeks looked like spies and informants.

"One ripple is a former astronaut candidate who suddenly quits her job and moves a few miles south for no apparent reason. A woman who pops up once or twice a week to buy a lot of groceries and do a lot of laundry. I took a glance in your backseat, Miss Sullivan, and you certainly do have a lot of dirty clothes back there. I'd say there's enough for four or five people."

"I didn't know the government let you snoop in someone's car."

His smile didn't waver. "I want us to be friends, Miss Sullivan. I've looked at your record, and it's very impressive. It's a shame your mission was canceled. All that hard work going to waste must have been a real blow. It probably hurt enough that you're willing to consider doing something drastic to make amends. I'm here to tell you that you don't have to."

Margot forced a smile. "I'm really not sure what you're talking about, Colonel... Boshears, was it? This sounds like a lot of stuff that has nothing to do with me. I'm just a pilot."

"At Magpie Air. You kept the name of your astronaut group. That doesn't sound to me like someone who has given up on her dreams." He faced her fully again. "The person we're looking for is planning something big and dangerous. And she's going to need a pilot if she wants to succeed. Someone who received the training to be an astronaut but had the opportunity cruelly snatched from her is a perfect candidate. She might have preyed on your emotions to make you do something you really don't want to do."

Margot looked down at her plate. "I made a mistake."

"It's not too late to fix it."

"You're right." She lifted her hand to get the attention of a waitress. "Can I get a to-go box for this, please? I think I'd rather eat alone in my car. With all my laundry."

The woman went to get a box, and Boshears chuckled quietly to himself. "Miss Sullivan..."

"Margot, please. We're all friends here, right?"

He looked up at her. "Help me stop Colleen Eckles and I'll guarantee you a spot on the Mars mission."

Margot felt like a metal spike had just been shoved through her. Boshears picked up on the shift in her posture and leaned in.

"What she's doing is reckless and has an extremely low possibility of success. There's no chance that she succeeds. Zero. All you're doing is stealing an incredibly expensive piece of technology and killing yourselves in the process. Stopping her keeps you safe and gets you what you've deserved for so long. You'll be one of the first women on Mars. Maybe *the* first. History would remember you forever."

She stared at him without blinking, even though tears were making her eyes sting. "You want me to trade something I don't have. That's... that's cruel, Colonel. And I'm done with this conversation."

The waitress appeared with a to-go box. Boshears was silent as she put her food in it and left money tucked under the plate.

"I would like it very much if this was the last time we ever spoke, Colonel."

She walked out, not waiting for his response. She didn't breathe until she was back in her car, takeout forgotten on the passenger seat, both hands gripping the wheel with a white-knuckled grip. She watched the front of the restaurant but Boshears didn't come out. Finally she started the car and pulled away from the curb, driving toward the center of town. She was grateful she had the laundry. It would be a good distraction and give her time to process what had just happened.

The laundromat had a wall of windows facing the street. Once she started the first load, she sat in a chair that let her see the intersection. She had just gotten settled when she saw an old drab green sedan, the kind that would have looked outdated twenty years ago, pull up to the stop sign. The windows were tinted so she couldn't see the driver, but she could feel eyes on her. It couldn't have been more conspicuous if they'd printed PROPERTY OF THE US GOVERNMENT on the hood. She watched as the car sat and waited, then finally rolled on.

She took out her phone and dialed a number she'd never expected to actually use when Colleen gave it to her. It rang once before it was answered with a clipped, "Yes?"

"Hey, Jessica Simpson. I need your help."

Twenty minutes later, the back door of the laundromat opened and Jessie rushed in. Margot stood to greet her, glancing out the window to make sure Boshears' car hadn't returned.

Jessie said, "He's parked in front of a church two blocks north of here. He won't be able to see the front door, but he'll see when your car leaves. Trade shirts with me."

"What?" Margot said.

"This is the plan. We're going to finish the laundry. Then I'll lead him away in your car. You'll take mine. It's parked at the convenience store down the street. Wait ten minutes before you leave, and leave through the back door. Go directly back to the Garage. Don't break the speed limit but don't dawdle, either."

Margot said, "What are you going to do?"

"Just lead him on a wild goose chase. Hopefully I can throw him off the scent. But I *hate* that he's here. Damn small town gossips." She put her hands on her hips and looked at the machines. "How long do the clothes have?"

"Uh... hours, probably."

"Not if we use multiple machines."

"What if someone else comes in?"

Jessie looked around the empty space, and at the wall of ten machines. "I'm willing to take the risk. Come on, give me any coins you have."

Margot took off her shirt and traded Jessie for hers, grateful they were close enough to the same size to make it work. They sat across the room from each other, just in case Boshears did a drive-by and saw them through the window. Jessie picked up a magazine and thumbed through it. Margot tried not to constantly watch the street, but every time the sun glinted off something, she thought it was their adversary swooping in.

"You're twitchy," Jessie said. "Stop it."

"Sorry. Not really looking forward to ending the day in a military prison."

Jessie flipped a page. "Boshears isn't going to arrest anyone. He doesn't have that authority. Well." She looked up and thought for a second. "He might have the authority to arrest Colleen and Iris. But he's not going to find them, so relax."

A car passed and Margot looked at the window.

"I'm not cut out of this clandestine stuff."

"This is what you signed up for."

"I signed up to fly a ship."

Jessie said, "Illegally, with stolen technology. This was always part of it."

"Was seducing me in a bar always part of it?"

Jessie rolled her eyes. "You really should let that go."

"How far were you planning to go with that? I'm just curious."

"I would have gone as far as necessary."

Margot said, "You would have done that for a mission?"

"No," Jessie said. "It wasn't... entirely for the mission."

Margot thought she saw a crack in the other woman's steely façade. She smirked. "You actually wanted to sleep with me, didn't you?"

"Yes, I did." She looked up from her magazine. "But don't worry. I won't try to sabotage what you have with Colleen."

"Good. Glad to hear it."

Jessie watched Margot for another moment, then shifted in her seat. "If... I seem cruel or cold, it's because... I'm... jealous."

"Jealous of me or Colleen?"

"I'm not sure, to be honest."

Margot said, "That's fair."

When the laundry finished, they loaded everything into bags without bothering to fold anything. Jessie had brought a baseball cap to cover the fact she had dark hair, not blonde, and checked her watch. They traded keys.

"Ten minutes after I leave. No sooner."

"Got it."

"Good luck."

"You too."

Jessie left through the front door, ducking into the car as quickly as she could. Margot ducked out of sight and watched her back away from the curb and then head south. A few minutes later, Boshears' passed as well. Margot held her breath while he was in view, as if that would make her invisible, and then looked at her watch. Ten minutes. Easy as anything. Just ten minutes of anxiety and fear, alone with her thoughts.

A guaranteed spot on a Mars mission. Or as guaranteed as some random officer could give her, assuming nothing else went wrong, assuming she wasn't blacklisted for aiding and abetting Colleen as much as she has. But that wasn't even the real issue. The real issue was turning on Colleen, a woman she'd grown to care immensely for. If this was just about going to space, she would have probably taken the time to debate the pros and cons of Boshears' offer. But as it stood, she couldn't even consider it a real possibility.

The Professor had asked her, *Would you kill to protect Colleen?* Her brain immediately went to the actual, real murder of a human being, but it was deeper than that. To protect Colleen, to protect the mission, she would have to risk the death of her dream.

She had to choose:

A guaranteed spot with a government-sponsored space program, with an entire team of scientists and technicians to back her up, in a flagship that cost billions of dollars.

Or Colleen, and her trash ship that stood a very real chance of blowing up when she tried to leave the atmosphere.

It was Colleen. It would always be Colleen, no matter what.

When the ten minutes were up, Margot checked the street and hurried out the back door. It took her five minutes to walk to the gas station. Once there, she stood by a fence for three minutes to make sure no one was watching Jessie's car before she risked approaching it. She followed Jessie's advice and drove back to the Garage as carefully as ever, checking her mirrors the entire time to make sure no one was tailing her. She drove a mile past the entrance just to be safe, then used the shoulder to turn around and head back.

When she got to the house, everyone except Jessie was already in the middle of what looked to be a very intense meeting. The visible relief on Colleen's face when she walked in made Margot's heart swell, and she immediately went to her for a quick hug and an almost-chaste kiss. Colleen put an arm around her, protective or possessive, Margot didn't care. She leaned hard into Colleen and tried to pick up the thread of the conversation.

The Professor was speaking. "We're fortunate that the current state of satellite surveillance means even the Air Force is unlikely to have eyes in the sky to look for us. But we still need to be cautious. We should remain indoors as much as possible, and no lights on after dark. Nothing that can be seen from a plane going overhead, let alone an orbiting camera."

"I'm still going to need light to work," Colleen said, "and I don't intend to stop after dark."

"Lanterns, and as few as possible, and the barn doors will remain closed."

Tracy said, "That could severely restrict her productivity..."

"So will being arrested," the Professor said. "We need to be cautious. Boshears getting this close so soon to the deadline is alarming to say the least. We have to react as if he's breathing down our necks because he very may well be."

Margot said, "What's going to happen to Jessie? Is she going to be arrested protecting me?"

Colleen started to answer, stopped herself, then shrugged and shook her head. "Honestly, we're not sure. When you called, she just ran out of here without discussing it. She said you were in trouble and she'd deal with it. We have to trust she knows what she's doing."

Margot's lips twisted and she squeezed Collen's waist. Colleen kissed Margot's hair and said, "We're running low on time. I'm going back to the barn. Will you come with me real quick...?"

"Sure."

They left the house together. As soon as they were outside, Colleen pulled Margot into a tight hug. Margot was startled, but returned the hug with equal strength.

"Are you okay?" Colleen whispered, her voice shaky.

"Yeah..."

"Are you *okay*?" Colleen asked again.

Margot stepped back and looked into Colleen's eyes. "Yes. I'm fine. A little shaken up, but unscathed. Boshears seems like a nice guy."

"Yeah, he seems like it. He's a one-man charm offensive. Patting your back one day and stabbing it the next with a 'hey, sorry sweetheart, that's business.' He's insidious."

Margot looked back into the house to make sure they were alone. "He offered me Mars in exchange for turning on you."

Colleen hissed through her teeth. "Margot..."

"I didn't even bother to say no. It's a non-issue."

"Margot," Colleen said again.

"This isn't a debate. I'm only telling you because it could come out and turn into a distraction none of us need. Especially if you thought I might have considered it."

"You really should consider it. Margot, it's your dream. Your dream since you were a *kid*..."

Margot said, "Kid dreams are stupid. Kids want to be Batman. I wanted to go to space and I didn't care how I got there. I thought getting there was the point, but it's not. I don't want a bunch of faceless bureaucrats sending me into space. I want to get there in a ship hand-crafted by a woman I... a woman I care for very much." She put her hand flat on Colleen's chest. "If I can't go into space with you, then it's not worth going."

Colleen blinked away tears. "Margot..."

"You don't have to say anything."

Colleen leaned in, kissed Margot's cheek, and whispered, "I'm going to get you to the stars, Margot Kathleen. I swear it."

"Then you better get to work, Joan."

Joan kissed her cheek once more, then stepped away from her. She lingered, staring as if trying to burn Margot into her memory, and finally turned to march back into the barn.

They had nineteen days before the engine left the base. Just under three weeks to get ready. Margot put her hands on her hips and looked up at the sky, squinting as if she could see any drones or satellites pinpointing their location. Eventually she looked away and went back inside, safe from any prying eyes.

Chapter Fifteen

THE HOUSE had never been loud, but it seemed eerily silent once the sun set. The lights remained off, though the Professor okayed the sparing use of cell phone flashlights. Jessie had come back close to ten o'clock, headlights off as she rolled slowly down the drive and parked in what had become her usual spot. She brought the laundry bags inside and quietly explained how she escaped Boshears.

"I just drove until I was almost out of gas. I pulled into the first Shell station I saw and waved at him when he passed. I didn't see him again after that, so I assume he gave up the chase. But Halcyon is one hundred percent burned. None of us are going back there for any reason. One of us can go up to St. Elmo and get supplies to keep us stocked until the day comes."

Tracy volunteered to be their go-fer.

"Be careful. If he knows about Margot, he's definitely got spies set up around town."

Tracy had promised to be careful, and then they set to work blacking out the windows. They cooked and ate dinner by lamplight. When the others started on the dishes, Iris announced she was going to spend the night in her car by the main road to keep an eye on traffic. Jessie promised to relieve her in a few hours.

Now Margot was lying in bed, staring at the ceiling, thinking about all the women sharing a house with them now, and wondering if she would get any sleep in the next three weeks.

She finally got up and went downstairs with a blanket wrapped around her shoulders, moving silently through the kitchen and slipping outside as quietly as she could. The barn was mostly dark, save for a small spot of light visible through the cracked-open door. Margot knocked before she went inside and saw Colleen sitting in the cockpit, hunched forward and squinting at something.

"Hey. Need a hand?"

"Yes, please. Can you aim a light at the place where I'm looking?"

Margot climbed up on the ladder and shined her phone's flashlight on the console.

"Ah, thank you, babe." Her hands began moving with more confidence. "I need a miner's helmet or something. Shadows are killing me."

"I don't think I'll be getting much sleep tonight, so I'm happy to lend a hand."

Colleen said, "How about we go for another hour and then we'll both try to get some rest?"

"Deal."

"How are you holding up? Just between us. Your first face-to-face with Boshears can be traumatizing."

Margot shrugged. "I was startled, but he didn't strike me as scary. Just dangerous."

"That's a fair assessment. He's a good man, in general, but he's on the wrong side of this. We disagree, and that makes him a threat."

"How far would he go? Would he have shot me?"

"God no. That's one thing we won't have to worry about. He won't surround the house with soldiers and empty a shit-ton of ammunition into it to bring us down."

"That's a relief, I guess." She looked at the control panel. "It looks great all installed like this. Weird after practicing on the bench for so long."

Colleen smiled. "Well, it's not installed yet. But we're getting there." She closed the panel she'd been working on, found a screwdriver, and sealed it shut. "We've got a lot of functionality, but we're not at a hundred percent yet. But close. Closer than we were yesterday. When we get the engine in, all I have to do is make a dozen or so connections and this candle will be ready to burn."

Margot used her free hand to pat Colleen on the shoulder. "Well done, babe."

"Thanks, babe. So have you thought about what you're going to name the ship yet?"

"I thought you'd name it. Since you're the one actually building it."

Colleen shrugged. "I'd be willing to let you have the honor. We have to call it something other than 'the ship.' Superstition." She leaned back in the seat. "Your planes are called Hawkeye and Hunnicutt, right? We could call this Hot Lips."

"Ew, no. No, I'm never going to call something I fly Hot Lips."

"Yeah, I see your point." She thought for a second and then smiled. "What about Magpie?"

Margot smiled. "That would be great. Fitting. And magpies have a reputation for stealing shiny things they see."

"Okay. Magpie-1." She ran her hand over the side of the cockpit. "Now it's going to have to keep you safe, because we treated it right."

"Can't argue with that logic. Where do you need the light next?"

They worked for another hour, as Colleen promised, and then she went to turn out the lantern. Margot stopped her.

"The house is full of people. If you go in for a catnap and then come back out in a little while, it'll only distract them." She gestured at one of the stalls and took the blanket off her shoulders. "Let's camp."

Colleen smiled. "I like that idea. I'll get the quilt to use as a pillow. It might have a little grease on it."

"I'm about to sleep in a barn. I'm not worried about a little grease in my hair."

They made a cozy little nest in one of the stalls and curled up together under the blanket. Colleen wrapped her arms around Margot, who used her as a pillow. From their position they could see the tailfins of the ship, shadowy and strange in the open space of the barn.

"Why are we called Sitting Ducks?"

"Because we're stealing something that only one person on Earth could possibly have a use for. It's like if a personalized shirt for Bojangles Schwartz went missing."

"I went to school with two Bojangles Schwartzes."

Colleen laughed and kissed Margot's hair. "We're not going to have a lot of plausible deniability when this is over. We're screwed. But if we succeed, it won't matter." She squeezed Margot's arm. "Do you still agree? Is all this worth the chance to spend a couple minutes in space just to come back and go to jail? Because you have an offer on the table—"

"Stop it." Margot sat up and twisted to look at Colleen. "I wanted space. I'm getting space. And as a bonus, I found you. At first, I thought it was just about sex. I thought if we slept together, it would scratch an itch. But it's more than that. I care about you. And being here with you, doing this, actually working toward my goal instead of letting a bunch of faceless techie nerds do all the work for me... If I'm trading a dream, then I'm trading up."

Colleen smiled in the darkness. "I'm glad I found you, too."

They kissed, and Margot curled up against Colleen's chest again.

"You know, we might have crossed paths and NASA and never even known it. You would've been hanging out with the cool kids. I would have been one of those faceless techie nerds."

Margot brushed her hand over Colleen's breasts. "I wouldn't have been looking at your face anyway."

Colleen laughed and swatted Margot's hand away. "I'm not fucking you in the barn."

Margot tensed and looked around. "Why? Are there spiders...?"

"No, no. Come on. Lay down on me. I like your weight on me."

Margot looked out at the ship again. "Just between us and the darkness. Can you do it? Are you going to be ready when they bring back the engine?"

"Yes," Colleen said. "It will be ready."

"You sound confident."

"Of course. I'm doing it for you." She kissed Margot again. "I can do anything with that kind of motivation."

From the daily journal of J. Colleen Eckles:

I don't know if I can officially call these 'daily' entries anymore. I've missed, what, weeks' worth of updates. But I've been busy as hell so I think it can be forgiven. The other Ducks are sleeping during the day and then spending their nights clearing the field so M can have a runway. IB doesn't seem to sleep at all. She takes ten-hour shifts watching the road and keeping notes on the vehicles she sees for any repeats. J helps her from time to time but mostly it's all her. She's a machine and she scares me, in a good way. We're lucky to have someone like her watching our backs.

No eyes in the sky so far. The satellite systems that could have spied on us from orbit are mostly all kaput, so if anyone does try to sneak a peek, we'll either see or hear them. That's comforting, to a degree. No more sign of Boshears, but we haven't left the property, so he could have Halcyon and St. Elmo annexed and we'd never know. IB hasn't seen any military vehicles, so we're holding out for hope on that.

M and I are doing really superbly well. We work together, we talk, we make love. We've discovered it's easier to take baths together than trying to shower. We're trying not to let it become a distraction.

Magpie-1 is progressing better than I hoped. I was expecting I'd have to lie to everyone, pad my successes and neglect to bring up any setbacks, but Boshears showing up lit a fire under my ass. I can see the endgame. I'm getting the important bits done and I'm confident I'll have time to go back and pick up the back-burner things before the shit hits the fan. Fingers crossed.

We have nine days until the engine is on the move. I have nine days to finish the ship to keep my woman safe when she makes history. Today I finished the last big task, and looked at what I have left to do. Barring any unforeseen problems, knock on wood, I've come to a thrilling conclusion.

I can do it in seven.

They had a runway.

Margot stood where the fence had once been, her T-shirt dark with sweat, breathing heavily as she squinted at the long flat terrain ahead of her. She tried to imagine how it would look from the sky, if a drone might pass overhead and some controller would think, "Hey, what an oddly uniform piece of land, I wonder if that's a runway for a spaceship." She decided there was no way to cover it up that wouldn't be even more suspicious, so she made the choice to stop worrying about it.

She left the runway and went to the barn. Colleen was sitting at the work table, writing something in the journal Margot realized she hadn't seen for a while. She leaned against the door and watched until Colleen sensed her and looked up, smiling when she saw who her guest was.

"I was just writing about you."

"Oh yeah? Mean things?"

"Annoying pilot who refuses to let me bathe alone," Colleen pretended to read. "Real pain in the ass. Hot, though, and good at making me squeal, so I think I'll put up with her for now."

Margot came inside. "I've had worse things said about me." She looked at the Magpie-1, which now actually looked like a complete ship. She walked closer and ran her palm over the paneling. It was perfectly smooth, cool despite the heat of the day.

"I want the other Ducks to sign the ship somewhere. Inside or out. I want this to be our ship. Unless that's sort of like signing a confession..."

"I think everyone would be willing to go along with that. Where do you want me to sign?"

Margot turned around and pulled down the collar of her shirt with one hand, tapped her upper chest with the other. "Right here."

Colleen laughed. "Don't tempt me. I'll find a tattoo gun somewhere." She stood up and walked over to the ship. "Can I tell you a secret?"

"Anything."

She gestured at the panels. "See how smooth and uniform this is? How pretty it looks?"

"I was admiring that, yes."

"It helps with things like wind resistance and structural integrity, but when the chips are down, it's mostly aesthetic."

"Okay." Margot started to nod, then realized what Colleen was saying. "Wait, you got all the vital things down?"

Colleen laughed and nodded, slapping her hand against the hull. "A whole week ahead of schedule. We have time to polish off the rough edges and catch all the things I put aside to make sure you survived the trip. Now the only necessary piece that's missing is the engine."

Margot grabbed Colleen and hugged her tightly, and Colleen responded by lifting her off the ground and spinning her.

"I haven't told anyone else I'm so close. I wanted you to be the first."

"Thank you. I'm sorry I'm so sweaty."

Colleen laughed. "Like I care."

Margot leaned against Colleen once she was put down. "Does this mean I can actually get some time at the controls without being in your way?"

"Sure." Colleen shrugged. "Nothing will work, but you can at least get comfortable with the actual layout."

Margot sighed happily. "Your ship. I'm so proud of you, babe."

Colleen's smile wavered, and she looked away.

"What? I'm sorry. What's wrong?"

"Nothing," Colleen said. "No one's ever, um." She wrinkled her nose and tried to wave it away.

Margot put a hand on Colleen's arm. "No one's ever told you they're proud of you?"

"The teacher who convinced my dad I should go to college said I had potential. That was the closest anyone's ever gotten. 'Proud.' I didn't... I didn't think..." She looked at the ground and shook her head. "It's silly."

Margot stepped closer and slid her arms around Colleen's waist. "Look at me, Joan Colleen Eckles." Those amazing blue eyes, with their thick black eyebrows, looked up. "You did something absolutely impossible. You built an engine that will change human history, and then you built a spaceship out of junk parts to test it. I am so, so proud of you and what you've accomplished."

Colleen laughed and a tear slipped free. "Thank you, Margot."

"You're welcome. You blow me away."

"Same."

They kissed, and Colleen returned Margot's embrace.

Now that they were sequestered, the days seemed to blend together while also stretching out endlessly. Margot would have lost track if Jessie hadn't been obsessively marking the calendar each morning. Tracy, Jessie, Iris, and Erica used the runway to jog - two in the morning and two in the evening to reduce their chances of being seen. The Professor spent her days going over Colleen's work to make sure the ship really was ready to fly.

One week before the engine was due to be moved, Margot woke just after the sun rose. She took the opportunity to use the bathroom and to start that morning's batch of coffee. While she was filling the machine, she looked out the window and saw Erica jogging alone on the runway. She got two water bottles out of the fridge and slipped on her shoes, then headed out.

Colleen was already hard at work, and it was difficult for Margot to direct herself away from the barn. She waited in the spot where the fence had once stood and waited for Erica to lap back around. Erica waved and slowed down, then jogged in place when Margot handed her a water.

"Morning," Erica said.

"Hi. Can't sleep?"

"I'd be surprised if any of us are getting much sleep. Final countdown." She hummed a song Margot didn't recognize under her breath and took a long swig of her water. "How about you? You doing okay? Mentally, physically?"

"All good," Margot said. "Maybe I could run a couple laps with you."

"Please. You're bound to be a better partner than Iris. That woman is a scary robot. And she makes me feel inadequate."

Margot took a long drink, put the bottle down, and motioned for Erica to set the pace. They kept to the edges of the runway. It wasn't clear if Erica had slowed down for her or not, but Margot was relieved that they could easily remain side-by-side without straining herself too much.

"Can I ask you a question? Well aware that you can only speak for yourself."

"Sure," Erica said. "If I can extrapolate to the other ladies, I'll give it a shot."

"Why are you all risking so much for this project? Obviously I'm grateful, and I know Colleen is as well, but it doesn't make much sense for you all to be taking such a huge gamble."

Erica smiled. "This is our project, too. All of us worked on it at some point, in some capacity. The engine might be Colleen's baby, but we all midwifed it. And we've all been in the scientific field long enough to know how often women get pushed aside so men can benefit from their contributions. Colleen's engine is too revolutionary to spend forever in a closet. One day that tech, or science built from that tech, will get us off Earth and to new colonies. We all know that it deserves to be known as the Eckles Engine."

"The Professor basically said the same thing. And don't get me wrong, that's a worthy cause, but we're talking about prison time."

"Sure. The alternative is just sitting back and letting it happen. When–"

It took Margot a moment to understand what happened. Erica was next to her, mid-word, and then suddenly there was a sharp crack and she was gone. Margot stopped and looked back to see Erica lying on her side, already up on one elbow. For a second Margot thought the crack had been a gunshot, and she reacted by dropping to her knees and scanning the area for a sniper. Colleen had insisted that Boshears wouldn't use shooters...

"Erica?" she said. "What happened?"

"Snake hole," Erica grunted.

Now Margot could see Erica's right foot, twisted around a lump in the ground. Her ankle was twisted at a strange and unsettling angle. Margot ran to Erica and put her hands on her shoulders.

"Shit. Stay still." She remembered the crack she'd heard. "Shit. Can you move it?"

Another grunt. "Nope..."

Margot twisted and looked toward the barn. "*Colleen!*" She moved down next to Erica's foot and gingerly examined the ankle. It was already bruised, and it was definitely not angled properly. When she looked up again, she saw Colleen running toward them at full speed.

"What happened?" Colleen asked when she was close enough to yell.

"I distracted her," Margot said.

Erica said, "Fuck off, no you didn't. I was watching where I was going. It was too early, I didn't see the fucking snake hole."

Colleen crouched down next to them. "Oh, God, that's broken."

"Seems to be. Yep." Her face was twisted in a mask of pain.

Margot looked toward the house and saw Jessie and the Professor were already running over. She got up and went to meet them halfway, quickly explaining what happened. The Professor ran a hand over her hair and turned away, moving in a quick and angry circle.

"That's just fucking fantastic..."

Jessie said, "Hospital?"

"We can tend to her here. Go get Iris, tell her what happened."

Margot watched Jessie run off, then frowned at the Professor. "Is that wise?"

"Our only options are Halcyon and St. Elmo, both of which are off-limits. The nearest hospital beyond those towns is at least two hours away. She's better off staying here with us. Iris has emergency medical training. She'll take care of it. The real issue is the fucking heist."

"We can worry about that later."

The Professor said, "No, we can't. Because in seven days, Miss Shearing was supposed to help three other women transfer the engine from one truck to another. The engine isn't terribly heavy, but it does require four people to move it."

Margot said, "Fine, uh, Tracy and Jessie are already in the truck. Iris will be there, too. They need a fourth? I'll go."

"We can't risk anything happening to you," the Professor said, "and the second Colleen's face shows up on a security camera, the government will cover the area like a swarm of bees."

Jessie and Iris came out of the house and ran past them without stopping.

The Professor said, "The facts of our situation are simple. We needed four able-bodied women to move the engine. We're down to three."

"I'm here," Margot said.

"No."

"If the choice is between failing and me taking a risk..." She realized who was being omitted. "Wait, why can't *you* go?"

The Professor rolled her shoulders and turned her head to watch the tableau playing out on the runway. Finally she looked at Margot again.

"Because, at the time of the engine's development, I was Boshears' commanding officer."

Margot's eyes widened. "You were military? That's how you made sure Boshears would be 'otherwise engaged' during the move."

"General Laura Durand, retired. But I still have some friends, favors I could call in. For forty-eight hours on either side of the heist, Mark Boshears will be inspecting a base in Milwaukee. I walked away after how they treated Colleen. That's one reason I've taken such an interest in seeing her project through to the end, and the main reason I cannot be seen at the truck. The soldiers may be required to describe the thieves, and we can't risk them identifying me."

"The plan ends with us all surrendering anyway, right?" Margot said. "What does it matter if they can describe you?"

"I won't force those boys to testify against a higher-ranking officer. Even if I am guilty, no soldier should be put in that position."

Margot was impressed. "A general. Wow. I really thought you were a professor."

"The girls call me that," she said, aiming for dismissive but unable to disguise her pride. "Colleen asked me to take charge, and that's exactly what I'm doing." She thought for a second and then returned to their original topic. "What about your friends at the airline?"

"Linnie and Rosie? You really want to bring in *more* people?"

"We don't have many options other than just giving up."

Tracy came out of the house, still in her pajamas. "What happened?"

"Erica broke her ankle," the Professor said. "We're debating what that means for the mission."

"The mission? Fuck the mission!" She ran to see what was happening.

The Professor stared after her with a sour look. "And that's what I was worried about..."

"What?" Margot said. "Compassion?"

"We can't afford compassion. I told you, we can't afford to risk the entire project for one person. If anything happens during the actual job, we have to leave people behind."

"God, that's cold."

"That's what you agreed to, Miss Sullivan. It's too late to get cold feet now."

She walked away before Margot could respond to that, leaving her to look out onto the runway where Iris and Tracy were tending to Erica's ankle.

CHAPTER SIXTEEN

FROM THE daily journal of J. Colleen Eckles:

We had a week, and it seemed like so much time, but now it feels like a straitjacket. Fuck. E is going to be okay, thank god, but not in time to take part in the heist. She's supposed to keep her weight off of it, and IB is banning her from even going upstairs unless absolutely necessary. And everyone is bugging out over the Professor's reaction to it. We all knew we were "expendable," but to actually see her so willing to leave someone behind in the dust was eye-opening.

I think M is having second thoughts. About this. About everything. She's not coming out to the garage. She's not talking. We're sleeping in the same bed, but we're just sharing the blanket right now.

Five days.

Fuck. Fucking snake holes.

Margot was brushing her teeth when Colleen appeared in the doorway behind her, revealed by the mirror. She spit out the toothpaste and turned around. They were both already dressed for bed. Margot appreciated Colleen going through the motions even if she only planned to spend a fraction of the night in bed. It was a touching gesture, and she looked really cute in a plain T-shirt and sweatpants.

"Hey."

Colleen had her hands in her pockets, almost cringing. "Hi."

"I'll be out of your way in a second."

"You're not in my way." She came into the bathroom. "I came up here to look for you. I was writing about you in my journal and it made me sad."

"Sad? What are you writing about me?"

Colleen came into the bathroom and closed the door. "We haven't really been the same since Erica's accident. Or I guess technically since the Professor talked to you afterward. I wanted to make sure we're okay."

"Yeah. Yes." She rinsed her mouth, spit, and then turned to hug Colleen. "I'm just shaken. We're so close, and then to have something stupid like this get in the way. And to think about if I'd been on her left instead of her right, it would've been me who broke my ankle, and then we'd all be screwed."

"We'll figure something out."

"I already have. But no one is willing to listen to it."

"You're not helping out on the heist."

Margot stepped back. "Who else do we have? You and the Professor can't show your faces, and we're too close to D-Day to bring in anybody new. I've barely done anything to help out during all of this. Let me pull my weight. Literally! Literally, let me carry the weight Erica was going to carry."

Colleen pressed her lips together in a thin line.

Margot put a finger under Colleen's chin and forced her to make eye contact. "We can't think of this as two dreams anymore. The engine was your dream, going to space was my dream, but we're past that now. This, what we're doing, it's all part of *our* dream. Let me do whatever I can to help."

"You have to wear a mask when you're actually at the truck."

Margot nodded. "I will."

Colleen rolled her eyes and rested her forehead against Margot's. "God. Yeah, yes. Okay. I'll convince the Professor to let you go along."

Margot angled her head until their lips met. "Thank you, babe."

"Be safe."

"I will. Now... we're running short on time. We're probably not going to have a whole lot of time together afterward, so now's your chance. Is there anything you want to do?"

Colleen said, "Like what? Sexual?"

Margot shrugged. "I'm game. But honestly, anything you might want to do with me that you haven't had a chance to do. Might not get a chance again."

Colleen started to say something, probably a denial, but then Margot saw an idea form. She smiled slightly and then the smile grew wider. It made her look like a kid.

"Yeah," she said. "There actually is something. Do you have any overalls?"

Margot was thrown. "I don't... think so. I can ask one of the other ladies, but I haven't seen anything in the laundry. Overalls...? Is this a farmer's daughter thing?"

"No, no. It's fine. Just... a dress, then. A nice dress."

"I can do that."

Colleen kissed her, then pulled away. "Change into it, then meet me in the barn."

"Should I tell the others to plug their ears?"

Colleen laughed as she left the bathroom, already moving down the hall. "They might do it anyway. I'll be waiting in the last stall."

Margot raised an eyebrow, unsure what she should expect but definitely willing to find out.

Margot paused at the entrance of the barn and listened for signs of life. The light was on in the last stall, and she approached cautiously. Colleen was crouching next to a little table, poking at a device which she'd propped up next to two small speakers. Margot knocked on the post. Colleen twisted, smiled, and finished what she was doing. She had changed out of her pajamas into a tank top and a pair of baggy jeans, probably Tracy's. The cuffs were rolled up almost to her knees, and she was barefoot.

"Tank top," Margot said. "You know I'm a fan."

"I'm aware, mm-hmm." Colleen stood up and turned to face her. "Promise you won't think less of me after what's about to happen."

Margot narrowed her eyes. "No promises."

Colleen sighed dramatically. "Okay, then. We had a good run." She bent down and tapped the device.

A mournful violin began playing. To Margot it sounded Irish, like a traditional folk song, but it only stayed that way for a few seconds before a drumbeat overpowered it and the melody picked up. Colleen rocked her head and shoulders to the beat, snapped her fingers, and began to shuffle from side to side. Margot recognized the song just before the band sang the title.

"Come On, Eileen?" she laughed, coming into the stall. "Seriously?"

Colleen raised both arms over her head and began two-stepping, crossing her right leg over the left, then reversing it.

"I grew up with this song," she said. "It was the closest I ever got to hearing my own name in a song, so I felt like it was mine. And I've always wanted to dance to it with someone, but I was always too embarrassed to actually follow through in public."

Margot began swaying to the rhythm with Colleen, fighting the urge to laugh. "What do overalls have to do with it?"

"The band wore overalls in the video," Colleen explained. "There was a cute blonde in it. She was Eileen. It's fine. The dress looks amazing on you."

"And the song mentions a dress, so there's that." Margot raised her arms like Colleen and tried to copy her two-step move. She couldn't help but laugh. "This is what you want to do together on what might could be our last night together?"

"Disappointed?"

Margot laughed and shook her head, now confident in the moves. Colleen jumped up and down to the beat, rocked her head back and forth to whip her hair, and Margot danced a circle around her. They laughed, sang along, and clapped, working up a sweat as the song ran through for a third, fourth, then a sixth time. It was the perfect song for a marathon because after ignoring the intro and the fadeout, it was easy to pretend it was just one extremely long song. Margot focused on the sheer joy on Colleen's face and decided she was willing to dance to this silly, dumb song until one or both of them collapsed from exhaustion.

At that moment, they weren't worried about deadlines, snake holes, or swarms of military police circling them like birds of prey. The only thing that mattered was the song, and the laughter, and having someone to hold onto when they fell.

Margot woke up on the morning of the heist surprised that she'd been asleep. She would've bet money that she would have been as sleepless as Colleen, but at some point her brain must have decided it needed to be in top form in a few hours. She lay in bed, the sheet draped over her legs, and looked toward the window. The sun had just come up and the light felt fresh, new, promising. Or at least that was what she thought before she scolded herself for being overly poetic.

In a few hours, they would have the engine. They'd bring it home, Colleen would put it in, and then Margot would strap in. They'd tow it out of the barn and she'd taxi along the runway to get the speed necessary to lift off. Her hands were shaking just at the thought. She was going to fly today. It had been so long since she'd been off the ground, even in an airplane, and her body ached for it. The pressure on her chest, the weightlessness as the wheels first left the ground. Her stomach fluttered and she fought it back before it became nausea.

There was a good chance she'd lose consciousness as she gained speed, but she always recovered in under a minute during all the simulations at NASA. It had been a few years but she was confident she would still be okay. And then...

Space.

She got up, quietly thanked whatever deity was available that the bathroom was open, and knelt in front of the toilet right before she threw up.

She was still there when Tracy appeared in the doorway. "Hey," she said, casually. "Nervous about something?"

"I don't know, I haven't checked my planner." She wiped the back of her hand across her mouth. "I feel like there's something I'm supposed to do this weekend, but I can't..."

Tracy chuckled. "I'd be nervous about anyone who isn't tossing their dinner right now."

"Iris?" Margot asked.

"Well, no. But I think she's actually a robot, so she doesn't count."

Margot chuckled and stood up to fill a glass of water. She rinsed out her mouth and spit, then realized Tracy was still standing in the door.

"It was sweet of you to check up on me, but I'm fine."

"No, I need to pee."

"Oh, shit, I'm sorry." Margot hurried out of the room, ducking her head apologetically as she closed the door behind her.

Downstairs, Erica and Jessie were sitting at the kitchen table with the Professor leaning against the sink between them, arms crossed, eyes on the floor. Margot assumed Colleen was out in the barn going over the ship with a fine-toothed comb. The Professor glanced up as Margot appeared at the foot of the stairs and nodded to her, then gestured at Erica.

"Miss Shearing is trying to convince us that an insane idea isn't insane."

"What's insane," Jessie said, "is changing the plan less than twenty-four hours before we have to put it in motion."

Margot said, "Wait, what's changing?"

Erica looked at the Professor, who nodded for her to proceed. "I think I have a way I can be useful and ensure that Boshears is as far away from us as possible."

"He's supposed to be reassigned somewhere else, right?"

"Yes," Erica said, "but the fact he showed up in Halcyon is proof that we can't guarantee he'll be gone. The Professor has been cut off. Boshears could have had his orders changed or convinced the brass that he needs to be on the security detail just in case. They don't want to risk pissing off someone like Enver Crane, so if changing someone's assignment helps protect his new toy..." She shrugged. "All I'm saying is that we need a little extra insurance."

"By putting yourself in unnecessary danger," Jessie said.

"We're *all* putting ourselves in danger tonight except for me," Erica said. "Because of my damned foot. I want to feel useful."

The Professor said, "Gee, I hate to see that guillotine standing there gathering dust, I should stick my head in it just to give it something to do."

Margot held up her hands for peace. "What exactly is your plan, Erica?"

"We have to assume Boshears is lurking around Halcyon or St. Elmo waiting for you to pop up again. And we're passing through St. Elmo on our way to Colorado Springs. Right now Jessie is picking up the truck we'll be using the tonight. It has a big, heavy-duty trailer. He might be suspicious enough to follow it, if he isn't already in position at Cheyenne Mountain."

"Makes sense so far," Margot said, "but I'm sure Tracy is going to be aware of that threat. That's why she'll have Jessie as her navigator. Keeping an eye out for tails."

"And I'll evade them if I have to," Tracy said, coming downstairs to join them. "What are we talking about?"

"Erica has a plan," Margot said.

Erica sighed. "I can still drive. Tracy, you leave here and head for the rendezvous. I wait five minutes and follow you in Margot's car. I'll give you a big enough lead that I'll be able to see if anyone latches on. If I see anyone, then I make sure they can't follow you anymore by rear-ending them or running them off the road."

Margot said, "Wait, you want to rear-end someone in my car...?"

"You're worried about your car insurance right now?" Jessie asked.

"Well... I guess not."

Erica said, "And if we get to the rendezvous and Boshears is there waiting for us, I can be your backup."

"What exactly does backup entail?" Tracy asked.

"Whatever you need to finish the mission," Erica said. "Shooting out their tires..."

"So there *is* going to be gunplay?" Margot said. "I never exactly got an answer about whether or not we're going to have guns."

The Professor said, "Anyone directly engaging with the soldiers will be armed. There's every chance Boshears will be firing the first shots, if that comforts your conscience at all."

Margot twisted her lips.

Colleen came in then, sweaty and breathing hard. She looked at them all and pushed her hair out of her face.

"What's going on?" she asked.

Erica said, "I want to watch your backs on the road. We need to be absolutely sure Boshears isn't lurking, waiting to swoop in."

Colleen said, "Will her doing this get in the way of our plan?"

The Professor considered it. "No."

Colleen shrugged and continued through the kitchen. "Let her do it. We all want to feel useful, and it's better to be safe than sorry."

With that, she went upstairs.

The Professor shrugged. "Works for me."

Margot watched her leave as well, and realized the discussion was over. She looked at Erica. "Are you sure you can drive with your ankle?"

"Needs must," Erica said. "Under normal circumstances I probably wouldn't try it. But to help out the cause? Yeah, absolutely, I can drive a couple hundred miles. I can't let everyone else take all the risks. I'd never be able to live with myself if something went wrong."

"I get that," Margot said. "I guess I can't hold it against you. I would probably be going a little crazy if I was in your shoes. Thank you."

Erica nodded.

"Try not to ruin my car too much."

"I'll do what I can."

Margot reached across the table and squeezed her hand as she stood and went upstairs. The bathroom door was closed, and she heard the sink running. She knocked and poked her head in to see Colleen scrubbing her hands, which already looked red from the hot water.

"Hey. What's going on?"

"Washing up," Colleen said, her voice clipped.

Margot slipped inside and closed the door. "Is everything okay?"

Colleen nodded. She kept her eyes on the extremely clean fingernail she was buffing with her other thumb.

"Everything's fine," she said. "Up to spec. Perfectly A-OK, ten out of ten."

"So what's the problem?"

Colleen suddenly slapped her hand flat against the mirror, leaving behind a soapy print of all five fingers. She was suddenly panting, and red blossomed up from her throat and began spilling into her cheeks. Margot jumped from the slap, then reached out and put her hand on Colleen's shoulder.

"Joan," she whispered. "I'm here. Talk to me."

"The problem is," Colleen growled, "that ship is the only thing keeping you alive. If I make one mistake, one tiny and stupid mistake, you start bleeding oxygen, or there's a rupture, or you lose navigation, or the landing gear falls apart, or~"

Margot stepped in and embraced her from behind.

"Don't lie to me and say it'll be okay," Colleen said. "Don't tell me something you can't possibly know just to try and, and put my mind at e-ease." She shuddered and gripped the sink with both hands. "I can't send you up in that thing, Margot. I ca-can't send you up in junk, god, I was so stupid to think I-I..."

Margot could feel Colleen's breathing become rapid, too rapid, and turned her around.

"Breathe. Honey, you need to breathe. Calm. Deep breaths. In..." She counted to ten. "Out." Another ten. "In." Ten. "Out."

The tension faded from Colleen's body. She opened her eyes and looked at Margot. Tears suddenly filled her eyes.

"I can't watch you die, Margot. But that means I can't be looking when you take off. I have to look away."

"I understand." She cupped Colleen's face. "I'll still feel you there with me. Holding me, keeping me safe. Whatever happens, if anything goes wrong, I will know that you did everything humanly possible to keep me safe. That's as much of a promise as I need. Please stop torturing yourself."

Colleen took a few more deep breaths, eyes closed and leaking tears down her cheeks. Finally, she nodded. She brought her hands up and covered Margot's with them.

"I love you, Margot."

Margot's heart leapt, her breath caught, and her eyes burned with tears. "I love you, too."

Colleen opened her eyes. "I swore I wasn't going to say that to you. What with... everything, the consequences. I thought it would be better to never say it. But it was getting so fucking hard, and I had to let go of something, and~"

"I think you chose well, babe," Margot said. "It's been on the tip of my tongue for a while, too. But I hate being the first one to say it. But I love you. I do. So much."

They kissed, embraced, and Colleen exhaled against Margot's shoulder.

"It's killing me that I might not see you tomorrow."

"Me too." She stepped back and took Colleen's hand. "So we should make the most out of today, don't you think?"

Colleen smiled, letting herself be led to the bedroom.

CHAPTER SEVENTEEN

FROM THE daily journal of J. Colleen Eckles:
T-Minus three hours until the troops head out. The next time I see them after that, they'll have the engine, and I'll be racing against the clock. And then...
And then...

Iris came back with the truck they'd use to transport the engine. The cab was a massive block with a wall of glass as the windshield. Behind the cab was a platform that looked large enough to carry a sedan, covered with a frame curtained by cloth that rippled in the breeze as Iris parked it next to the house. She hopped down and walked over to the Professor, who immediately filled her in about Erica's addendum to the plan. Iris listened, was apparently told the question had already been decided, and nodded once.

Margot and Colleen had spent the morning and a bit of the afternoon in bed, making up for time they had to assume would be lost soon. Now that they'd rejoined the rest of the group, Colleen seemed reluctant to venture more than ten yard from the ship for any reason. Margot even had to bring her lunch out to the barn to make sure she ate. Everyone was killing time, playing board games or pacing the house, too anxious about their part in the plans to sit still very long.

Margot went for a walk on the runway, getting as far from the house as she could before she took her phone from her pocket. There was a risk to what she was about to do, but she knew it had to be done. She didn't want to go into this mission with any regrets. She bit her lip, praying Boshears didn't have a tracker on the number, and dialed.

"Hey, speak of the devil," her father said when he answered. "I told someone last night that it had been ages since I heard from you."

"Phones go both ways, you know," she said, tears already brimming in her eyes.

"Considering the talk we had last time I saw you," he said, "I assumed you had enough to deal with and didn't need me checking in. You okay?"

"Yeah. I'm great." She looked back at the house, the barn. "I've been really busy. I... I met someone."

"*What?*" He laughed. "Well, that's absolutely worth a call. Tell me about her."

Margot sighed. "Her name is Colleen. She's a genius. Tough. Stubborn."

"God, what a pair you two must be."

She laughed and rubbed her eye with her knuckle. "I love her, Dad."

"Good," he said, sincerely. "It's about time you had someone like that in your life."

Margot took a deep breath. "Do you remember last time we talked and you said the real crime would be having a boring daughter?"

"I remember and stand by it."

"You might regret it over the next few days."

"What's going on?"

"I can't tell you. But even if everything goes right, it may not paint me in the best light. I wanted you to be prepared for that."

He considered. "Are you doing something criminal?"

She weighed the pros and cons. "Yes. But not harmful to anyone but me."

"Oof, kid, you're a handful."

"I'm in a derby car at the top of the hill. But I'm wearing pads and a helmet, and I've thought this through. I just wanted to tell you this time so you won't worry."

"Hell, kid, I'm going to worry either way. But I appreciate the heads-up. Be as safe as you can. And be smart. And tell Colleen I approve of her, as long as she makes you happy."

Margot smiled. "She's giving me everything I ever wanted and more. I wish I could tell you more. But you'll know the whole story soon enough."

"I'll take your word for it. I'll keep my fingers crossed for you, Margot."

"Thanks, Dad. Love you."

"Love you, too."

She sniffled as she hung up, waiting until her tears dried before she started back toward the house.

It was almost six o'clock when everyone but Colleen gathered in front of the house. The Professor was checking her watch every five minutes. The sun was starting to set, and long shadows stretched across the property.

Finally she looked around the group and nodded.

"Are we ready?" she asked.

"As we're ever going to be," Iris said.

Colleen came out of the barn. The group turned toward her, and she gave them a nod. "Magpie-1 is ready to fly."

The Professor clapped. "Then let us get underway."

Colleen had given Margot a cloth surgical mask, sunglasses, and a baseball cap to wear during the actual heist. Jessie and Tracy were also going to wear bandanas, but Iris opted to go without a disguise. Margot realized if most of them were going to be masked, the Professor could have helped out after all. She decided not to bring it up this late in the game and climbed into the back of the truck with Iris. The walls were cloth, but there were benches along each side where they could sit relatively comfortably facing each other. The center space had a large platform where they would strap the engine once they'd retrieved it.

Colleen helped Erica get to the car, which she'd driven up and down the driveway a few times to prove she could do it without issue.

The Professor stepped back. "Good luck tonight, ladies. Godspeed."

Colleen looked like she was about to throw up. Margot winked at her and nodded, and Colleen nodded back to her, lips pressed together in a thin line.

"See you in a few hours." The Professor reached up to release the cloth flap, tying it down. Margot and Iris gripped the benches as the truck lurched forward and began to roll up the driveway.

Iris said, "One hour to Colorado Springs."

Margot wasn't sure if the comment was directed at her or just a vocal reminder, so she didn't respond. Her palms were sweating and she was working hard to control her breathing as the truck rolled out onto the main road. Iris settled against the back of her bench, shoulders straight and hands loosely holding onto the bench on either side of her legs.

"No turning back now," she said, this time clearly talking to Margot.

"I'm ready," Margot said.

Iris nodded once. "I know you are. I wouldn't be here if I thought you weren't."

Margot looked at her watch and closed her eyes.

Iris' phone chimed just before they arrived in Colorado Springs. She answered and put it on speaker. It was hard to hear over the noise from the road, but she could still make out what was said.

"You ladies doing okay back there?" Tracy asked.

"Nice and cozy," Iris said. "Any problems?"

"Smooth sailing, knock on wood. Erica texted and said she hasn't seen anything suspicious on the road so far. St. Elmo was quiet. I'll feel better about it once we get into Colorado Springs, but for now we're cautiously optimistic. We'll keep in touch."

Iris said, "Thanks for the update."

Margot had been sitting with her eyes closed, trying to meditate. Her hands weren't sweaty or shaking anymore. She had a sense of calm, released from the anxiety of some scary thing in the future. The moment was here, and there was nothing for her to do but follow through. She was prepared. The other Sitting Ducks were prepared. And she had a feeling any one of them would have called her out if they thought she wasn't up for it.

The waiting, though. She could do without this endless waiting.

They pulled over on the south side of Colorado Springs for even more waiting. Tracy called back after fifteen minutes.

"We got a pin drop from Norm and Colin. They're on the road. We should see them in about five more minutes."

Margot frowned. "Who are Norm and Colin?"

"The soldiers driving the transport," Iris said.

"Right. The guys we're blackmailing to help us. I didn't know they'd be such an active part of the event. Why didn't they just tell us which route they were taking?"

"They probably didn't know themselves until the very last minute. Security precaution."

Margot said, "Smart. Considering."

"Mm."

They kept the line open as they waited. Finally, Tracy spoke again. "I have eyes on the truck. We'll give them a few minutes and then fall in line."

Iris said, "Text Erica to let her know."

"Jessie's already taking care of it. Okay, hang tight ladies. We're on the road again."

"Call back we make the turn," Iris said. "I want to know where we'll end up."

Tracy said, "Roger."

Margot said, "Still hoping for the mountain route?"

Iris nodded. "It makes the most sense and grants us the most cover. I don't want to risk doing this out in the open. We'll know in about an hour and a half."

"Geez," Margot said, rolling her head on her shoulders. "This plan is going to be twenty-four hours of tedious and five minutes of intense terror."

Iris actually cracked a smile, the first Margot had seen from her. "Welcome to the military, Miss Sullivan. Perhaps we should have brought music."

"It's probably worse for Colleen and the Professor back at the Garage. I can't imagine being out of the loop all night like this."

"Mm," Iris agreed.

Margot looked at her watch. It would be half past eight when they finally reached I-70. Then, according to the maps she'd seen, another ten minutes to the rendezvous point. She assumed it would take ten to twenty minutes to get the engine off the military truck and into theirs. After that it would be another two and a half hours back to the Garage. They would get there at midnight, and then however long it took Colleen to put the engine in.

So six hours. She started bouncing her foot on the floor, but she stopped as soon as Iris shot her a look. She crossed her arms over her chest and looked at a spot above Iris' head, where the framework of the trailer threaded through the cloth. She closed her eyes and dozed. She was never fully asleep, because she was aware of Iris shifting on the other bench as well as the sounds of other cars on the road with them. The hum of tires on asphalt was hypnotic and she willingly let it soothe her anxiety.

Finally, Iris' phone rang again. Margot was instantly awake, leaning forward to hear over the road noise.

"Brace for a big turn, ladies," Tracy said. "We're going into the mountains."

Iris and Margot smiled at each other.

Ten minutes into the mountains, the truck noticeably slowed. Tracy was still on the phone. "We're pulling in now. The truck is parked right where they said it would be."

"Any sign of the guys?" Iris asked.

"Negative. They've hopefully already gone inside."

The truck rocked over a rough shoulder and then hit the gravel of a well-traveled parking lot before it came to a stop. Iris ended the call and motioned for Margot to follow her out of the back. Margot slipped her mask on, put on the glasses and cap, and hopped to the ground. She took a second to get her bearings. They were in the parking lot of a bar and grill that looked like it was nestled in the elbow of two mountains. The lights were on and there seemed to be a decent number of people inside, but no one glanced outside to see what was happening.

Tracy and Iris approached the military truck, a clone of the one they had just left. Tracy had just untethered the cloth flap when the driver and passenger doors opened and two men in fatigues jumped out. Iris immediately went into soldier mode, holding her arm out to shepherd the others behind her as the men marched toward them. Jessie and Tracy had neglected to put on their masks, which left their faces exposed to the men.

"Everything okay on your end?" one man, the driver, asked.

Iris said, "Until this very second. You're supposed to be inside."

The passenger said, "We thought you might need help. This thing isn't exactly lightweight."

"We'll be fine," Tracy said.

The driver squinted at Margot. "What's up with that one?"

"She's the Lone Ranger. Go inside. Let us deal with this."

The driver and passenger exchanged a look. "We want to help. Really. It's no trouble."

"Shit," Jessie said, and pulled a gun from the back of her belt. She aimed it at the driver. "Go inside. Now."

The driver slowly raised his hands. "Calm down, girls. This can be nice and easy."

"It was supposed to be," Jessie said, "but here you are, fucking things up. Don't make me fuck it up even more. Go inside. Get a hamburger. Forget you ever saw us."

Another thirty seconds of tense silence. Then, as calm as anything, Iris said, "Wife or mother?"

Everyone looked at her. She was holding her phone up as if she was about to take a photo, her other hand poised over the screen. She stared at the men, calm, patient, waiting for their answer.

"Your wife," she said to the driver, and then to the passenger, "or your mother? Which one am I sending the email to?"

The driver grunted. "She's bluffing. They're all bluffing. They pull the trigger, they don't have anything else to threaten us with."

"Hell of a trigger, though," Iris said.

"I don't know if you want to stop us, or if you were about to extort us. Money or sex, whichever you were hungrier for. But we had an arrangement. You're getting in the way of that arrangement. We have ammunition of our own to fuck things up, but there's still time to salvage it. But I want to know which one of you will suffer the consequences of changing the script. You have thirty seconds or I send them both."

Driver swallowed hard, then reached out a hand toward Passenger. "Let's go get a burger."

Passenger whipped his head around. "Wait, what?"

"C'mon," Driver said quietly. "Let's just go."

Passenger looked between Driver and Iris, then something clicked. "Wait. If you go with them, that means *my* shit gets sent!"

"To your *mother*," Driver said, "I think you'll fucking live."

Passenger lunged. Driver swung and clipped the other man's jaw, and the two men went down in a flurry of fists and elbows. The scuffle didn't last long. Driver got his arm around Passenger's throat and choked him to unconsciousness. When the fight was over, he pushed himself up onto his feet and looked at Iris.

"You won't send mine?"

"You have my word." She put the phone away. "Put your friend in the cab of the truck and go inside."

"Get a hamburger," Driver said.

Iris nodded.

They waited as he put his unconscious partner in the truck, then crossed the parking lot. As soon as he was gone, Iris snapped her fingers and motioned the others forward.

"Move, move, move. We lost a lot of time with that bullshit."

They climbed into the back of the military truck, which was full of crates and metal boxes. None were labeled, but it was easy for Margot to tell which box held the engine. It was easily the largest box, strapped onto a platform exactly like the one in their truck. Iris unfastened the straps and the four of them took positions around the box. Iris put her hands flat on top of the box and looked at everyone.

"This is going to be heavy, so just take your weight. Don't expect to take it all on your own. Have any of you ever tried to pick up a car?"

"Gas or electric?" Jessie said.

"Think electric. It's doable, but it's no fun. On three."

Margot braced herself. On three, she lifted. It felt as if every muscle in her body turned to stone. It felt like she was trying to move a house. Her arms strained, her back sent warning alarms out to every extremity, and her legs immediately began to shake. Panic rushed through her, fear that she was literally the weak link that would ruin the plan.

And then...

Iris was right, it wasn't easy. But once all four of them were throwing their weight into it, she was confident she could do the job. Tracy was the one with the hardest part: walking backward toward the edge of the truck platform. They took it one step at a time. Iris said, "And step. And step. And step." They moved together fluidly. Margot wondered why they'd never practiced this; there was a freezer at the house they could have used, but it seemed like it wasn't necessary.

The transfer was rough, she wasn't going to lie to herself about that. They were all sore, sweaty, and ached by the time they got it into their truck. Margot was grateful for the long drive back which she now saw as a chance to recover. But the task was done and the engine was successfully strapped down, ready to go to Colleen.

Jessie said, "We should swap positions. Margot and Iris up front, me and Tracy in the back. Those guys saw our faces, so they might call descriptions of us to the local cops."

Margot said, "I'd think the truck is more of a sore thumb than either of you."

Tracy said, "Yeah, but you deserve a comfortable seat considering you have to do the next step by yourself. We want you in top form."

Iris said, "Agreed. I'll drive."

Margot decided she wouldn't waste time arguing. The thought of a cushioned seat sounded like heaven after the long drive and carrying the engine. Iris took her phone out again. "Texting Colleen and the Professor to let them know we're on the way back."

"Are you going to mention the complications?"

"Best to tell them about that in person. I'm going to wait until we're back at the Garage to send the blackmail, too."

"Probably wise."

Tracy checked her watch and looked down the road to the east. "Hey, guys...? Shouldn't Erica have caught up to us by now?"

The drive back felt like a funeral procession, despite their victory. Iris kept her eyes on the road, her entire body tense. Jessie had texted Erica several times on the drive up, but she never responded. They chalked it up to driving safely, but now her silence seemed ominous. When had she gone missing? Was she hurt, or had someone gotten to her? If it was Boshears, why would he grab Erica and not their truck? There were too many questions and no way to get answers, so Margot focused on the scenery.

The roads were carved into and, in some places, seemed to actually emerge from the hunkering rock cliffs on either side of them. To the left, the stones were bare and prehistoric, with the occasional patch of tall, dry grasses. To the right, the mounded hill was carpeted by thick evergreens. It was gorgeous, and she wished she could have seen it in daytime. But it was likely the last bit of nature she would see for a long time, so she cherished every bit of it she could see in the wash of their headlights.

"I'm sure she's fine," Iris said when they left the mountains and headed south again.

"She could be in custody," Margot said.

Iris shrugged. "In a few hours we'll probably all be in custody. That's the plan." She paused. "All except for you, of course."

Margot's lips twisted and she looked out the window.

"Keep an eye on our mirrors," Iris said. "Let me know if you see anyone following us."

"Yeah, okay," Margot muttered.

She tried not to think about where Erica was, but she kept her eyes peeled for her car on the side of the road with the hazards on. The car never appeared, and the road behind them remained empty of repeat followers. None of them seemed like military vehicles. Pick-ups, minivans, tiny sports cars, and cars that were at least ten years old. Definitely not official tails.

St. Elmo was dark when they rolled through. The town always went to bed early, some places closing at eight-thirty. Margot almost asked Iris to take a detour so they could pass the airport, but she knew time was of the essence. She settled for waving goodbye at the cross street they would have taken. Iris noticed but didn't comment on it.

"Almost there."

"Yep." Margot took out her phone and dialed Tracy. "Hey. Everything okay back there?"

"Fine and dandy," Tracy said. "Jessie has been sleeping for most of the ride. Me, sitting next to this thing feels like being strapped in next to a bomb, but I'm glad she can get some rest. How far from home are we?"

"We just left St. Elmo, now it's just a straight shot. No sign of tails yet."

"Good to know. You still good?"

"Ready and raring to go." Margot wasn't sure, to be completely honest, but she felt good enough to lie. "Talk to you soon if there are any changes."

"You're ready," Iris said when Margot hung up.

Margot looked over at her. "Yeah? You think so?"

"I've been watching you. Part of my assignment was to let Colleen know if I thought you weren't up for the job. We had a backup plan."

"She told me."

"She didn't know about this one. The Professor didn't want to bet all our chips on one hand. We took the second choice from Colleen's list and spoke with her. We didn't tell her what exactly the job was, but we had her in reserve in case something went awry."

"So I could have been replaced at any time."

Iris nodded.

"Is that supposed to make me feel better?"

"No," Iris said, sounding confused as if that was the last thing on her mind. "I just wanted to let you know that we were never, at any time, stuck with you. Colleen may have thought you were the only option, but that wasn't the case. You're here tonight, right now, because you truly are the best option."

Margot relaxed. "Oh." She considered it for a second, and then nodded. "That does actually make me feel a little better."

"Good. Because all this has been building up to one moment, and it's yours alone."

Margot swallowed the lump in her throat. She suddenly didn't feel good anymore.

Chapter Eighteen

The barn was lit up like the launchpad when the truck rolled down the driveway. The ladies left behind had apparently filled the time setting up lanterns inside the work space so that light spilled out of the open door. Margot saw Magpie-1 gleaming in the pseudo-sunlight and felt a surge of possessiveness. *That's mine,* she thought. *That is my ship, and isn't it glorious.* Her skin pebbled with goosebumps. Colleen jogged out to meet them, waving her arm over her head in greeting. Iris turned the truck around and carefully backed into the barn door with the Professor guiding her.

They disembarked, and Margot flew to Colleen for a hug. "You okay?" Colleen whispered against Margot's ear.

Margot nodded, squeezed, and then stepped back to watch as the Professor jumped up into the truck bed. Iris jogged to the back of the barn and came back pulling a tall crane-like mechanism with a dangling chain. She'd seen it before, both here and another one like it in Rosie's corner of the hangar, but she hadn't paid much attention to what it was until this moment: an engine house. She was relieved that they wouldn't be required to use brute muscle to get their engine onto the ship. The Professor directed everyone's movements, pointing to where they needed to be as she shouted instructions. Colleen took Margot's arm and took her to the other side of the ship.

"Hey," Margot said, just before Colleen's lips covered hers. She relaxed into the kiss, her hands on Colleen's hips. She felt like a sail going slack when the wind finally dies down, and all the tension of the past few hours evaporated.

"I love you," Colleen said.

"I love you, too," Margot said.

Colleen wet her lips and kept her eyes closed. "Don't come back."

Margot frowned. "What?"

Colleen twisted and pulled a folded map out of her pocket. She pressed the paper against Margot's chest. "This map shows an abandoned airfield in British Columbia. I know someone who lives nearby. All the information is on the paper."

"Colleen..."

"I've been thinking about this all day. If this works, the rest of us are screwed no matter what. Boshears is already clawing at the door. It's a matter of time before he finds out the engine has been stolen, and there's a very small radius of where we could have taken it. He's already as close as Halcyon. He'll be here soon enough and the rest of us will go to prison. But you can land anywhere. Bring the ship back to Earth, land in Canada, and walk away. My friend will help you. She owes me one. Just disappear. Don't come back here just to get handcuffs put on you."

Margot wanted to scream, argue, fight, but she knew it wouldn't do any good. She understood where Colleen was coming from. Hell, part of her wanted to rip out a Colleen-shaped hole in the cockpit and stow her away in it so they could both run away.

"It's not fair that we met like this."

"No," Colleen said, her voice breaking. "But I'm glad we did meet."

Margot smiled. "I got two dreams for the price of one." She stroked Colleen's cheek. "Joan Colleen Eckles. Thank you for giving me space."

"I haven't done it yet."

"Close enough."

Margot took the map, looked at Colleen, and then put it in her pocket. Colleen sighed with relief, her shoulders sagging. She cupped Margot's face.

"Thank you."

They kissed once more, only returning to the group when the Professor called for them. She was standing behind the truck with Iris and Jessie. "What's this about Erica going AWOL?"

Margot shook her head. "We haven't heard from her since we left. I was kind of hoping she'd come back here, but..."

The Professor looked like she was holding a mouthful of something foul, but she finally shook her head.

"There's nothing we can do for her short of going out and covering two hundred miles in the dark looking for where she might be. Colleen, you need to get to work attaching this engine. Margot, it's time for you to suit up."

Margot brought Colleen's hand to her lips and kissed it before they parted ways. Margot went into the house and retrieved her suit. She brought it back out to the barn, intending to change in the back stall. She wanted to be among the others as much as possible during the next vital hours.

The engine was out of its crate, dangling from a chain. There were three circular orange panels arranged like a pyramid with a shiny white frame, looking almost like a wide-eyed face with a mouth open in surprise. This was Colleen's baby, the thing she dedicated her life to, the baby she was risking everything to make sure it fulfilled its purpose. Margot thought it was the most beautiful thing she'd ever seen. Colleen was up on the ship, guiding Tracy and Iris with the hoist.

Jessie's phone rang, and everyone in the room spun to look at her. It felt like the air had been sucked from the room. She took it out and looked at the screen, her face pale.

"Erica."

The Professor jabbed a finger at Colleen. "You, don't stop." She swung the finger around to Jessie. "Answer."

Jessie answered the phone. Before she could say anything, Erica shouted, "You have two hours. He's coming. Boshears is on his way to you *now*, and you have *two hours*."

The Professor moved closer. "Where are you? What's happening?"

"Cheyenne Mountain." Erica's voice was strained. She was almost panting, wheezing. "Saw military convoy on the road. In Colorado Springs. They weren't following. Made a judgement call. Followed them." She cried out. "They're at the mountain. Mobilizing."

"How do you know all this?"

A weak laugh. "Hiked. I know, I'm a dumbass, and my ankle might never be the same. Fuck it. Got close enough to see. Boshears definitely knows where they're going. He's ordering people around like a fucking general."

The Professor looked at the ground, eyes dark as her mind worked. She suddenly looked up, spinning to face the engine accusingly.

"Fucking fuck, he put a tracker on it."

"Two hours," Erica said. "I'm going to try to slow them down, but I don't know how much I can do without being arrested."

The Professor said, "You've done your duty, Miss Shearing. Keep yourself safe."

Colleen hadn't stopped her work. "We're not going to take it apart looking for a tracker."

"No, it wouldn't do any good now. I'm certain he's already got the latitude and longitude memorized. We have a bullseye on us." She walked closer to the ship. "Miss Eckles, can you finish this job in under two hours?"

"Yup."

"Do not be glib in this matter, Miss Eckles, we~"

"*Yes, General*," Colleen snapped, not even looking up. "So stop fucking talking to me and let me do it."

The Professor wasn't thrown by the retort. She turned to Jessie. "Take the truck up and block the gate with it. Make them work for it."

Jessie saluted, either muscle memory or sincere respect, and ran for the truck. A minute later, it rumbled to life and pulled out of the barn.

Margot stood among the madness, the suit still draped over her arm. The Professor saw her and pointed at the back stall.

"Change. Now. We need you in position the second we're ready to go."

Margot hurried to comply. She stripped down to her underwear, put on the jumpsuit that went under the actual spacesuit, and carefully geared up. She ignored the tremor in her fingers. She knew she wasn't hyperventilating, even though she could almost feel her heart in her throat. She was extremely careful as she pulled the suit on. No rips, no tears, no mistakes. Not at this juncture. She checked every seam, every point where the pieces of her suit came together, checked the pressure on her emergency oxygen, fitted the earbud and angled the microphone down in front of her mouth.

The only thing she lacked was her helmet, which she wouldn't put on until she absolutely had to. She walked out to the main room. Iris was on her back under the engine, up to her elbows in something. Colleen was directly above her on top of the ship, lying flat, digging in the ship's guts. Margot moved the ladder and climbed up into the cockpit. She sank down into the seat, which molded around her like a glove thanks to Colleen.

She looked at the console, planning to check the systems to make sure they were all as expected, but she was caught off-guard by the photo tucked into the altimeter's frame. It was a candid shot of Colleen, much younger, wearing clear-rimmed glasses and an MIT sweatshirt that had to be two sizes too big for her. Her hair was shorter and she had bangs. She was striking a pose in front of a fountain, arms out to either side, mouth open in a carefree grin. Margot slipped her fingers over the glossy image, kissed it, and put it back.

She relaxed. She focused her mind on what had to be done. When she got the go-ahead, she would taxi forward out of the barn. Bear right. Out onto the runway. Build speed. Ascend.

Margot opened and closed her hands, feeling the stiffness of the gloves fade until they felt like old leather. She rolled her shoulders against the seat. She stretched her legs out in the compartment.

"Margot?"

"Copy," she said, resisting the urge to turn toward Colleen's voice.

"I need you to test the responsiveness of the engine. The green button on the base of the console."

Margot found the button and pressed it. A panel flashed red. "Improper attachment of port A," she reported.

"Fuck," Colleen grunted. "Hold on. Try it now."

The panel flashed again. "Check connections, port A."

"Fuck!" The sound of a fist on metal, and then grunting. "Now."

Margot hit the button. "Port A Connected!"

"Hell yeah," Colleen said. "Okay, now we're making progress."

The Professor and Tracy left the barn. Margot assumed they were on the way to help Jessie shore up their defenses in some way or another. She was glad that wasn't part of her duties. All she had to do was sit here and wait for all systems to go green and then...

She wasn't going to stand up again until she'd been in space.

She couldn't think like that. She refused to think like that. She gripped the yoke, a two-handled version, and used it to center herself.

"Port B should be connected now," Iris said.

Margot checked. "Red."

No reaction from Iris until thirty seconds later. "Now?"

"Port B connected!"

Again, no reaction. She hoped the woman had some kind of internal celebration. Either way, they were two-thirds of the way there. She checked the chronometer on the console. One hour and forty minutes left. Unless Boshears and his men moved faster than Erica's predictions. She inhaled through her nose and let it out through pursed lips. Calmed herself. Relaxed. Stayed centered.

The whole console went dark.

Margot stared at it, unwilling to breathe or speak in case it had been caused by something she'd done. After ten seconds without it coming back, she croaked, "Uh, Colleen...?"

"Hm?"

"I-I seem to have lost power here."

"What?" Thumps on the ship as Colleen moved to crouch behind the cockpit, looming above Colleen's seat. "What the fuck. Iris, did you do something to the power?"

"I don't believe so."

"If she gets up there and the fucking power dies..."

"I'm checking," Iris said, still calm.

Colleen reached down and rested her hand on Margot's shoulder. "We'll get it. We've got plenty of time, baby."

"I know."

The console lit up again and Colleen told Iris of their success. "Sorry," Iris said. "It was a bad connection. I've shored it up now. It won't happen again."

"It better not," Colleen said, then thumped back to the engine.

Time continued ticking by on the chronometer. Connections were made as the ramshackle ship was tied into the state-of-the-art engine. Soon there was only an hour left. Margot tried not to imagine a fleet of army vehicles speeding down the road toward them, but it was impossible to banish the thought. Forty minutes left. Colleen yelled at Iris, and by that point even the unflappable Iris seemed frazzled. Colleen only asked for the time once, when there was half an hour left.

"This is going to be sloppy," Colleen said at one point, "but it'll hold." Her voice was so soft that only Margot could have heard it, but she didn't know if that was intentional.

With ten minutes left, Colleen moved back to the cockpit. She stretched out on her stomach and pointed at the control panel.

"We've been over this, but for my own peace of mind. Port A will give you just enough power to taxi. It'll get you in position and that's where you build speed. When you hit the threshold, activate B and C for thrust and uplift. Everything else should be familiar to you from flying planes. It's basically just a big Cessna that can go into space."

"I've had dreams like that."

Colleen smiled. "Look up at me. Give me a kiss for luck."

Margot tilted her head up and they kissed. Colleen pulled a strip of cloth from her pocket. Margot reached for it and Colleen pressed it into her palm.

"What's this?"

"Piece of my tank top."

Margot laughed. "Perfect."

"If you have to abort the mission for any reason, you do it. Understand me?"

"Yes, ma'am. It's now or never, and never isn't an option."

Colleen climbed down and began clearing the area around the ship. Margot tied the strip of tank top around the center of her yoke, letting it hang like a little white flag. Colleen had just started pushing the hoist back when the truck's horn began blaring.

They both froze for a heartbeat before Colleen ran to the workbench. She grabbed Colleen's helmet and ran to the ship with it. She tossed it gently up, and Margot caught it easily.

"Go," Colleen said.

"I'm..."

"Go."

Margot put her helmet on. She reached over the top of her head, tapped a button, and the canopy slid into place over her head. A yellow light on the console flashed to indicate it was secure. Colleen had run to the barn door but turned back to look at her.

Margot held up her hand: forefinger, thumb, and pinkie extended in the sign for "I love you." Colleen's face twisted with emotion as she copied the gesture, then put her palm against her heart. Then she turned and disappeared into the darkness.

Margot wet her lips. She could hear her breathing inside the helmet. She flicked the switches, watched the indicator lights come on. She felt the ship hum around her. Suddenly it was a living creature, an extension of her body. She took a second to run her hands over the sides of the cockpit.

"Maybe you are Hot Lips after all. Or maybe Houlihan..." She smiled. That sounded right. "Okay, Houlihan, let's see how you handle on your maiden voyage, huh?"

10

She could hear the countdown in her head. She advanced forward.

9

The ship rolled through the open doors of the barn. From her position she couldn't see the ground, the hull blocking most of the ground floor of the house. But to her left she could see a fleet of headlights at the head of the driveway. People were standing in the beams, and she saw other silhouettes of people kneeling on the ground, hands on top of their heads.

8

Margot banked right. The tires rolled across uneven ground as she picked up speed, her foot sinking the pedal. She watched the arrows climb on her gauges.

7

There was a muffled commotion behind her. Shouting, blocked by the canopy.

6

Truck horns blaring. She saw beams of headlights bounce across the ground, trying to keep up.

5

She gave it more speed. In her peripheral vision, she saw trucks pulling up on either side of her.

4

Margot ignored them, eyes forward. She could just barely make out the line between sky and mountains at the end of the runway. The darkness made it look like a ramp.

3

The trucks fell behind, unable to get in front of her. Houlihan was racing across the ground, shaking and rocking her in the seat, kicking up fantails of dirt behind her that she hoped would blind her pursuers.

2

One last quick sweep of her indicators, all in the green. Five-by-five. She checked her speed.

1

"Liftoff," she whispered to herself.

Margot felt the familiar sinking of her stomach as she broke gravity, her body pressing hard into the seat. She didn't know she was smiling until she felt the strain in her cheeks as she gained altitude, a laugh bubbling up in her chest. She flexed her fingers on the yoke and wet her lips, the smile immediately returning. She needed speed, she needed the angle, and she couldn't get those right if she was too busy being giddy. Break atmosphere at the wrong angle and she would just crash back to Earth.

Every lesson from NASA came back to her, like it had been waiting behind a door that she just had to kick open. Her hands moved effortlessly across the controls. Her breathing was calmer than it had been all week, and her heart was steady. This is the moment she'd been waiting for. All she had to do now was follow her instincts a~

She opened her eyes, swimming back to consciousness like rising up through molasses. She blinked at the controls in front of her with a fleeting moment of confusion before she remembered where she was, what she was doing, and what still needed to be done. The G-forces had pushed the blood to her feet, but fortunately it was just a brief grey-out and she was already getting back to normal and her hands confidently worked the controls to keep her on course.

The ship shuddered around her, and she glanced out once or twice to make sure all her paneling was still in place, but she was confident it would hold together. She could feel a flawed ship, knew in her bones if something wasn't trustworthy, and Houlihan was worth her faith. Colleen was worth her faith.

And then.

Stillness and silence.

Margot held her breath and let go of the yoke, watched her hands float away from it, weightless.

"Hah..."

She swept her eyes up, through the visor of her helmet and the glass of the canopy, and she saw stars. A vast spray of stars. She laughed again, and this time tears came with the sound. She grabbed the yoke and squeezed tightly, her laugh venturing into screaming sobs before it came back around to plain hysteria. She blinked rapidly to clear her eyes, reaching up to wipe the tears away before she realized the helmet would prevent her from doing so, and she laughed again.

"Finally," she whispered. "Finally, finally."

She pressed her head back against the seat and screamed as loud as she could: "*I'm here!*"

She closed her eyes and let go of the yoke, relaxed her legs, and felt herself floating against the harness. She was here. She had finally made it.

Margot Kathleen Sullivan was in outer space.

Chapter Nineteen

FROM THE daily journal of J. Colleen Eckles:

You were fucking phenomenal, baby.

I don't know who I was originally writing this for, posterity or the news or for people on social media to pick apart, but this is one hundred percent for you, Margot. I want you to know what it looked like when you took off.

Jessie and Iris did their best to block the road, but Boshears was relentless. He brought a whole battalion with him. I swear there had to be a hundred people in khakis climbing over the fence and rushing the property. The Professor told us that the only smart move was surrender. She doubted Boshears knew how many of us there were, and lining up like that would confuse him. Tracy came up with the idea of wearing old astronaut helmets to disguise our faces so it wouldn't immediately be obvious you weren't part of the group. We must have looked insane kneeling there in space helmets, but if it slowed them down for even a second, it was worth it. We were all bound to be arrested anyway, why not give them a show? So we got on our knees, laced our hands on top of the helmets, and waited. Boshears ordered us to be taken into custody, and then he ordered men to clear the house and barn.

That's when you came out. That shining ship, that Magpie-1, as you rolled her out. I watched you build speed. I watched those trucks try to catch you and our ship left them in their dust. It was like watching a wild animal break free while Tonka toys tried to corral it. Boshears yelled for everyone to hold their fire. I don't know if he was concerned for your safety or just didn't want to damage the engine, but I owe him for that, at least.

And then, baby, you soared. You lifted up, and it looked so unreal that I almost didn't believe it was really happening. My ship, OUR ship, the thing I built one piece at a time, and it was alive and free and god it was so beautiful, Margot. The engine

GLOWED. It was alive and it was finally doing what I'd built it for. You shot straight up and I swear the wings caught the moonlight. I saw you gleam and shine as you went up, as you became smaller and smaller, until you were gone. I sobbed then. I didn't give a fuck, I cried like a damn baby.

I knew whatever happened next, no matter how this all ended, at that moment, you were glorious.

Margot slowly and carefully took care of the minor tasks, checking on the systems designed to keep her alive and ensuring they were all in the green before she allowed herself to flip the ship so the planet was "above" her. She smiled up at it with wide-eyed awe, incapable of words or any kind of sincere thought. She was above America, could see mountains and rivers, could see the Pacific coast, swirls of clouds and storms and the web of lights that revealed cities across the nighttime landscape.

The radio crackled. She looked down at the display and tapped to open her line. "Receiving."

"Margot Sullivan," Boshears said. "What a surprise."

"Hello, Colonel."

"You sound extremely calm for someone who just took the last joyride of her life."

Margot smiled and looked up again. "You'd be calm too, sir, if you were looking at the same view I am. Hard to feel anything but calm up here."

"We have your friends, Miss Sullivan. All of them are in custody, and I have a feeling the next bit of their lives won't be very pretty."

Margot took a deep breath of recycled air and let it out slowly. "That's one story."

There was a long pause from the ground. She imagined him on the ground, hunched over Colleen's work station, using her radio and trying to parse her comment. She hadn't told Colleen about this idea, hadn't even really formed it completely until she was actually sitting in the cockpit waiting for the engine to be connected. An hour is a long time to sit and stare and wait for the go-signal, and she'd used it wisely.

"How do you figure?" he finally asked.

"People are going to know what happened tonight. I imagine a bunch of amateur astronomers picked up the launch, and who knows how many people recorded it. Someone's going to have to explain what shot up into the night sky, and why a large military force was called out to a farmhouse in the middle of nowhere. There are two answers you can give." She thought. "Well, three. But I think society is way past cover stories at this point, don't you?"

Boshears said, "Okay. What are the answers?"

"The first answer is the one you already have. A group of women managed to steal a high-tech engine from the US military. They built a spaceship and sent someone to space before the military even knew where they were. But in the end, you win. All the women are taken into custody. They get the book thrown at them. The military gets their expensive toy back. And we spend the rest of our lives in prison."

Boshears said, "Seems like a reasonable story to me."

"I'm sure it does, Colonel. But appearance is everything. Who do you think the villain of that story is?"

He didn't answer.

"There's a second story..." She wet her lips, knowing this was a gamble but also that they had nothing to lose. "The military had a toy they spent an insane amount of money to develop, and it was just sitting in a closet gathering dust. It hadn't even been tested yet to make sure it worked. But then, a rich and powerful man named Enver Crane came along, and he wanted to borrow the toy. He wanted to take it apart and see how it worked so he could copy it. That left the military with a problem. What if they accepted Mr. Crane's money and the engine *didn't work*? What if it had been a dud this whole time? Maybe that was the real reason it was mothballed. That would be a huge embarrassment for the military. It would be bad enough admitting they had this engine just sitting in storage, but for wunderkind inventor Enver Crane to report that it was just a hunk of junk...? Bad PR, Colonel Boshears. Really bad look for you."

Silence from the ground. Margot looked up and saw she had drifted north, and she corrected her course a bit.

"Are you still reading me, Colonel?"

"I hear you." He sounded contemplative.

"So," Margot continued, "the military decided that it would be in everyone's best interest to shake out the mothballs. A dry run of the engine just to be sure it worked as advertised. They put together a group led by the woman who came up with the engine in the first place and quietly arranged for a test flight. They even got a former astronaut candidate to be their pilot. But they kept it quiet because it's the kind of potentially disastrous thing that would lead to more bad PR if things went wrong. Dead astronaut. Never good to see in the news."

Boshears said, "So that would make you all some kind of heroes, huh?"

"No, not heroes. Just scientists. Engineers. Pilots. People doing their jobs. But for that story to hold water, I have to come back to Earth. I have to land at the Garage, shake your hand. I have to hand the engine back over to you rather than you taking it from me. That was always the plan, by the way. We have no use for it ourselves, and we never intended to sell it to anyone. Colleen just wanted to know the damn thing worked. She wanted everyone to know she had succeeded. When it was over, no matter the consequences, she always intended to surrender. Did she fight your men when you got to the Garage?"

"No," he said. "No, they did not resist."

Margot swallowed. "Here's what's going to happen next. Because no matter what story you decide to tell, this part stays the same. I'm going to do a lap around this gorgeous planet of ours. Take in the sights and record how the engine performs. It's five-by-five across the board so far, by the way. My baby made an amazing engine. It's going to make history.

"When I get back to Colorado, I'm going to land this thing right back where I took off, give or take a few yards. Right now I'm traveling at about five miles per second, so I'm due back here in about an hour and a half. You have that long to decide if you'll take me into custody when I land."

He didn't say anything.

"Either way, Colonel, I'm about to leave range. So I'm going to wish you good luck and hope you can wish me some back. I'll see you in a little while."

She turned off the radio before he could respond.

"Give my love to Colleen," she said quietly, then set in her course to begin her orbit.

She soared.

There was really nothing for her to do other than maintain her heading and keep track of her vitals. The ship was running smooth as silk, her oxygen was perfect. She kept an eye out for debris, but Colonel Laurie had done a good job of clearing out the junk. It wasn't exactly clear skies, but there was enough of an open road that she didn't have to risk playing bumper cars. In the end, she didn't really have to do anything but sit back and enjoy the view.

And what a view. She was still low enough that the planet looked impossibly huge, but each individual piece was still so tiny. She skimmed over the Pacific Ocean, saw dusk in Asia, and crossed from India to Spain in about twenty minutes. Ships moved along the Atlantic, creating impossibly small wakes as they traveled from one shore to the other. It was still night in America, but she could see dawn creeping up on the east coast. Several times during the trip she caught herself holding her breath and forced herself to exhale. This was no time to hyperventilate.

Now, in fact, was the time to begin reentry procedures. She reluctantly flipped Houlihan back around. No point in landing on her head; it was going to be rough enough the right way. She'd been told by other astronauts that she could prepare for reentry, but she'd never actually *been* prepared, so she tried to brace herself for whatever was about to happen. She checked her angles so she wouldn't skip off or burn up like an asteroid, tightened the straps holding her in, took a few deep breaths, and began her descent.

The heat was immediate and overwhelming. The air racing past the canopy burned orange, then red, and she heard the panels being pulled and tugged by the sudden presence of atmosphere. One or two broke off and whipped past, but she didn't pay them much attention. She couldn't pay them much attention, because a ten ton stone had just landed on her chest and was trying to push through to her back. She pursed her lips to suck in air, forcing her lungs to expand against ribs which were suddenly reluctant to move.

She could barely make out her instruments, saw that the ship was still flying straight and true toward Colorado. In the meantime she was cutting a swath through multiple airspaces and probably drawing attention from dozens of agencies who thought they were seeing a real-life UFO. She saw the Rockies and knew she was almost home, whatever that might mean following her ultimatum to Boshears. It didn't matter to her, honestly. She'd had one gambit and if it didn't work, she was fine with the alternatives.

The ground rushed up to meet her. She braced for impact but was still unprepared for the violence of smacking into the hard, rocky ground. It was like being rear-ended and sideswiped at the same time, and she was thrown forward against the harness, rattled like a pebble in a tin can. The ship skidded for what felt like minutes, but was probably only seconds, before it came to a stop.

Margot slumped forward against the harness, hands limp at her sides, eyes closed. She took deep, slow breaths. She was trembling, she felt heavy and shattered. Tears had dried on her face but fresh ones poured free to cover their tracks. She was aware of movement outside the ship but didn't want to spare the strength to look up and see who it was or what they were doing. She only reached up and hit the button to release the canopy. It popped open and she reached up, arms like rubber, and shoved it high enough to let it fall over the side.

Someone was climbing on the side of the ship. She looked up and saw a pre-dawn sky enhanced with the beams of what had to be four or five trucks that were encircling the ship. The person who had climbed onto the hull was silhouetted and, though she had only met the man once, she knew it was Boshears.

She smiled weakly and lifted her hand to block her eyes. "Hello, Colonel."

"Hello, Miss Sullivan," he said. "Welcome back to Earth."

The silence between them grew until it was almost unbearable. Finally he held out his hand.

"Let's get you out of there. Mr. Crane is very eager to hear how the engine performed."

"He's not mad that we took it out for a spin?"

Boshears made a noise that was more sigh than laugh. "I'm going to let you explain it to him. You can be very persuasive."

Margot's smile widened.

When Margot felt steady enough to walk, with Boshears offering his shoulder for support, he escorted her back to the house where the rest of the Sitting Ducks had been sequestered. She'd landed almost half a mile away from the property. Not exactly landing on a dime, but damn close enough to be proud. She was trembling and sweaty by the time he opened the door for her. She found the other women crowded around the table. Erica was there, which brought her great relief, and Colleen had her head down on the table, using her folded arms as pillows.

The Professor offered a wan smile. "She passed out almost immediately after we got locked in here," she said in a quiet voice. "I think all these months of preparation and stress finally got to her."

Margot crouched down next to Colleen and gently plucked the hair away from her face. She lightly brushed her fingertips over the curve of Colleen's cheek.

"Hey," she whispered. "Hey, sleeping beauty..."

Colleen's eyelids fluttered, then opened, and slowly focused. Margot had spent years dreaming of seeing Earth from space, but now that she could make the comparison, the color of Colleen's eyes was the clear beauty winner. Margot smiled, and Colleen choked on a gasp as she sat up and threw herself at Margot. Margot was rocked back on her heels but managed to stay upright, putting her arms around Colleen.

"You're back. You're okay. Are you okay?"

"Bruised and beat-up, but good."

She kissed Colleen's neck, and Colleen pulled back to give her a proper kiss.

The Professor cleared her throat. "Perhaps you could clear something up for us. Boshears had us in custody. We were literally handcuffed and placed in the back of trucks, separated from one another and guarded by men with guns. Then he went into the barn, presumably spoke to you on the radio, and ordered his men to release us and move us into the house. Do you have any idea what prompted his change of heart?"

"Yeah." Margot cleared her throat. "Sorry. I sort of changed the plan. And judging from how he's acting now, he decided to go with it."

Tracy said, "So we're not all going to end up in prison or dishonorably discharged?"

"No," Margot said. "No, in fact... I think we might end up being considered heroes."

The Professor sat back, crossing her arms. "Explain."

"Well..." Margot looked for a seat and, when she didn't find one, sat down on Colleen's lap with an arm across her shoulders. "A lot of people just saw a spaceship come zipping through the atmosphere. There are going to be questions. I told him he could give one of two answers..."

It was morning by the time Boshears came into the house. Margot and Colleen had relocated to the living room, curled against each other on the divan, while the rest of the group had scattered to various locations in the house to lie down as well. They all reconvened in the kitchen where Boshears placed a tablet on the counter and tapped the screen to activate a call. The face of Enver Crane, familiar from countless interviews and magazine covers, appeared on the screen. He smiled broadly and waved.

"Hello! Can everyone hear me?"

"They can hear you," Boshears said, sounding annoyed to be reduced to this kind of servitude.

Enver smiled. "Fantastic. Hello to the Sitting Ducks!" He laughed. "Colonel Boshears informed me of everything that's transpired over the past twenty-four hours. And when I say everything, I mean he's told me the whole story. Including the version that will be given to the public. May I ask which of you is Joan Colleen Eckles?"

Colleen lifted her hand. "That's me."

Enver looked like a kid meeting a celebrity. "You... built a *spaceship*... out of *garbage*. You, Miss Eckles, are my new favorite person. And it actually flew? It *flew?*"

Margot smiled and squeezed Colleen's hand. "Oh, it flew. Yes, sir."

Enver's eyes moved to her. "And you! You must be the fearless Margot Sullivan. I don't know which of you is more impressive, the woman who built a junk ship or the one who trusted it to take her into the vacuum of space. But I also don't see why it has to be a competition. You are both amazing women, and if Colonel Boshears hadn't agreed to your clever little plan, I would be trying to think of a way to help you out."

The Professor said, "So you're not angry we stole what is, essentially, your property?"

"Upset?" Enver said. "*Upset?* Ma'am, I am in awe, humbled, and completely in love with what you managed to pull off. This is the sort of shit I could only dream of doing as a young man. I fully support the official version of events, without hesitation. You ladies were working on a project of the utmost secrecy to ensure the viability of the Eckles Engine."

Colleen stiffened. "The what?"

Enver grinned and winked. "We can negotiate on the name, of course, but I think it has a nice ring to it. And of course, it goes without saying that we'll be offering you a position at Astraea to continue your work on this project."

"You... i-it does," Colleen said, frowning as if she didn't understand.

"We'll discuss the terms of your employment at another time. In fact, I think all of you could have a spot at Astraea given the skills and tenacity you displayed during this heist." He looked at Margot again. "We could always use a pilot with guts like yours."

Margot squeezed Colleen's hand again. "Sure. We can talk."

He winked at her. "For now, there's a lot of work to be done to make sure everyone's stories match. But I have a feeling everything will work out for all of us. Even Colonel Boshears will come out smelling like roses for coming up with such an ingenious scheme."

Boshears cleared his throat and looked at Margot. "Of course. All my doing."

Margot was perfectly willing to let him take credit for the idea if it got him onboard with the plan.

"Okay, ladies," Enver said, already doing something on his phone. "I'll speak to you all later, I'm certain. Thank you, Colonel."

Boshears disconnected the call and closed the tablet. "There you have it, ladies. The brass agrees with Mr. Crane. They don't see much reward in detaining you for your actions. Despite the fact you stole an incalculable amount of resources from your various bases, despite the fact you compromised two of our soldiers, despite the unauthorized use of military property, we have decided that..." He sighed heavily. "This is... easier... for everyone. And the optics are better. It gives us a victory instead of making us look like the bad guys punishing a female scientist for using her own engine."

Margot said, "For what it's worth, I want to reiterate that we were willing to suffer the consequences for what we were doing. None of us went into this expecting to go unpunished."

"I'm not sure that really helps. I put a lot of time and effort into stopping this little operation. I called in a lot of favors. Really put my ass on the line." He let the comment hang for a moment, then allowed himself the smallest of smiles. "But it's impressive. I have to admit that much. What you accomplished here...?" He chuckled. "Damn impressive."

"Thank you," Colleen said.

He looked around the table. "Sitting Ducks? What's the name of the ship? Did anyone name it?"

Margot said, "Houlihan," before anyone else could answer.

Boshears nodded. "I like it."

"What will happen to it?" Colleen asked.

"The engine is Astraea property, and every piece of that ship is something the military was going to throw out anyway, so in our records I suppose it would still be listed as garbage. I would take it up with Enver Crane. Better him than me. I'm done with all of you." He started for the door, then turned to the Professor. He offered her a salute. "Ma'am."

She nodded to him.

Boshears looked at Margot, chuckled, shook his head, and muttered, "Houlihan..." before he left the kitchen.

They sat in silence, no one wanting to be the first to move or break the silence. Finally Jessie pushed her chair back and went to the window, craning her neck to see around the curtain.

"It looks like... they're leaving."

Colleen looked at Margot, then scanned the faces of the other women in the room. "What just happened?"

The Professor looked confused as well. "I think we got away with it."

Erica was the first to laugh. The others stared at her, and then one by one joined in. Even the Professor relaxed her hard-edged mask and gave a relieved smile as she sagged back against her chair. Colleen was laughing hard when she pressed her lips to Margot's cheek.

"Looks like you're stuck with me after all."

"You better start building me a new spaceship or else I might get bored."

Colleen's eyes sparkled. "I'll see what I can whip up. Any requests?"

Margot nuzzled Colleen's cheek. "The Moon."

EPILOGUE

THE SITTING Ducks became an overnight sensation. As Margot predicted, social media exploded with sightings of a shooting star over the Midwest. Grainy video showed Houlihan streaking through the sky, and there was no questioning that it was a ship. There were no outer markings so naturally everyone made the immediate leap to aliens before Enver and Colonel Boshears could issue a press release explaining their version of events. The FAA was absolutely livid that they hadn't been alerted, pointing airspace violations and risks of commercial flights, and Enver was appropriately apologetic to them both publicly, privately, and monetarily.

When the fervor died down, the only thing that remained was the admiration for seven women who joined forces to make an experimental spacecraft in a barn. They were booked on talk shows, podcasts, interviewed for magazines and blogs, and had their faces plastered all over the internet. The Professor was the first to bow out of the coverage, only participating in a single interview before she declared her part to be finished. Jessie followed almost immediately afterward; she had no interest in answering the same banal questions over and over again with a fake smile plastered on her face. Iris remained, rarely speaking unless directly spoken to, until her presence was no longer requested.

Tracy and Erica started doing separate interviews unrelated to the mission, focused more on getting Black and Hispanic girls interested in pursuing STEM careers.

By the end, Margot and Colleen were left alone, the face of what the press eventually decided to call the Secret Seven. Margot could think of many better names - her favorites were Houlihan Heist, Space Pirates, or

Ocean's Seven - but they all involved knowing the true story and the fact they'd stolen the engine for the test flight, so she didn't bring it up.

During the set-up of one interview, the reporter noticed Colleen holding Margot's hand. "Oh, I didn't realize you two were... Is that a topic we can cover?"

Margot shrugged, and Colleen laughed. "Sure, why not."

After that, with public interest reignited by the love story twist, they were subjected to a new round of publicity from LGBT organizations and the whirlwind started all over again.

They were put up in various hotels around the country during their press tour, and invited to stay at various Astraea institutions when possible since they were now officially representatives of the company, but eventually the requests slowed down and they were forced to think of a more permanent place to stay for a while. Margot had given up her place in St. Elmo, but her father had kept a spare room open for her just in case, and he was incredibly eager to meet "that cool scientist lady from the news and, oh yeah, my daughter's partner."

The night they arrived, after a huge dinner her father cooked for them, Margot and Colleen squeezed into the twin bed together and held each other under the thin blanket.

"It's so quiet," Margot said sleepily. "It feels like we haven't stopped moving since the launch."

"We really haven't." Colleen kissed Margot's forehead. "And forget about time alone. All those press people and the robots telling us where to stand, where to look, how to speak. And thank god we never have to share a hotel room with Iris ever again."

Margot said, "I know! Such a quiet woman, who knew she snored like a lawnmower."

Colleen chuckled and burrowed closer. "I'll take spending the night with you in your childhood bedroom over the fanciest hotel any day."

"I never lived in this house..."

"Sh, sh, let me imagine."

"Okay."

They lay in silence for a bit. Finally Colleen broke the silence.

"I really thought the launch would be the end of this."

Margot tensed but kept her tone light. "Disappointed?"

"No, god, fuck, no." She tightened her hand on Margot's hip. "No. That's not what I meant. When it had an end, when I knew there was a finish line, I was relaxed. Now it feels like a bonus, like I'm in overtime, and it could end at any second. It's scary."

Margot said, "I can only speak from my point of view, but you don't have to worry about the end coming any time soon."

"No?"

"No. You built me a spaceship. You gave me something I've wanted my entire life, and once I was up there, all I could think about was how I could stay with you. The way I see it, we finally get to have a normal relationship. Dates. Getting annoyed with each other. Maybe living separately for a little while when you go to work in California. But even if we don't share a house, I still want to be with you."

"I want to be with you, too."

Margot kissed her. "I love you."

"I love you, too." She brushed her nose against Margot's. "I feel a lot better about this bonus time."

"Yeah? Good. Because it's going to keep going a long, long time."

Colleen smiled and moved her head to Margot's shoulder. Then, as she had been doing more frequently since Houlihan's launch, she fell into a deep sleep.

Hawkeye and Hunnicutt stood shining and beautiful outside of the hangar, their hulls catching the last light of the setting sun. Margot had just finished washing them and they looked glorious and brand new. She was now sitting in a lawn chair with her feet up on a cooler of drinks. Colleen was at the grill, flipping the burgers and looking like a suburban dad in her long shorts and Hawaiian shirt. Linnie and Rosie, the ladies of the hour, were taking a walk together down the length of the runway.

Margot and Colleen had been witnesses at the wedding. It was still a little hard to imagine Linnie as a married woman, but Rosie was the perfect woman for her. A gearhead, funny, smart, tough. She was exactly the type of woman Linnie needed to keep her in line. And as a bonus, she would always have someone around to help if the plane started acting up. What more could someone ask for in a spouse?

Colleen came over with two plates stacked on top of each other. She paused to offer one to Margot before taking her own seat.

"I didn't trust myself to keep everything separate, so we're all having veggie burgers."

"I'll try to cope." Margot leaned forward and got drinks out of the cooler. She handed one to Colleen, keeping a grape soda for herself. "When we decide to call it a night, I want to take you up. Show you the mountains."

Colleen smiled. "Cool. I love flying with you."

Margot had worked out an arrangement with Astraea and Magpie. She would work for Enver as a test pilot on a case-by-case basis, flying to California whenever he needed someone for a shakedown of a new ship. The rest of the time she would stay in St. Elmo and fly with Linnie. She'd missed the airline when she was at the Garage, but she'd considered it a chapter of her life that had to be closed. Now that the future was open to her again, she realized how important it was to her. She was proud of her business and, now that she wasn't blinded by her dreams of space, she could truly appreciate what she had accomplished.

The only downside was that Colleen had been offered, and obviously accepted, a permanent position with Astraea. It meant she had to relocate to Mojave, California, just over a thousand miles away. It wasn't ideal, but it also wasn't the end of the world. They could make it work. They *were* making it work. They began their relationship crammed together in a house, and it was doing them good to spend a little time apart. It made the time they had together more special. Margot could see the day when she officially left Magpie for good, when she packed her bags and relocated to Mojave, but not yet. Not right now.

She let her hand drop off the arm of her chair. Colleen, without looking, reached down with her hand to link their fingers. She nodded at the newlyweds in the distance. Linnie and Rosie had reached the end of the runway and now seemed to be dancing together despite the lack of music. Margot smiled at the sight and shook her head.

"You know they didn't speak to each other for a week when I hired Rosie? Everything went through me. 'Could you tell the new mechanic...' or 'do you or Ms. Payton need anything before I go...' They finally got sick of using me for a middleman."

Colleen said, "Good thing, too. That would've made the vows really long."

Margot laughed.

Colleen raised her bottle to them. "They make a cute couple."

"They're great together," Margot said, joining in the toast. "I'm really happy for them."

Colleen tilted her head back to examine the sky. "A lot of clouds. Will we be able to get high enough to see any stars?"

Margot looked at Colleen, smiling, content.

"Maybe. Maybe not. Stars are actually pretty overrated."

Collen grinned.

They ate their dinner, drank in silence, and as the sun set and cast the valley into darkness, neither of them wasted any time looking up.

Read More from Geonn Cannon
Can You Hear Me?

Can You Hear Me received Honorable Mention at the 2018-2019 Rainbow Awards.

For the next two years, Colonel Noa Laurie - the sole survivor of a disaster which destroyed the International Space Station - will be orbiting Earth in an experimental craft called ODIE. Her mission: to clear away the treacherous minefield of space junk that has accumulated around the planet and endangers future missions. Her only lifeline during this mission will be the radio connecting her to the command center and whoever happens to be assigned to the communications desk. Or so she thinks.

Because tucked away and almost forgotten in an Indiana woodshop is an antique radio. Its owner, Jamie Faris, occasionally uses it for eavesdropping on the truckers passing by on the highway. One day in the third month of Noa's mission, Jamie uses the radio to vent her frustrations by screaming into the ether. She screams and rages and curses into the thick static knowing it won't matter because no one will hear, but she's wrong... someone is definitely listening. And she's about to say hello.

"Cannon's prose is beautiful. This isn't the most plot-filled of his novels but highlights the splendour of everyday life that it's so easy to take for granted. It's there to remind us that love can sometimes happen, not at first sight, but through the captivation and enmeshment that comes from truly listening and being heard by someone out of reach." - Jo at Goodreads

Into the Furnace

Kelly Lake comes from a family of firefighters, but she still had to prove herself to her brothers and her father before they accepted her as one of their own. On her days off she tends bar at the firehouse hangout across the street and spends time trying to breathe life into a relationship she knows is doomed. Her life is cruising along just fine until the day her squad responds to a horrific arson that will cause her carefully-orchestrated balancing act to come falling down around her. The blaze claims the lives of eleven people, half of them children, and the fire department takes the blame.

Kelly soon finds herself at the center of a media firestorm when she inadvertently becomes the poster girl for the incident. The trauma of the fire is compounded by her personal house of cards collapsing. Her relationship begins showing its cracks at the same time long-buried family secrets rear their ugly heads. Attacked from all angles, Kelly starts thinking the only place she'll be safe is running headlong into the furnace.

"Easily one of the best samplings of queer fiction I've had the pleasure to read in a very long time. I could not recommend it more, and sincerely hope that upon its release in November Into the Furnace will light the same fire in each of your hearts that it has already lit in mine." - Tabitha Beth, The Rainbow Hub.